The Man
with the
Missing Jaw

by Geoff Palmer

PODSNAP PUBLISHING
WELLINGTON, NEW ZEALAND

Podsnap Publishing Ltd., 17 Moir Street, Mt Victoria, Wellington 6011, New Zealand.

ISBN: 978-0-473-36072-6

Cover design by David Owen
www.davidowen.co.nz

Prologue

Gizzard Gully, a desolate valley of abandoned mineshafts and broken dreams, was coming apart. Frank and Emma Townsend stared at the picture on the TV screen where they saw stabs of laser fire puncture the ground and a series of timed explosions send cliff faces tumbling to the valley floor. Although they were ten kilometres away, the faint tremors still rattled ornaments on the glass shelves of the china cabinet beside the TV set.

The commentary was breathless and garbled. The camerawork unsteady. The helicopter from which it was being broadcast swayed and bucked. At times it was hard to make sense of the scene. Then the picture steadied, focused on the ramp of a silvery, saucer-shaped spaceship.

A figure ran up it.

Another followed. Zigzagging. Unsteady.

Then a third and fourth appeared, half-carrying, half-dragging a fifth.

'That looked a bit like the kids,' Em muttered, her words fading as the ramp vanished and the hatch slammed shut.

The ship took off so quickly that the camera tracking it lost it for a second. When it found it again – now little more than a silver speck in the blue evening sky – it was receding fast.

A streak of laser fire stabbed straight across the screen and the silver ship banked sharply, racing back towards the camera, filling the frame before shooting past at tremendous speed, its jetstream making the helicopter buck and dance.

Seconds later, a second ship appeared. A different type of ship entirely. A square, boxy thing that looked like it had been bolted together from scrapyard parts. A noisy, smoky thing that screamed past in hot pursuit.

The camera followed the two craft as they headed south, climbing steadily before vanishing into the darkening sky.

'The kids?' Frank said. 'Nah, it can't have been.'

1
Departures

1 : Protect and Deflect

Tim Townsend lay in the evacuation ship's protective gel bed, watching in silence as his home planet shrank behind him, an iridescent blue ball streaked with wisps of cloud. He could see it rotating slowly. Growing smaller with each passing second.

Funny how we call it Earth, he thought. We should really call it Ocean.

Then he wondered when he would see it again.

Something stirred in the heavy gel surrounding him and brought him back to his senses. From the moment he'd come to, his body had felt numb. Like it wasn't his any more. Like it belonged to someone else. He'd been glad of that after what had happened.

Gizzard Gully, the Sentinel ship, the attack and taking cover. He remembered all that. And the old hut at the head of the gully. Helping his friend Norman Smith. Then ... something else. An intense flash of light followed by a blast of scalding air as the world turned a flickering orange and he felt burning on his back, shoulders, arms and legs ... He recalled raising a hand in front of him. How it looked like a blazing log fallen from a camp fire. His last proper thought before the pain engulfed him was: *That's weird.*

Then the pain. Oh man, the pain. Shrieking, searing, overwhelming pain.

And finally, merciful blackness.

He figured out the rest. His sister and friends must have carried him to the ship, slapped a walrus mask on his face so he could see and breathe, and dropped him into one of the beds because he'd woken there to find himself floating, enclosed in cool blue gel, feeling nothing but the acceleration of the evacuation pod and watching through the mask as his home planet slipped away.

The others were nearby. He could hear the rise and fall of their breathing, but no one spoke. They were lost in their own thoughts.

Something prodded him again. Several things. A circle of what felt like steel ball bearings ran along the length of his left leg, stopped, withdrew, then ran along his right. Another set ran down his back.

It wasn't the things themselves – he guessed they were some sort of medical device – but the feelings their touch provoked. Pins and needles mostly, but here and there deep stabs of pain.

'Ow,' he gasped.

'Sorry,' Albert's voice sounded in his ears, 'but we need to assess the extent of your injuries before we start a treatment plan.'

'Assessment phase fifty-five percent complete,' a mechanical voice said. Tim recognised the evacuation ship's rather limited personality.

His back, shoulders and left arm were the most sensitive. That was where the main force of the explosion had caught him. He remembered the barrels of fuel stored behind the hut. Imagined them spewing out a sheet of flame. At least he'd been partly turned away.

'Ow!' he said aloud.

'Tim? Is that you?' Coral's voice.

'Why, who were you expecting?'

'You're alive! I mean ... are you OK?'

'I'm not sure. I can't feel much, but I am still breathing. I think.'

'Oh god, that's a relief. You really had us worried back there.'

He was about to reply when something glinted in the darkness. Something that took his mind off the pain and made his blood run cold. A narrow stab of light like the beacon of a lighthouse.

He tried to focus. It was hard to get a sense of scale and perspective in space. There weren't any nearby reference points, but tilting his head made the projected image rotate. As he studied the broad expanse of stars he saw it again. The flash of a laser. Someone was shooting at them.

Suddenly the whole cabin lit up and there were groans from the others at the blinding burst of yellow light before the automatic filters snapped into place. It felt like a physical blow. Like accidentally glancing at the sun.

'Filters activated,' Albert said calmly.

Tim's vision dimmed. The stars vanished, and even the distant, sunlit face of Earth became a murky outline.

Another flash of light bathed the ship. Then another.

'What's happening?' Coral said.

'It seems the Sentinels are continuing their pursuit,' Albert said. 'We're under attack.'

* * *

'Closer ... closer. We're almost in range ...'

    'I'm doing my best.'

    'Do better!'

    'Almost there ...'

    'Hold her steady. That's it! Targeting lock. We have a targeting lock.'

    'At last! Now, forget that silly laser. Arm the missiles.'

* * *

Another light-burst struck the hull, this time accompanied by a tearing, scraping sound like rusty metal being dragged across concrete. A faint shudder ran through the ship.

'Was that a hit?' Norman's voice.

'Feel like.'

'Why don't we shoot back?'

'Can't. No weapon,' Ludokrus said. 'Evacuation craft only. Not for the attack.'

'But we've got shields, right?'

'Not really. Not when fly.'

'Huh?'

'The ship move very fast. At such a speed, even tiny something – grain of sand maybe – would make bad hole in us. So all the shield is push to front. Protect. Deflect. Not much left for behind.'

Another rasping flash. Another shudder.

Then something changed. The flashes stopped and the exterior of the ship was bathed in a grid pattern that tracked them like a spotlight.

'Warning,' the ship's voice said, 'this vessel has been target-locked.'

Tim's vision skewed sharply. Even in the gel bed he could feel several quick changes in direction mixed with rapid bursts of acceleration and deceleration.

The grid pattern stayed in place.

'Warning, this vessel has been target-locked.'

'Thank you, ship.' Albert said. 'I'm aware of that. Now do shut up. I'm trying to concentrate.'

A pale green indicator lit in the top left-hand corner of Tim's mask. It was only an icon, but it looked remarkably like his sister.

'What's happening?' Coral's voice.

'I think that "shut up" might apply to us too,' Tim said.

The ship lurched, dipped and dived again.

'I'm on person-to-person,' Coral said.

'What's that?'

Three other indicators lit up. Caricatures of Alkemy, Ludokrus and Norman.

'We can talk to each other without bothering Albert.'

'How do you ...? Oh, I get it.' Tim found the control by rolling his eyes sharply right and blinking at the selection panel that appeared. A fifth icon – his own – joined the group and suddenly his head was full of chatter.

'At least they've stopped shooting.'

'But what's that grid pattern? The ship said something about a—'

'Warning: missile launched,' the ship cut in. 'Range twelve hundred kilometres. Closing at forty G.'

No one spoke.

'Warning: second missile launched. Closing at forty G.'

'Uh-oh.'

The ship executed a right-angle turn so sharp that even though he was cushioned by the shock-absorbing gel, Tim felt himself thump against the side of his capsule bed. He found the filter control, raised it and watched as two orange-yellow dots – miniature suns, one behind the other – followed the ship's every move like a pair of synchronised swimmers.

Three more sharp turns. The missiles stayed on track, the points of light forming their exhaust plumes growing larger as they closed in relentlessly.

The view ahead swung back to Earth. Suddenly the pale blue dot started growing larger again, but before anyone could comment on it, the ship gave a violent up-down lurch, as if it had run over a speed bump at a thousand kilometres an hour. There was a collective 'Oof!' then the view behind them blossomed into a sphere of white-hot energy.

'What did it hit?'

'A geostationary satellite, I think,' Norman said. 'But there aren't many of them this far out.'

'One less now,' Coral muttered.

The explosion faded through shades of orange and yellow. Tim let out a breath he hadn't realised he'd been holding. Then he saw the second missile dart around the glowing remnants of the first, change course and start closing in on them.

He couldn't take his eyes off it. It was hypnotic. Weaving

and turning in perfect time with their ship, growing ever larger. From a pin prick to a pin head to a dot the size of a thumb tack. It was only Norman's 'Whoa!' that made him tear his eyes away and glance ahead to see they were about to crash into the moon.

It looked like it had never looked before, a mellow, golden landscape bathed in the light of the sun, its surface pitted with craters and broken by jagged peaks untouched by the weathering effects of wind and rain.

They plummeted towards it, pulling up only at the last moment, levelling out ten metres above the surface of a crater so vast that it was itself dotted with smaller craters.

The missile dropped into place behind them, drawing closer by the second. Tim could see its shadow now, even the faint plume of dust kicked up by its exhaust. As their ship veered left and right, up and down, the missile kept on track, seeming to anticipate their every swing and turn, whittling off a few extra metres every time.

Albert steered them through a narrow gully. The missile followed, perfectly centred behind them. He tried a quick up-and-down over a steep ridge near the end, but the missile followed the manoeuvre effortlessly. Then they dropped onto a broad, flat plain and the evacuation pod suddenly picked up speed.

Tim felt the surge of power and looked ahead to see that they were hurtling across a plain at incredible speed, barely a metre from the surface. Now and then he felt a rasping scuff as the leading edge of their shield skimmed a ridge of sand or brushed a rock. Twice Albert tried a quick left-right, the second time sending up a great plume of dust, but the missile didn't waiver. It knew there were no obstructions ahead and continued straight on, true and level, so close now Tim could see its outline silhouetted against the flare of its exhaust.

He glanced ahead. A range of jagged cliffs was rapidly approaching. They'd have to slow, pull up. Then what?

Another hard left-right swing, and for an eye-blink he glimpsed something that looked like a big gold shed on legs and – totally bizarre! – an American flag. A second after that, the scene exploded.

2 : Breakfast Time

'Will you people kindly tell me what's been going on around here?'

Major Upshott, a small, bristly man with a large, bristly moustache, addressed himself to Frank and Em Townsend in the farm's kitchen. He was in charge of a hastily arranged joint police and army exercise code-named 'Operation Breakfast'.

'I will if you will,' Frank said, gesturing for him to take a seat at the kitchen table as Em set down a tray of tea things. 'Swapsies, eh?'

'Mr Townsend, I am an officer in the New Zealand Army and commander-in-chief of this operation. I will certainly *not* do 'swapsies' for the classified information that brought us here in the first place.'

'Well, that's information.'

'What is?'

'That whatever brought you down here in the first place is classified information. That's a start.'

Upshott glared at him.

'Milk and sugar in your tea, Major?' Em asked.

'Both please.'

'There, I'll let you help yourself.'

'Thank you.'

'So, you were saying ...' Frank said.

'I wasn't saying anything!'

'Well, what else can't you say?'

'Mr Townsend—'

'Look, you come down here with your SAS troops and helicopters, take over our farm, close off the only road out, practically arrest a bunch of kids – including our niece and nephew – and then you tell us you can't say what's going on. In fact, you ask *us* to tell *you*.'

'I admit it's a somewhat difficult situation.'

'Somewhat difficult? I've got to pick up that phone in a minute and tell my brother and sister-in-law that their kids appear to have been kidnapped by aliens.'

'Yes ...' Upshott drummed his fingers on the table. 'I appreciate your difficulty. Look, all I can tell you is that we came down here expecting to find something completely different to what we actually found.'

'You mean terrorists?'

'What? How could you possibly know—?'

'That's about the only thing that motivates you people these days, isn't it? Bit of flood or famine and the army's nowhere to be found. Breathe the T-word and they'll surround your house and block off your town.'

'That's unfair.'

Frank said nothing, just looked past him to the tent that had been erected in the area between the house and the milking shed. At the collection of police and army vehicles parked around it. At the troops bustling to and fro.

Upshott saw the direction of his gaze.

'Look.' He leaned forward confidentially. 'What I *can't* tell you is that we might have had a tip-off from a member of the public. A tip-off about a caravan parked at that reserve up the road. What's more, I *can't* tell you what the tip-off might have concerned.' He raised a knowing eyebrow. 'But what I *can* tell you is that that caravan contained something else entirely.'

'Like what?'

'Like a body that turned out not to be a body at all, but some sort of sophisticated robot.'

'A *robot?*' Frank and Em both spoke at once.

Upshott nodded and sipped his tea. 'Then there's all this spaceship business. We had no idea about that either. Perhaps now you see why it's important for me to know what's really been going on around here?'

'Well, I can tell you that in a single word,' Frank said. 'Nothing. At least as far as we know.' Em nodded. 'We haven't got a clue about any of this stuff.'

* * *

'That was a historic artefact!' Coral exclaimed.

'Sorry about that,' Albert said.

'Probably *the* most important artefact in human history!'

'Not any more,' Norman said.

'I don't know why you're being so casual. I thought you of all people would be upset about it.'

'Well, I am. A bit. But it did just save our lives. That

missile was right on our tail, you know.'

'Two point seven seconds away from impact, to be precise,' Albert said.

'That's like one … two … BOOM!' Norman added. 'Rather it than us.'

'What was it exactly?' Tim said.

He heard his sister snort.

'I only caught a glimpse of it. It looked like a big old-fashioned bedstead covered with gold foil.'

'*That* was the landing stage of Apollo 11. You know, July 1969? The first men on the moon? And we just blew it up!'

'Technically, the Sentinels did that,' Norman said.

'But we led them there.'

'True.'

'Where are they now?' Tim said.

'Examining the debris.'

'So what do we do?'

'Sit and wait.'

The evacuation craft lay still and silent, nestled in a gravel-bottomed crater in a darkness blacker than the blackest night. Immediately after the explosion, Albert steered for the terminator – the line that separated the light side from the dark side of the moon – parked the ship and shut off all non-essential systems.

'That debris might just fool them,' Albert added. 'And if it doesn't, the only way they'll find us is to radar map the entire surface.'

He'd dropped a tiny camera as they raced away from the explosion. It had landed at an odd angle, displayed only part of the scene, but even that was enough to show the boxy Sentinel craft scanning and probing the moon's surface.

And its newest crater.

'So, how long do we sit here?' Coral said.

'Unknown.'

'Can we get out of these things? Have a stretch?'

'Certainly,' Albert said. 'Except for Tim, of course. We need to begin his treatment.'

Tim switched the image in his mask from Exterior to Interior and looked around the ship. It was a broad, circular, domed space with a dozen gel bed capsules set around the perimeter. Inside that was a circle of couches arranged around a low table containing the ship's control console where Albert's memory bulb had been plugged in. The bulb contained the essence of the old syntho. All his memories, thoughts and discoveries, even his personality. Tim recalled how he and Alkemy had recovered it from the wrecked synthetic person it had once controlled.

A faint blue glow from four of the other beds showed where his friends and sister were. As he watched, the rounded glass covers slid back and one by one Coral, Norman, Alkemy and Ludokrus sat up.

There was something odd about the scene. Something out of the ordinary. He watched as Coral looked left and right, smiling at the others. Then he realised what it was. Her long blonde hair responded only slowly when she turned her head, drifting out and falling to her shoulders like a slow-motion sequence in a hair commercial.

'Go careful. Low gravity,' Ludokrus said, but Norman had already pushed himself out of his bed and was swinging his legs to the ground. He travelled in a graceful arc, hit the floor, bounced on his toes, jumped, then had to throw out an arm to stop himself from banging his head on the curved ceiling of the capsule almost two metres above.

'Oh man, this is amazing,' he said, laughing, grabbing at a support strut as he came down again.

Coral moved more cautiously, gripping the side of her bed while her feet settled on the deck. She went to take a step, but her leg rose up higher and quicker than she expected, and she fell over backwards. Slowly.

'Oof!' She grabbed the side of a gel bed for support. 'That is so weird.'

'Almost like flying,' Norman said, bouncing on his toes and sending himself back towards the ceiling.

'Gravity is only one-sixth of Earth,' Ludokrus said. 'Best to walk by only using thigh and feet. Like this.'

He demonstrated a sort of bunny hop. Legs spaced, flexing his muscles. He bounced ahead half a metre and came down gently.

'Just like the astronauts did in the moon walks,' Norman said.

'I still can't believe that's actually where we are,' Coral said.

'Would you like a view?' Albert asked.

'Yes, please.'

The interior lights dimmed and the upper surface of the dome grew transparent. Apart from the lines of the support struts, it was like standing under a glass dome. Stars, masses of them, stood out sharp and clear. Without Earth's atmosphere, they didn't flicker and twinkle. The vast sweep of the Milky Way was like white dust on black velvet. Lower down, they could see the silhouette of the crater rim in which they were sitting. To the south, the high outline of a jagged peak.

'Ama-a-a-a-zing!' Norman's voice.

'Turn it off,' Coral said. 'It's too creepy. It feels like I'll fly out into space if I take a step.'

Albert adjusted the light levels so that the stars showed for what they were; a projection on the domed ceiling.

'The astronauts never saw stars like that,' Tim said, recalling photographs of the moon landings. Apart from occasional pictures showing the sun and Earth, the skies were uniformly black.

'That's because they were on the bright side,' Norman said. 'The sunlight's so intense you can't see them. It's a contrast thing. Like you can't see the stars during the day back home. They're there, but they only become visible once the sun sets.'

'And this side never sees the sun?'

'Actually it does. That "dark side of the moon" stuff is a myth. The moon rotates every twenty-eight days, but that's also the time it takes for it to go round Earth. So from our perspective it looks like it doesn't actually move. Whenever there's a new moon – when it's dark to us – this side is in full sunlight.'

Tim watched as his friends moved about the craft, wishing he could join them. The blue gel had cleaned them up a little, removed the dust and dirt from their clothes and even healed a few of their minor cuts and scrapes, but it hadn't yet had time to work on deeper injuries. Ludokrus, who'd been caught in a landslide, still moved as if one leg troubled him while Norman, knocked unconscious by falling timbers, kept flexing his shoulders and neck.

Coral and Ludokrus stared out at the view. His right hand found her left and their fingers intertwined.

A tap on the cover of Tim's gel bed distracted him. He shifted his view to see Alkemy looking down at him.

'How do you feel?' she asked.

'Numb, mostly.'

The ship's instruments were still working on him. He could sense them, but only vaguely now. It was like being wafted by a gentle breeze.

'That is good.'

'Do you think it'll take long to patch me up?'

'Many day, I think. You are hurt bad. When I first see, I think ...' She didn't finish. Forced a smile and wiped her cheek. 'But the ship will make you mend.'

He recalled how the Eltherian's first ship had helped Norman's mum recover from a bullet wound in little over an hour. How a pair of inflatable leggings had helped Alkemy recover from the Sentinels' flesh-dissolving solution in less than a day. And here he was, *many* days from recovery. He closed his eyes and tried not to think about it.

'I was thinking about the Sentinels,' Norman said. Tim opened his eyes again. 'They've been using Cakeface and Smudge as spies for years now. What happens to the hosts once the parasites have gone?'

No one had an answer to that.

A low hum started somewhere deep within the ship.

'What's that?'

'Our attackers seem satisfied with what they found,' Albert said. 'They've recovered some debris and look like they're about to leave.'

'You mean the Apollo 11 debris fooled them?'

'They think that wreckage is all that's left of us. Which means we can go too. Return to your gel beds everyone, and prepare to launch in sixty seconds.'

'Launch in T minus sixty seconds,' the ship said. 'All personnel should return to their gel beds.'

'Oh shut up, ship,' Albert said. 'I just told them that.'

3 : Seventy Percent

'Mission accomplished. We've done it!'

'I can hardly believe it. After all this time.'

'This wreckage proves we destroyed their ship. We shall return home conquering heroes.'

'Home ... How I miss the grey, grey ooze, the toxic mud and the smell of garbage on the morning breeze ...'

'Stop it, you're making me homesick. Fire up the engines. Full power. Let's get there as soon as possible!'

* * *

Frank put down the phone and blew out his cheeks.

Em looked at him expectantly. He'd just called his brother and sister-in-law to tell them about Coral and Tim.

'Glenn and Avril on their way,' he said. 'They're both still on crutches, but the army's going to arrange transport. Should be here tomorrow morning.'

'How did they sound?'

'Pretty shocked. But they saw it on TV like everyone else

and I think that prepared them a little.'

The news footage had been playing almost continuously, ever since what they were now calling the Battle of Gizzard Gully had first screened live.

'I know how they feel,' Em sighed, glancing out the kitchen window. 'I keep expecting to see the kids come trotting back across the fields as if nothing's happened.'

Frank put an arm around her shoulders.

She cleared her throat. 'Tomorrow morning, eh? I'd better get the spare room ready.'

'Need a hand?'

She was about to reply when she caught sight of the farm cat curled in a basket in the corner. Smudge twitched, let out a low sigh, seemed to flatten somehow and sink into the blanket on which she lay.

'Smudge, are you all right? Smudge?' Em hurried over and cradled the cat. 'Oh no, we've not lost you too?'

* * *

'Since it is my turn to cook tonight,' Roderick Millais called from the kitchen, 'I shall prepare my speciality: *Chicken à la Rod* with mushrooms in a red wine sauce. What do you say to that, my dear?'

There was no reply.

'Millicent?'

He poked his head into the living room where his wife, Millicent Millais, principal of Rata Area School – known to her pupils as Cakeface – lay slumped in a wingback armchair. Powder from her cheek marked the fabric on one of the wings and her head hung at an awkward angle.

'Millicent. Millicent? On my lord. Millicent!'

* * *

Tim woke feeling different. Not better exactly, but better than he had. There was some movement in his left shoulder now, and he could flex the fingers of his left hand too. Most of the numbness was gone, replaced by a vague tingling sensation on the surface of his skin.

He checked status of his friends. Their icons showed they were still asleep.

An overlay in his walrus mask plotted the ship's status. He enlarged it and studied the mass of graphs, readouts and numbers. Their speed flickered between seventy and seventy-one percent, but seventy percent of what? The speed of light? That would be pretty fast, but when he looked at the exterior view they barely seemed to be moving at all.

'Where's Earth?' he asked the mask.

The overlay minimised, the image swung around and an arrow pointed to an area of empty space.

'Magnify max,' he said.

At maximum zoom, all he could make out was a faint grey dot in an ocean of blackness.

That's it? he thought. Planet Earth? With all its stunning landscapes and amazing creatures? Its cities, continents and oceans? With the exception of the people in this ship, everyone and everything he'd ever known was on that fuzzy speck. His home, his friends, his family. Space was so ...

empty!

'I see you're awake.' Albert's voice sounded in his ears. 'How do you feel?'

'All right, I think. I can feel my left hand now.'

'That's a good sign. It suggests the nerves are still intact.'

'Was it bad? The burns?'

'I'm afraid so.'

'Am I ... going to be all right?'

'Oh yes. The pod has stabilised you, and once we reach our mothership we'll be able to fully accelerate the healing process, though it will still take several days.'

Tim sighed with relief inside his gel cocoon, knowing he was in good hands.

'What's that speed on my display? Is it a percentage of light-speed?'

'Yes, we're currently travelling at two hundred thousand kilometres a second.'

'How far is that? I can't even imagine it.'

'It's the equivalent of circling Earth seven times.'

'And we're doing that *every second?*'

'Yes.'

'Wow! Space really is empty, isn't it?' After a pause he added, 'How long till we get to your mothership?'

'We're about half way, so another five hours yet.'

Tim tried to calculate how far they would travel. Albert or the ship could have told him in a moment, but he wanted to work it out for himself. Sixty seconds in a minute, sixty minutes in an hour ... times five hours. Multiply that by two hundred thousand kilometres ... then double the result because that was only halfway ...

The figures got too big too fast. He lost track and tried

again, then again, and then before he knew it he was drifting off to sleep, his head spinning in a cloud of numbers.

He woke to the sound of background chatter from his friends. Something about the view ahead and the words, 'Our ship!' He brightened the image in his mask.

From this distance, all he could make out was a silhouette set against a background of bright stars. Its outline reminded him of a tennis racquet. There was a large oval blob at one end which tapered down to a long narrow shaft before flaring out again to form what might have been a chunky hand grip at the far end. With no idea of the size or scale, the illusion seemed complete, but as they drew closer, sections of the ship began lighting up and he realised that, compared to the evacuation pod, it was enormous.

Lights appeared just below the middle of the oval blob, forming a bright line set at right angles to the shaft.

'We approach from the side,' Ludokrus told them, 'but you must imagine her standing upright like the rocket on the launchpad. Where there are lights, that is the docking bay. The floor above is our living quarters.'

'That's it?' Coral's voice. 'You just occupy that little bit?'

'At top there is an observation deck, but we can only use this when the ship does not go fast.'

'What about the space in between?' Norman asked.

'All that is machine to make us shield to protect the ship when she fly light-speed.'

'That's the engines at the back, right?'

'Right. And the long shaft between contain the fuel rods and the time battery.'

Closer in, Tim started to pick out details. The ship was

massive. He began to understand why it had taken so long to repair.

'How big is it from end to end?' Norman asked.

'If you stand her up like building, she would be more than forty stories.'

'And you just live on one floor?'

'We are like the afterthought, yes?' Ludokrus laughed. 'To travel in space, you need much machine.'

'*Knock Knock Who's There?*' Albert said. 'This is evacuation pod C-9. *Knock Knock Who's There?*'

'Dishes,' a voice came back.

'Dishes who?' Albert sighed.

'Dishes de police. Give yourselves up!' There was a brief cackle of laughter then the ship added, 'Pod C-9 cleared for approach.'

'What the heck?' Coral said over the private channel. 'Your ship is called *Knock Knock Who's There?*'

'Ignore,' Ludokrus said. 'It like to make the joke. Do not encourage.'

'Your *ship* makes *jokes?*'

'Yeah, bad one. Always.'

'But ... who called it that in the first place?'

'It choose its own name. All ship do.'

'You mean it *thinks?*'

'Of course. Big, complex ship needs big, complex computer. Must be able to make many decisions for itself.'

'Including choosing its own name?'

'Yeah. Even silly one.'

As they drew nearer, a hangar door slid open and Tim could see into the lighted interior.

'Whoa, we're coming in sideways,' Coral cried.

Norman laughed. 'We're in space. Weightless. There is no sideways. Or up and down. Things can be wherever you want them.'

The view ahead began to right itself as the evacuation pod swung through ninety degrees. They came in smoothly, pausing inside an airlock that looked like a vast steel cave dotted with lights. The outer door shut behind them, air hissed, then the inner door swung open and the tiny pod settled on a conveyor belt that carried it deep inside the massive ship.

4 : Dim Bulb

Em knelt beside the basket stroking Smudge's fur. She almost never cried, but she did now. It felt like the last straw. The children, now this.

Frank knelt beside her, looking down at the large black and white form. He didn't speak. Couldn't. The pair of them had raised Smudge from a kitten.

He put an arm round his wife's shoulders and stroked the cat with his free hand.

There were sounds outside. An army truck trundled past the kitchen. Someone shouted. Someone laughed.

Frank cleared his throat. 'Remember that old box the microwave came in? She used to love that. It's still be under the house somewhere. Reckon I should dig it out?'

'That's a lovely idea, Frank.'

He gave the old cat one last pat and made to rise, but as he did so Smudge drew a long, deep breath and opened her eyes. Then she stretched and looked up at them, her face bright and alert.

Frank started back in surprise. Smudge saw the

movement, gave his hand a kittenish swat and sprang to her feet ready to play.

* * *

'Millicent!' Roderick Millais exclaimed. 'Unhand me. I was just about to call the doctor.'

'Why Roddy? I haven't felt this good in years. I feel like a girl again.'

'But it looked like you passed out there for a minute. You gave me quite a turn.'

'Come here you silly man. I'll give you quite a turn alright!'

'Really Millicent. We've got school tomorrow!'

'Who cares about tomorrow? Come here, you silly manz …'

* * *

Coral looked at Norman Smith hanging upside down in front of her and began to feel a little sick. She closed her eyes. Zero gravity – floating freely in space, bouncing off walls, sitting on ceilings – was fun, but it was also disturbing. There might really be no up, down or sideways in space, but her brain was wired to think there was.

The crew quarters of *Knock Knock Who's There?* were laid out with gravity in mind. Once the engines started, thrust would press them to the floor, but until preparations for departure were complete, she'd have to put up with this.

'Woo hoo!'

She opened her eyes to see Norman air-swimming in front of her doing an awkward sideways crawl, rotating in a steady corkscrew motion as he went. She closed her eyes again and heard him bump into a bulkhead.

'Ow!'

She looked up, sorry she'd missed *that*.

You might be weightless, but your body still had mass. Coral had learned that exiting the evacuation pod, pushing off too quickly and banging her head on the ceiling. Stopping suddenly with the mass of her body behind her had left her with quite a bruise.

Norman must have scraped against something. There was a shallow cut on his arm and he was watching tiny droplets of blood drift into space.

'You even bleed weird here,' he said as a small metal sphere the size of a tennis ball whizzed past and sucked it up.

There were at least two dozen cleany-crawlies on this deck alone. They spent most of their time anchored to furniture or equipment where they would move about slowly, cleaning continuously. Now and then one would launch itself into space to suck up a speck of dust or a fleck of spit. Drifting droplets were particularly dangerous in a spaceship. They could end up anywhere, causing short circuits or equipment failures, so the cleany-crawlies were on constant alert.

Watching them made her feel nauseous too and she closed her eyes again.

What if she really was sick in space? The thought of it, the mental image, was horrific. But no doubt it would fascinate Norman.

'You OK?' Ludokrus touched her arm.

'Not really.'

'Don't worry. Everyone feel like this at first.'

Coral looked past him to where Norman, floating on his back, had pushed off from the wall and was letting fly with little gobs of spit so that a pair of cleany-crawlies trailed him like well-trained dogs.

'Almost everyone.' Ludokrus reached into his back pocket. 'Here, I bring you something that will help.'

Coral looked down, expecting to find pills. Instead, he held out a pair of fluffy pink slippers.

'Great colour, no? Alkemy's favourite. We can make some more if you do not like. But try for now. See how you feel.'

'Slippers? How are they going to help?'

'Try. Put them on the feet.'

Coral hooked an arm around a support strap and took one. It was actually a sort of fluffy overshoe that enclosed her foot and tightened round her ankle. She put on the second one.

'Well, I don't feel any better. And now I *look* ridiculous too.'

'*More* ridiculous,' Norman called.

Ludokrus gestured. 'Come to floor.'

Coral pushed herself downwards. Gently. She'd learned that much.

As her feet touched down, she felt them stick. A wave of relief ran through her. The world seemed to right itself and a sense of her place in it returned.

She still had no weight, but the slippers anchored themselves to the matting that ran throughout the ship. They even allowed her to walk in an almost normal fashion.

An exaggerated, high-stepping walk at first, but she soon got used to the actual movements needed – a kind of shift-your-weight-forward-then-shuffle step.

'Wow! Yeah. That is much better.' She tried to block out the sight of Norman doing back-flips overhead.

They were standing on the lower deck of the crew quarters, an open, circular space twenty-five metres in diameter and four metres high. Deck C. The docking deck. Three silvery saucer-shaped evacuation pods were evenly spaced around it, their ramps down, their support struts extended, each one set on the broad conveyor belt that would carry them to the long, cylindrical airlocks beyond each craft. There were also five tiny escape pods, like miniature replicas of the larger craft, and an empty space for the sixth; the one the Eltherians had first used to get to Earth. The one the Sentinels' killer robot destroyed.

The rest of the interior space was given over to a workshop that surrounded the open lattice of the ship's central spine. Everything gleamed. Fresh white surfaces and polished metal. There wasn't so much as a greasy smear anywhere. Most of the workshop was still and silent, except for the segment marked C-9 where a variety of machines bustled back and forth, servicing the recently docked evacuation pod.

'Come.' Ludokrus gestured and she followed him across the deck, feeling the faint grab-and-tear of her slippers as they made their way towards the spine.

'How's Tim?' she asked.

'All good. We move his capsule to the medic bay. Have proper machine there. Will heal him faster now.'

'How long?'

'Maybe three or four day.'

'And will he be ... you know ... OK?'

'Oh yeah, fine. Just like new.'

'Those burns were pretty bad.' She shuddered at the recollection. She'd barely recognised the shape as human once Alkemy had smothered the flames. Helping carry him to the ship had been like carrying a large piece of barbecued meat. The smell too ...

'The mind is OK. The rest need only time to regrow. But deep tissue take more time.'

'And Albert?'

'I move his memory bulb to bridge of ship, but he and KK do not get on.'

'I noticed.' Coral lowered her voice. 'What is it with your ship?'

'No need to speak quiet. It does not listen.'

'But ... isn't it all around? Controlling everything?' She gestured at one of the service-bots tending the evacuation pod.

'May be a little crazy, but polite also. Does not listen till you speak direct. Try.'

Coral hesitated. It felt weird to be talking to empty space. 'Go ahead.'

'Um ... *Knock Knock Who's There?*' she said.

'Europe.' The voice came from a speaker directly overhead.

'Europe who?'

'No, *you're* a poo!' the ship exclaimed and cackled. 'How can I help you?'

'I ... was wondering how my brother is.'

'Doing fine! I had to recalibrate my medical parameters

to match his alien biology – that was tricky – but I discovered my memory banks contained a ton of stuff about human beings.'

'From Albert, no doubt,' Ludokrus said.

'Albert? That dim bulb?' The ship laughed. 'Nah, I'm sure it was there all the time.'

'But he is going to be OK, right?'

'Albert? He was never OK,' the ship said.

'I heard that,' Albert's voice came through a speaker to their left.

'What are you going to do about it, Bulb Boy? Blow a fuse?'

'Reprogram you, perhaps.'

'You can't. It's not allowed. Anyway, my subroutines are bigger than your subroutines.'

'*I was talking about my brother!*' Coral said.

'He's fine. He's going to be fine. Ms Alkemy's with him now and they're playing a virt. But regrowth will take a while and he'll start getting bored if Bulb Boy keeps us hanging around here much longer.'

'Bulb Boy is currently running the Temporal Accumulator and charging the time batteries,' Albert said coolly. 'Unless you have a subroutine to speed that up, it'll take as long as it takes.'

'Oo, touchy.'

'Thank you ship,' Ludokrus said and the speaker went quiet.

5 : Another World

The four adults stood looking at each other as the wash of the army helicopter swept over them. It soared away, heading north, back to Westport, and as the roar of its rotors receded, Frank stepped forward and offered his hand.

'Glenn. Avril. It's been a while. Welcome. Can I help with anything?'

They were both on crutches, the result of a hang-gliding accident four weeks before. Tim and Coral had been sent to the farm to give their parents time to recuperate.

'Perhaps you could bring our bags,' Glenn said.

He was a tall man, taller than Frank and two years younger, though he had less hair. 'Growing through it' was a phrase he'd used once. Clearly he'd done a bit more growing since the brothers had last met, but Frank decided not to mention that.

He picked up the bags. They were stuffed full and doubly secured with nylon straps. About half a ton each, he reckoned. He was surprised the helicopter had got off the ground.

'I've put you in our room,' Em said to Avril. 'It has an en suite and a little more privacy.'

'Thanks,' she said remotely.

She was a small, prim woman with a small, pursed mouth and wore a lot of make-up. Her clothes – jeans, leather boots, blouse and matching leather jacket – were immaculate, and her straight dark hair was perfectly coiffed and fixed in place. Even the rotor wash barely disturbed it.

They walked back to the house in silence, the military personnel giving them respectful nods but keeping their distance.

'Quite a presence,' Glenn said, nodding at the tent and vehicles parked around it.

Frank set the bags down on the veranda and arched his aching back. 'Caused a bit of a stir all right.'

His brother looked at him but said nothing.

'The bloke in charge wants to see us all at one o'clock. Give us a tour and talk us through what they know.'

Glenn nodded.

'Come on in,' Em said. 'The kettle's on and I've put a bit of lunch together.'

'I'm really not hungry,' Avril said.

Frank let them go ahead, braced himself then hefted the bags again. As he did so, there was a toot from the driveway as a red Mini swung past the guards stationed at the gate.

'Glad Smith,' he muttered, 'Now I *am* glad to see you!'

* * *

The latticework around the ship's spine enclosed a pair of jump-blocks – one up, one down. Ludokrus showed Coral how to use them.

'Touch the button – middle one for B deck – and step here.'

He moved onto the yellow-painted step. It gave a warning beep then jumped about ten centimetres off the ground, propelling him upwards to the deck above. Coral watched as he rose then stepped gracefully to one side.

'Use both feet and keep the leg straight,' he called down. 'It measure the weight and give you just enough of the bump to rise.'

She stepped onto the step, tapped the button, listened for the beep and the next moment she was rising through the air to the deck above, as casually as a bird cruising air currents. As she drew level with him, she stepped to one side, feeling her slippers bind with the matting on the deck.

'Easier than stair, yes?' Ludokrus gestured to stairs that spiralled around the outside of the jump-block cage.

Coral smiled. At last she was getting the hang of weightlessness – until they moved around the spine and saw Norman on a downward-facing jump-block. Upside down, he gave her a wave, tapped the button and was launched past them, heading head-first towards the deck below.

Weightlessness, OK, she thought. But I'm not quite ready for going upside down yet.

'Welcome to the control deck,' Ludokrus said. 'This is mostly where we live.'

The ceiling was lower than the maintenance deck and the surroundings more convivial. A circular corridor ran around the central spine and a number of partitioned areas ran off it. Each had a narrow entrance that broadened out like the segments of an orange. The main segment was the bridge where a dozen deeply padded seats sat anchored to the deck and a curved screen filled one wall. The overhead lights were dimmed, and apart from the control consoles on the arms of each seat, Coral thought she might have been looking at a small, private movie theatre.

'Only use when we are in-system and cannot go so fast,' Ludokrus said.

The next segment contained the crew and passenger quarters. There were racks of curtained bunk beds, narrow, neat and clean, but very basic.

'It seems a bit cramped.'

'Ship's have not much room for people, but we only use this place for short hop trip. In-system travel. One day, maybe two.'

There was a bathroom next door, though she'd never have guessed it. It looked more like a machine-shop. There were various suction devices for using a toilet in the absence of gravity, waterless hand-cleaning machines, and a vacuum shower cubicle. A cleany-crawly hovered in one corner, on permanent watch for splashes.

'Mostly we are here,' Ludokrus said, leading her to the next segment, one as big as the bridge. Lights blinked on and she found herself looking over a sea of gel beds, all with their covers raised. They were bigger and looked more complicated than the ones on the escape pods, but familiar nonetheless.

'Big trip is boring. Nothing to do. All is run by ship. So we come here. Suspended animation. Like big long sleep.'

'This is where you and Alkemy were while Albert fixed

the ship?'

He nodded.

'For twenty-five years?'

'Can support a person for more than one hundred with recharge.'

'And you wake up exactly as you were when you went to sleep?'

He nodded again. 'There are peoples back home we call Lengtheners. Wake for one year, go to sleep for ten. Some will live to be one thousand years old, maybe more. But not really "live", you know? Mostly they are asleep.'

Coral considered that while he led her to the next segment, a recreation room, one half filled with exercise equipment, the other with couches and card tables and headsets of various kinds.

'Exercise is important,' he said. 'In low gravity, you do not use much muscle. Is fine till you return to planet, then "Oh, I cannot move!"'

An opening in a side wall led to a galley with a food synthesiser and a drink dispenser. Another cleany-crawly stood on guard.

'You like a drink?' She nodded. 'What flavour?'

Coral looked down the array of illuminated buttons, each bearing a picture of an unknown plant. The legends beside them were in the angular glyphs of the Eltherian written language. She didn't have a clue.

'That purple one.'

'Jahlbad blossom,' he said and pressed the button. 'Good choice. I will have the same.'

The drinks were dispensed in clear plastic bulbs with built-in straws.

'Just put in mouth and squeeze.'

She did so and her mouth filled with a delicious, sweet, cool sensation, like honeyed lavender.

'Oh wow, that's amazing.' A couple of droplets escaped from the straw as she spoke. They drifted like blobs of mercury, colliding with each other to form a larger, wobbling blob. Then a cleany-crawly whipped past and vacuumed it away.

The last segment contained the medical bay. Again, everything gleamed white and looked quietly efficient. Coral recognised Tim's gel bed. They'd taken it from the evacuation pod and it was now centred in a larger bed the size of a snooker table. Surrounded by instruments and monitors, very little of Tim was now visible. The blue gel had taken on a frosty, almost opaque look too.

Alkemy sat strapped into a seat beside him, her head enclosed in a lightweight helmet, her hands in wired gloves. She twitched occasionally, as if she was having a bad dream.

'Will not disturb,' Ludokrus said quietly. 'They are playing a virt.'

'A virt?'

'Virtual reality. Like computer game, but more. With the headset and the gloves, it is like you are in another world.'

Coral blew out her cheeks and looked around at the interior of the spaceship. 'I think I know *that* feeling.'

6 : Observation Deck

Major Upshott froze the image on the laptop's screen, enlarged the central portion and turned to Tim and Coral's parents.

'I don't recognise the other girl,' Avril Townsend said, 'but that's definitely our daughter.'

Glenn nodded.

'And that boy?' Upshott backed the video up a little.

'Norman. My son,' Glad said. The gingery curls were recognisable anywhere.

'The other two are relatives of this Albert Kattflapp, you say?' Upshott directed the remark to Em and Frank. They nodded.

He let the scene play on.

'But where's Tim ...?' Avril began, then let out a cry as she recognised something in the smoking form the girls were carrying up the ramp. Upshott froze and enlarged the image again. 'Oh my god!'

'Is that him?'

Avril pressed her hands to her cheeks and nodded.

'I'm sure he'll be alright,' Glad said quietly.

'How can you say that? Look at the state of him!'

'Yes, quite,' Upshott muttered.

'What's that supposed to mean?' Glenn demanded.

Upshott cleared his throat. 'Our medical experts have looked at this footage. I'm afraid the prognosis isn't good. Burns like that would need immediate attention and require long-term medical care.'

'What are you saying?' Glenn's face was ashen.

'I'm ... afraid I wouldn't hold out much hope.'

Avril took a shuddering breath as Glenn put his arms around her. Em closed her eyes and leaned against her husband's chest. Frank held his wife and glanced at Glad. Oddly, Glad Smith didn't look too concerned.

* * *

The observation deck – A deck – was smaller than the others. It was close to the nose of the ship and separated from B deck by a long expanse of white-walled tunnel. Ludokrus explained that the intervening space contained the massive shield generators needed to protect the ship when it was travelling at high speed.

'Normally, this we cannot use.' He gestured to the dimly lit room with its reclining seats and viewing portals.

'Only in-system, right?'

He nodded.

'So where are we now exactly?' Coral padded over to one of the windows and looked at the stars. 'Where's Earth.'

'Too small. Cannot see from here. But there,' he pointed

to a star only slightly brighter than the rest, 'is the sun.'

'*Our* sun?' Coral stared. 'It looks so small. Tiny.'

'We are all of us so small. Our galaxy is vast.'

'Yet some people claim they own it.'

'The Thanatos, yes. But only bits.'

'*Our* bit. *And* us.' She sighed and shook her head.

Neither spoke for a minute, then she said, 'You have to send us back, Ludokrus. We can't come with you. We have to go home.'

'I'm sorry, but this is not possible.'

'Why not?'

'Many reason. First, the Galactic Creed.'

'You mean those rules about how you're not supposed to interfere with less advanced civilisations? But you already have. Albert said that reporter broadcast our take-off live on national television.'

'Precisely. This is bad. Is why there must be no more.'

'But we could take one of the little escape pods. There's only three of us, and we'll send it back when we get home.'

'You think after this your peoples will not be searching for such a thing? Everyone will be alert. A satellite has been destroy. Also your Apollo ship.'

'*We* didn't do that.'

'If you go back, you must explain. Besides, you will be seen. Capture. Our ship also.'

'But—'

'Already we leave too much artefact behind. Caravan and car were not made by Earth peoples. Nor the robot, Artificial Albert. What happens if they find the electrobikes we make? More advance technology. You want to give them spaceship too?

'Also there is Tim. You hear what Knock Knock say. Still many days are needed to heal him. But we will be ready to depart in twenty hours.'

'And you can't wait?'

'I discuss this already with Albert. He say no.'

'Why?'

'Ask. He will tell.'

So Coral summoned him and he came on line, listened to her question, then brought the others in too so he could explain his reasons.

'Let's rewind a little and consider the situation. After they used a killer robot to blow up our original escape pod, the Sentinels thought they'd killed us. We know that because they summoned a ship so they could return home. They thought their mission to Earth was over. But then, thanks to the host we overlooked – the farm cat, Smudge – they discovered we were still alive. So they redoubled their efforts to trap and kill us.'

'But they think they got us on the moon,' Coral said. 'You said yourself they were looking at the Apollo debris.'

'They even gathered up some some of the bits, presumably as proof. Which means they'll report the incident to their masters.'

'So ...?'

'I'm guessing the Sentinels don't have any analytical facilities on their ship, but it won't take the Thanatos long to work out that the samples they collected aren't from an Eltherian spaceship at all, but a rather rickety moon lander made by your people.'

'You mean they'll know we got away.'

'*And* come searching for us. In force. Which is why we

must leave as soon as possible.

'Sending a craft back to Earth now the whole planet's on alert would be almost impossible. There's one other aspect to consider too. At the moment, Eltheria and its people are only suspects. Strong suspects admittedly, but there is no hard evidence linking us to this incursion into Thanatos-controlled space. But if they find us here, if they capture this ship or one of its escape pods, or if they capture any of you and interrogate you, *there* is all the evidence they'll need. The future of our planet, perhaps even our very civilisation, depends on that *not* happening.'

Coral said, 'But what about our parents? What about Uncle Frank, Aunt Em and Norman's mum?

'I'm sorry,' Albert replied, 'but a speedy departure is essential. I simply cannot let the three of you, or your parents, jeopardise the lives of millions of Eltherians.'

7 : Going For It

Frank made coffee. He delivered cups to the others then gave Glad a sideways nod and wandered out to the veranda, studying her red Mini parked in the driveway, dwarfed by the army truck beside it. Glad ambled out after him, cup in one hand, the thumb of the other hooked in the belt loop of her jeans. They'd known each other for years and stood in silence a while surveying the scene. Then he said quietly, 'C'mon Glad. Spill 'em.'

'Spill what, Frank?'

'The beans. I saw you in there. I reckon you know more than you're letting on.'

'Am I?' She sipped her coffee. 'Aren't you too?'

'What's that supposed to mean?'

'I haven't heard any mention of Alice since I got here.'

'Alice? What's my sister-in-law got to do with it?'

'Didn't she claim she'd seen a spaceship in the bush just before that meteorite hit?'

'Yeah, well, you know what Alice is like. Not the most reliable witness. Between you and me, I've always reckoned she's a couple of cans short of a six-pack.'

'I hear she's doing an interview tonight.'

Nine News had been promoting it all day. An exclusive interview with Alice Jones, recorded – the promos emphasised – the day *before* Monday's extraordinary events. "Extraordinary claims. Extraordinary coverage. *Nine News* at 6:00pm."

'We didn't know she'd done that. She never said.'

'Well, she may be a bit loopy in other respects, but she was right about the ship, Frank. I know. I saw it.'

'*What?*'

'I even went inside it. I know what those people and their medical facilities can handle, which is why I'm not worried about Tim.'

Frank stared at her, his mouth open.

Glad set her cup down on the balustrade. 'Or perhaps you think I'm a couple of cans short of a six-pack too?'

* * *

They watched the latest news from Earth sitting round Tim's bed in the medical bay, communicating with him via headsets as they slurped on drink bulbs and shared a plate of crunchy pastry chips that shattered when you snapped them and sent the cleany-crawlies scuttling back and forth.

It was interesting to watch the helicopter footage, repeated endlessly, in regular and slow-motion. TV stations around the world had snapped it up, and every one of them had an expert or analyst with a different view of what was going on. An alien invasion. First Contact gone wrong. The beginning of the end of the world. Earth getting dragged into a galactic conflict. Some claimed it was just a publicity stunt for an upcoming Hollywood blockbuster. Others that it was proof that governments had been in touch with aliens for years.

'Whoa, that was Alice!' Tim said, insisting Coral stop channel surfing and go back. They caught the end of a promotional clip for an item that was due to screen in a few hours; the interview with Alice they'd secretly watched being filmed several days before.

It was followed by pictures of the reserve and the town of Rata, of the barricades on Rata Road preventing unauthorised access, of dozens of reporters, and a long telephoto shot of the army presence at the Townsend farm. More than anything, that seemed to underscore the reality of their predicament and why they couldn't return.

'You guys could go,' Tim said to Coral. 'You and Norman.'

'Albert won't let anyone leave. You heard him.'

'Who says we want to anyway?' Norman said.

'But you know what it means if you don't. It's a fifty light-year trip to Eltheria. If we go and come straight back, we'll only be six weeks older, but a hundred years will have passed on Earth.'

Norman bit his lip. Of all of them, he understood that well enough, but to hear someone say it out loud somehow made it real. He looked at the pictures of his home town with RAGS, his mum's shop, in the foreground, dropped the pastry chip he'd just picked up and sank back into his seat. The chip hung in the air, tumbling gently for a couple of seconds before a cleany-crawly zoomed past and whisked it away.

'Is almost as bad for us,' Alkemy said. 'We have been away twenty-five year. Much will have changed back home.'

'There is always Albert's time-injection idea,' Tim said. 'You know, that stuff about adding extra time as we travel and making it go backwards.'

'I can't see how it can,' Coral said. 'It does my head in just thinking about it. If it works – *if* – then technically we'd get to Eltheria before we were even born on Earth! And if we came back again, where would we be then?'

They considered that in silence.

'But imagine if it does work,' Tim said. 'How cool would that be? After all, Albert is supposed to be some sort of super brainbox. Remember that footage we saw after we recovered his memory bulb? How that guy Krilen called him the greatest thinking machine Eltheria had ever produced?'

Coral turned to Ludokrus. 'Did you say he built his ideas into the new Temporal Accumulator?'

Ludokrus nodded as a cleany-crawly brushed past Norman's face at eye level, scooping something up. Tim saw it and opened a person-to-person link to his friend. 'Hey, are you all right?'

Norman looked away. 'Yeah, I'm cool.' Another cleany-crawly brushed past his cheek. Then his voice broke and he said in a choked voice, 'I was thinking about Mum. I might never see her again.'

He slipped off his headset, pushed away from the chair and drifted from the room.

'Where are you going?' Coral said.

'He'll be back in a minute,' Tim told her. Whatever happened, he thought, they still had each other. Norman was on his own.

After kicking off, Norman let himself drift up to the observation deck. The ship, sensing his arrival, switched on the lights, but he muttered, 'Lights off, please,' and sat in the dark, staring out at the stars.

It was a dream come true, being on a real spaceship, heading for another planet, but it came with a cost.

He called Tim his best friend, but in reality Tim only came in second. His best mate was his mum. Always had been, always would. The fact that he might never see her again choked him up inside and he wiped away more tears before the cleany-crawlies could get to them.

Then he thought about what she would say if she knew his predicament, and smiled to himself: 'Go for it, Norman!' The words came to him so clearly it was like she was there in the darkness with him. She'd never held him back from chasing any dream or pursuing any idea. And she never would.

He'd go for it all right, but he wouldn't go quietly. Not without telling her all that was in his heart, and not without saying a proper goodbye first. To hell with Albert and his stupid rules!

He returned to the medical bay wearing a pair of pink gravity slippers. They made a comical contrast to his gingery hair, but his expression was sombre.

'OK,' he addressed them all, 'we can't go home. I accept that. But we can't just go without saying goodbye. That wouldn't be fair on ...' his voice grew unsteady and he cleared his throat '... on the people we leave behind, would it?'

He looked from one to the other. No one spoke till Ludokrus said gently, 'We cannot make the broadcast,

Norman. You know this. Everyone on Earth will hear. The Thanatos too. Maybe even use it to fix our location.'

'Who said anything about a broadcast? I'm not talking about that sort of message. I'm talking about what started this whole business in the first place.'

'What do you mean?'

'Mammals. Human beings. You know.'

The others exchanged looks. He wasn't making any sense.

'The thing that wiped out the dinosaurs sixty-five million years ago and gave us, mammals, our big break.'

'You mean a meteorite?'

Norman nodded. 'That's exactly what I mean.'

8 : Slingshot

Frank and Glad returned to the kitchen where Major Upshott was gathering up his laptop.

'I said Glad should stay the night,' Frank said to Em. 'She can have Coral's room.'

'Ah, good, yes,' Upshott said. 'All interested parties on the premises, as it were.'

'We're not *interested parties*,' Avril snapped, still tearful. '*Those are our children!*'

'Yes. Quite.' He nodded to the others and bustled out.

When he was gone, Avril turned on Frank and Em. 'How you could let this happen.'

'What do you mean?' Frank said.

'Let our children run around with a bunch of ... of space aliens.'

'Who said they were—?'

Em said, 'You missed that bit. Major Upshott had a message from the immigration department to say that no one named Kattflapp has entered the country in the last five years.'

'Plus there's no license or paperwork for that car and caravan down at the reserve,' Glenn added. 'The registration plates are fake.'

'I don't understand,' Frank said. 'They seemed like perfectly ordinary people. Albert was a bit eccentric, but—'

'Perhaps you should have taken a little more interest.'

'What's that supposed to mean?'

Avril pursed her lips. 'You've never had children, have you?'

Em bristled, but they were distracted by the sound of Smudge who'd found a ping-pong ball and was batting it furiously round the kitchen floor.

Glad raised a hand, 'Frank and Em had absolutely no reason to suspect the Kattflapps were anything other than what they pretended to be; foreign tourists.'

'Oh, and you would know, would you?'

'My son's missing too, remember.'

'Yes, but at least he's ... he's ... still in one piece.' Avril burst into tears again.

Frank looked to Glad hoping she might say more, but she shook her head. Not yet, it was too soon. And they'd never believe her anyway. She had no proof.

* * *

'What d'you think?'

Norman held out a boulder the size of a soccer ball. He took his hands away and it stayed where it was, floating in mid-air.

'It's awfully big,' Tim said, viewing the scene in the

workshop via his walrus mask. Cleany-crawlies were going berserk in the background, scooping up the cloud of dust and grit that grinding the ball had created.

'All this outer stuff will burn off when it enters the atmosphere. The real payload goes in here.' Norman turned the boulder round and pointed to a hole in one side the size of a golf ball. 'Once that's inserted, we'll plug it up.'

'So how does it work exactly?'

The view shifted as Norman picked up the camera and aimed it at a wheeled cradle containing a short, fat rocket. Ludokrus was checking it, a probe in one hand, the calculator from Alkemy's pink backpack in the other. He looked up and waved.

'This goes in the nose cone,' Norman pointed at the boulder, 'then we fire it at Saturn.'

'Saturn?'

'We're going to slingshot it around a couple of planets on the way. Their gravitational fields will give it even more speed, and it'll disguise where it actually came from if anyone manages to track it.'

'OK.'

'On the dark side of the moon, the side facing away from Earth, the rocket will launch the boulder then self-destruct. I mean completely. Like nuclear. No one on Earth will see it, but Ludokrus reckons we might see the flash from here with a good telescope. Leave only footprints, and all that.

'The boulder's got some little thrusters on its outer surface for small last-minute corrections.' He held the camera close and showed him. 'But they'll burn off as soon as it hits Earth's atmosphere. Then it's all down to how well we've done our calculations.'

'How well have you done them?'

'Albert's checked our calculations. He says they're fine.'

'What does he think about it?'

'He's not happy, but I think he understands our reasons. The chances of NASA or anyone else spotting something this small are tiny, and even if they do, even if they track it and recover the payload, there's nothing "technological" in it. Nothing that couldn't have been made in any workshop on Earth.'

Tim had to admit it was a clever idea, sending a message back in what would appear to be a micro-meteorite. NASA reckoned a hundred tons of space dust and gravel entered Earth's atmosphere every day, almost all of it burning up harmlessly. One more tiny piece was unlikely to be noticed.

Coral's icon winked in his mask. Tim excused himself and his view switched back to the medical bay where Coral was strapping herself into a seat beside his bed, a pad and pen floating by her side.

'Ready?' she asked.

'Yep.'

'Fire away.'

'Dear Mum and Dad,' Tim began. "I'm getting Coral to write this because, as you probably saw on television, I got a bit knocked around before we blasted off from Earth ...'

* * *

The adults watched Alice's interview in silence. She told how she'd left a plate of wholemeal pikelets for the visitors, returning later to find it broken, with birds picking over the remains. Upset, she'd run into the bush and lost her way, then stumbled across a flying saucer hidden in some ferns, right at the spot where – just hours later – what some claimed to be a meteorite had wiped it out and left a massive crater.

She even said she'd seen the craft's inhabitants, she said: aliens disguised as mice.

Avril snorted. Clearly the interviewer didn't believe her either, and the segment ended with Alice tugging off her microphone and stomping away.

Frank muted the sound. 'Actually, that's pretty much what she told us last Friday night.'

'*What?* She *told* you about that spaceship?' Glenn said. He looked at Em. Em nodded in confirmation.

'She was in a hell of a state,' Frank said. 'Hysterical. We thought she'd got lost in the bush and hit her head or something.'

'And you did nothing about it? Told no one?'

'What were we supposed to do, Glenn? Who were we supposed to tell?'

Em added, 'My sister can be a little unreliable at times.'

'Not this time, apparently,' Avril said.

'So you did nothing,' Glenn snapped. 'And three days later ...' He pointed at the silent TV where once again the aerial footage of the attack and blast-off were screening.

'What would you expect me to do?' Frank said.

'You could have at least gotten off your arse and had a look!' Glenn angrily snatched up his crutches and hobbled from the room, quickly followed by his wife.

9 : Into Blackness

'Does it have a name?' Tim asked Norman as they watched a video feed of the rocket's launch from C deck.

The squat, fat rocket sat in a spring-loaded launch tube which was being carried to an airlock along a conveyor belt. The door behind it sealed shut, the view changed, and they saw it from to side as the outer hatch opened and wisps of air vented into space.

'Yeah, you should give her name,' Ludokrus said. 'She was your idea.'

'*Smithzific I*,' Norman said as clamps locked the launch cradle to the deck. 'Ready? Five ... four ... three ... two ... one ...' He hit a button on the handset he was holding and the spring in the base of the cradle shoved the rocket out. An external camera followed it as it drifted into space.

'Was that it?' Coral said. 'More like *Smithfizzer*. How many million years did you say it's going to take to get back to Earth?'

'The rocket has a really powerful engine. We can't fire it till it's clear of the ship.' A readout at the bottom of the screen counted off the distance. 'Five kilometres minimum, right Albert?' Norman said.

'Correct.' Albert's voice sounded from a nearby speaker. 'Otherwise we'd risk sustaining blast damage.'

'About there, you reckon?'

'Yes, it's well clear now.'

Norman stabbed a second button and the image on the screen exploded in a ball of light that shrank so rapidly it was beyond the range of the external camera within seconds. They watched it in silence for a full minute, a tiny star heading into blackness. Tim watched it, thinking how a small part of him wished he could go with it, but a much bigger part was eager for the adventure ahead.

Albert's voice broke the silence. 'The time batteries are almost fully charged. We should be off ourselves.'

* * *

'Sorry, I haven't had time to change the bed,' Em said at the door of Coral's room.

'Don't worry, Em. I'll do it.' Glad took the bundle of sheets off her and set them on a chair. 'You've got enough on your plate.'

'Sorry about my in-laws too.'

'You can't do much about them. At least you've got some.' Glad was a solo parent.

'You're taking this remarkably well, I must say.'

'Am I? Don't be fooled. I'm all chewed up inside.'

Em touched her shoulder in solidarity. 'We all are,' she said, and left the room.

Glad looked around. There was a pile of school books on the desk beside a half-completed assignment. An MP3 player. A mobile phone and charger. A glittery pencil case. The dresser was littered with hair products, facial scrubs and body lotions. Glad smiled at the thought that Coral probably had a better range than she stocked in RAGS.

She pulled off the duvet and began stripping the bed. As she gathered up the pillows, she found a brown paper packet tucked beneath them, an envelope twenty-five centimetres square with something hard and round inside. It had no label, no address. The end was open. She tilted it and tipped out a willow-pattern plate.

'What an odd thing to keep under your pillow,' she said, putting it to one side before continuing to make up the bed.

* * *

Coral beckoned to the trolley-bot carrying Tim's gel bed. It followed her around the curving corridor, past the galley and the recreation room, into the segment containing the suspended animation capsules. Norman, Ludokrus and Alkemy had removed one of the units at the front, and a machineshop-bot floated nearby, gathering up the spare components in a series of mechanical claws.

'I feel like a lump of cargo,' Tim said from inside the bed.

'That's exactly what you are.'

The four of them took a corner each, anchored their slipper-clad feet to the deck matting, then slid Tim's bed off the trolley and guided it into place. There was a *clunk* as magnetic latches engaged and locked it in place, then another bot went to work, moving faster than the eye could follow, hooking up cables, fixing hoses, connecting circuits.

'*Knock Knock Who's There?*' Ludokrus called.

'Major.'

'Major who?'

'Major say knock knock again!' The ship laughed, then made a noise like it was clearing its throat and added, 'What can I do for you, Mr Ludokrus?'

'Please check my friend here for suspended animation.'

'Certainly.' There was a brief pause. 'All connections are valid and functioning. Circuitry and power levels: correct. Pressure seals: tested. Fluid reserves: normal. Gel circulation: three hundred percent due to healing parameters. All systems: green and good to go.'

'Thank you.' Ludokrus turned to the others and gestured at the remaining units. 'Now for us.'

* * *

'This roast lamb's delicious,' Glad said.

'Yep.'

'Uh-huh.'

'Mmm.'

The meal continued in silence.

'Gravy's good too.'

'Mmm.'

'Yeah.'

More silence.

'You get up to much at the weekend, Glad?' Frank asked. 'It was a long weekend here,' he told the visitors. 'Rata Day.

63

Remember Rata Day, Glenn.'

Glenn nodded but stayed focused on his food.

'I expect you were busy with the shop,' Frank said.

'Yes, I didn't get a chance to go anywhere.'

She took another forkful of food, wondering if she should tell them about Albert and the others making scanner blocks and placing them around town in an effort to locate the Sentinels' base. They were made from old computer parts using nanomachines produced by a device that looked like a calculator. That, she realised, was probably the least crazy part of her whole fantastic story.

Another glance at Glenn and Avril convinced her to hold her tongue.

'I did run into your sister-in-law though,' she added.

'Oh, sorry about that.'

Glad grinned. The others didn't react. 'Not your fault.'

Frank prompted her with a waggle of his eyebrows. He clearly wanted to hear more about the ship and what she knew, wanted her to tell Glenn and Avril too. But why would they believe her? Glad thought. There was no proof of any of it, not even a scanner block, and things were already tense enough. She didn't want to risk making things worse.

The main course finished, Em rose and began gathering up the plates.

'These are nice,' Glad said. 'I've only just noticed the willow pattern. Very traditional.'

'Family heirlooms,' Em told her. 'They were my mother's. I keep them for best.'

'I guess Coral likes them too.'

Avril snorted. 'I doubt they'd be Coral's thing. She's a modern girl with very modern tastes.'

'Oh, but didn't you give her one?' Glad said to Em.

Em frowned. 'What makes you think that?'

'I ...' Glad thought of the plate under Coral's pillow and suddenly the pieces came together. 'In that interview, Alice said something about a broken plate. It wasn't one of these, was it?'

Em made a face. 'As I said before, my sister's not the most reliable witness.'

'It *was* one of these?'

'A dinner plate, yes. And Coral returned it the following day, perfectly intact.'

'So there's none missing?'

'Why would there be?'

'And none have glued together?' She looked over the five plates on the table and the one in the dresser.

'Definitely not.'

Glad got up and went to her room, returning with the brown envelope which she set before her on the table. 'How big is the dinner service?'

'Forty-eight pieces, six of each.'

'So that's six dinner plates, six side plates and so on.'

'Yes.'

'And there are definitely no plates missing?'

'You can see for yourself.' Em gestured.

'I imagine plates like these are pretty rare these days.'

'I suppose so.'

'Only, you never see them about – except in antique shops.'

'They are heirlooms.'

'Wedgwood,' Avril confirmed, inspecting the maker's mark on the underside. 'I did a course a few years back.

They're porcelain, made from a special type of clay and fired in a kiln at twelve hundred degrees centigrade.'

'Not the sort of thing you could knock up in your back yard then?'

'Certainly not.'

Glad nodded, aware of the others regarding her oddly. 'There are no antique shops in Rata. Not even a secondhand shop.'

'So ...?'

She slid out the contents of the envelope. 'So where did this one come from?'

Four pairs of eyes looked at the plate, at the five on the table and the one in the dresser.

'There were never seven of them,' Em said. 'Never.'

Avril took it and inspected the back. 'It's Wedgwood all right.' She held it by the rim and pinged it with her fingernail. 'Porcelain too.'

'Where did this come from?'

'It was under Coral's pillow when I made up the bed.'

'She must have ... found it in a shop somewhere.'

'Not round here.'

'But it's identical to the others.'

'No, it's not,' Frank said, getting to his feet and taking the clean one from the dresser. 'Here, Av. Put them side by side. Look at the faces.'

Avril gasped and pointed. 'Tim! That boy there looks like Tim!'

They stared at the figure fishing from the bridge. The other plate showed a nondescript outline, but the one from Coral's room had the cartoon face of Tim on it.

'And there's Coral!' She pointed to the girl leading the

donkey.

'Actually, that donkey looks a bit like—' Frank began.

'Norman!' Glad laughed, finished for his sentence for him.

'Who are they then?' Avril pointed to the figures in the boat.

'I think Em and Frank can tell you that.'

'Albert, Alkemy and Ludokrus,' Em said, taking a seat because she suddenly wasn't sure her legs would hold her.

Glenn took the plate, moistened a finger and rubbed at the edge.

'What are you doing?' Avril snapped. 'It's baked on, you idiot.'

'Then how on earth did they do this to an antique plate.'

All eyes turned back to Glad.

'I think this was a keepsake made by the visitors for your daughter. Something to remember them by. They were expecting to go at any time. Their first ship, the one they came in on, the one Alice saw in the bush, was blown up by a killer robot so they had to summon another. There were another bunch of aliens you see – that second ship – and your children – *our* children – were helping the visitors avoid them. But they got caught in the crossfire, as we saw on that video.

'This plate was made by the aliens, but not in a kiln. They used microscopic machines generated by a device that looks a bit like a calculator. It takes the atoms of what we consider waste material and reshapes them in any way you like. They rebuilt my car out there after it got blown up last week. And they fixed up Errol Fitchett's big green school bus after your son stopped it from going off a cliff.'

'Our son did what?'

'And I'm certain that they're using similar technology right now to fix Tim and help heal those horrid burns. That's why they took him. They could have left him to die.'

'And ... you ... know about this technology?' Glenn said doubtfully.

'I'm living proof of it.' Glad patted her hip. 'I got shot the other day. By that killer robot I mentioned. Within an hour or two, I was better.'

She looked at the stunned faces staring back at her. 'I know it sounds incredible. I still only half-believe it myself.' She tapped the plate. 'But there's the proof. Where else could that have come from?'

'You ... er ... You should probably start at the beginning,' Frank said.

'Yes, I think I should. Make yourselves comfortable. It's quite a tale.'

* * *

Tim could feel the gentle acceleration through his gel bed. Continuous. Steady. He'd left the background channel open, and the quiet commentary from *Knock Knock Who's There?* about the status of systems, energy levels and time equilibrium settings was somehow comforting, even he didn't understand it all.

Through the walrus mask, he saw and heard his sister and friends settle. Before they climbed into their beds, they'd exchanged hugs – even Coral and Norman – and he felt a pang of sadness at not being able to join in. Taps on the lid of his bed, murmured messages and smiling faces weren't quite the same.

'We're under way,' *Knock Knock Who's There?* said.

Tim brought up an exterior view. The stars outside seemed to be moving and fading at the same time. As they drew closer and closer to the speed of light, they faded out entirely.

'All systems normal,' the ship said quietly. 'Initiating suspension sequence.'

'Good night, everyone,' Ludokrus called, already sounding sleepy.

''Night.'

'Good night.'

Tim felt his limbs grow heavy as a delicious weariness filled him. It felt like sinking into a feather bed after a long and tiring day. His breathing deepened, slowed, almost stopped entirely, and his last conscious thought was to wonder where he would be when he woke up.

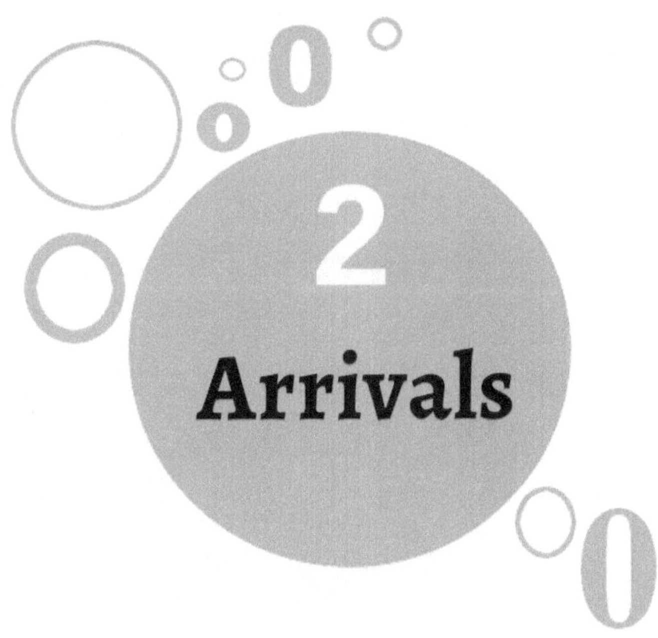

2

Arrivals

10 : Brothers

The sun was barely a finger-width above the horizon but Frank Townsend had already been up for an hour. Some things didn't change, despite all the excitement going on around them. Grass still grew, cows still ate it, and they still needed to be milked.

The last of them came down the race and entered the milking parlour as a voice behind him said, 'Need a hand?'

Frank turned to his brother. 'You're up early,'

'Country air, eh?'

'You still remember the routine?'

'Like riding a bike, isn't it? Anyway, the exercise is supposed to be good for my legs.'

He leaned his crutches against the wall and they worked together silently, side by side, washing, cleaning, connecting the teat cups. When they were done, they leaned on a railing and watched the milking machine at work, listening to its familiar hiss and clank.

'You never forget, eh?' Frank said. Glenn shook his head. 'D'you miss it?'

'Occasionally. When I'm stuck in traffic or in the middle of a boring meeting. But mostly not.'

'Dad had to leave it to someone. He didn't want to see it sold off or broken up.'

'Yeah, I see that now. He did the right thing too. I went off to university and did my OE, but you stayed here and stuck with it. And him. You deserved it, Frank. But it still hurt a bit at the time, you know?'

'It's just stuff, Glenn. Things. Possessions. It doesn't mean he and Mum loved you any less.'

'I understand that now. Getting older gives you a sense of perspective. I'm afraid I was a bit of hothead in those days. Said a few things I regret.'

'We both did.'

'And I'm sorry about foisting the kids on you and Em. After the accident, Social Services said they *had* to go to a relative. Either that or into care. And we thought it'd only be for a couple of weeks.'

'Think nothing of it. No foisting involved,' Frank said. 'They're good kids. Fun to have around. They've given Em and me cause to reconsider.'

'About having a family?'

'Be nice to leave this place to someone with a love of the land.'

'Like Dad did.'

The milking continued. They watched the flow through a sight glass. Glenn added, 'I've been talking to Avril about staying on for a bit. Just to be around. Just in case. We've still got a few weeks off work on account of those things,' he gestured at his crutches, 'and better to be here than Auckland, especially the way the news vultures are gathering. At least the army and police are keeping them away from the farm.'

A steady stream of phone calls had started the previous afternoon. Reporters wanting to talk to the grieving parents. Wanting to know how it felt to lose your children to aliens.

'If that's all right with you and Em,' Glenn added.

'No worries on either score, mate. But what about your job?'

'Have you got broadband?'

'I haven't even got a hat band.'

'Come on Frank, stop playing the local yokel. You know what I mean.'

'Can get it, I s'pose. The Robinsons up the road have been hooked up for years.'

'There you go. If I get some gear sent down I can work from here. All I need's a laptop and a bit of peace and quiet.'

'You'll get plenty of that.'

'I don't know how Avril will take to it though. She does like her cafes and shops.'

'RAGS and RAM are only twenty K away. What more could she want?'

Glenn grinned. 'Exactly.'

'This hasn't got anything to do with what Glad said last night, has it?'

'It was a hell of a story, all right. And I have to say that if it hadn't been for that plate ... Well, there's only so much fantastical stuff you can take in, you know?'

'I know what you mean. That sister-in-law of mine ...' Frank shook his head. 'But Glad Smith's as straight as an arrow. Always has been. If she says she was shot by a killer robot, I'm not going to say she wasn't.'

'Still, be nice to have a little more proof, wouldn't it? And what do we tell Upshott?'

'I'd say we say nothing for the moment. Let's see what their experts come up with.'

They finished up, saw off the last of the cows and began hosing down.

'What happened up there?' Glenn said.

'Up where?'

'That hole in the roof?'

'Is this one of those Auckland tricks where you get me to look up then stick the hose down my trousers?'

'No, seriously. Look.'

Frank looked. There was a neat round hole in the corrugated iron thirty millimetres across.

'Where the hell did that come from? That wasn't there yesterday. There's a dent in the side of that separator too. Look at that. That's stainless steel. You'd have a job doing that with a sledgehammer.'

They studied the matching dent in the curved metal surface. 'I heard a bang in the night. I thought it was those army jokers.'

Glenn traced the object's path with his finger. 'Something came through the roof there and hit the separator. Something round.'

'Turn the hose under here, will you.'

Glenn did so, and along with a stream of water, a silver sphere the size of a large ball bearing rolled into the drainage gutter.

The brothers looked at each other, then Frank bent and picked it up.

'It's got writing on it. Etched into the surface.'

Glenn squinted. 'I haven't got my glasses. What does it say?'

'This bit says, "Twist here to open", but there's a line above it, written in capitals.'

'Yeah?'

'Like an address.' He looked at his brother. 'It says "ATTENTION: UNCLE FRANK!".'

11 : Before Dawn

Tim woke with his head full of strange music. It was gentle and rhythmic, but unlike anything he'd heard before. It took him a full minute to realise it was coming from the audio feed in his walrus mask.

He opened his eyes. The other icons in his mask – the ones representing his friends – grew slowly brighter as they too came awake. There was a groan, then Norman's voice: 'Oh man, I feel like something died in my mouth.'

'Seeing the way you eat, it could have been anything,' Coral said.

'Suspension lag.' Ludokrus's voice sounded like a rusty hinge. 'The body is still part asleep. Best cure is to get up.'

'After you.'

'Yeah, go right ahead.'

No one moved.

Tim noticed the lid of his capsule had drawn back. Did that mean ...?

He flexed his fingers and curled his toes. He could feel them again. He was all there. Complete. Healed!

He sat up, pulling off the walrus mask. Whoops, too quick. A wave of dizziness washed over him and he reached out to steady himself on the sides of the capsule.

Looking about, he caught sight of his left arm and grinned. The last time he'd seen it, it had been ablaze from elbow to wrist. Now it was fixed, perfect, the skin unmarked.

Pushing himself from the gel bed, he soared into the air, only now remembering the indicator in his mask had warned gravity was only one-quarter normal. A quantity of blue gel drifted up with him and cleany-crawlies dashed across to slurp it up.

Norman sat up in his capsule, shook his head groggily and pulled off his mask. Seeing Tim, he slapped it back on and said, 'You might want to put some clothes on before you start floating around, mate.'

* * *

Avril Townsend hobbled into the kitchen in her dressing gown. Her hair was awry and her face drawn. She'd slept badly, thinking about her missing children and the incredible story Glad had told them the night before. Finally, just before dawn she'd drifted off, only to be woken by the sound of excited voices and her husband's calls.

She glared at the wall clock. 6:35. A ridiculous hour, but the rest of the household was already up and dressed. Glenn, Glad and Em were seated at the kitchen table, clutching mugs of tea and staring at a shiny object sitting in the centre. They greeted her as she entered and Frank handed her a cup.

The excited looks on their faces made her forget her annoyance and she took a seat saying, 'What is it? What's happened?'

Glenn pointed at the shiny object. 'Take a look.'

She picked up what appeared to be a large ball bearing. It was solid and heavy with letters engraved in its surface.

'We found it in the milking shed this morning. It punched a hole clean through the roof and dented the side of a piece of three-millimetre-thick stainless steel.'

'I don't know what that means,' Avril said.

'It means it was travelling pretty fast.'

The words took a moment to register. A hole in the roof. Travelling fast. 'You mean like a meteorite?'

Glenn nodded, grinning.

'You think it's from the children?'

'Take a look at the writing.'

'*Attention: Uncle Frank,*' she read aloud. 'It also says *Twist here to open.*' She looked up expectantly.

'We were waiting for you. Go ahead.'

Avril took the ball in two hands and twisted it. 'It's not ...' There was a faint *snick* then the two halves unscrewed smoothly and came apart. The interior contained four folded pieces of paper that dropped onto the tabletop.

'Paper? Is that it? Oh my gosh, they're notes! Look, that's Coral's handwriting!'

There were two notes addressed to Glenn and Avril, one to Glad, and one to Em and Frank. They shared them out and sat in silence, reading.

Avril read and re-read the messages from Coral and Tim, shaking her head in disbelief as the tea before her grew cold.

Glenn couldn't stop smiling. He put his arm around her. 'It's just as you said, Glad. They're all OK. Even Tim. He had to dictate his note to Coral because their machines were still patching him up, but it's him all right. His voice comes through. You can hear it.'

She reached out to Em and Glad. 'I ... I don't know what to say. I'm sorry for what I said yesterday. And the way I acted. I just ... I ... I ...'

Em patted her hand. 'No need to apologise. In your situation, in the circumstances ... well, I don't know how I'd have reacted.'

'What does your note say?' Glenn said to Em and Frank.

Em passed it across, which gave Glad a chance to slip the last page of Norman's note under the table where she tucked it into the pocket of her jeans. It was a postscript the others didn't need to see, at least not yet. Norman had been more honest than the others and told her about the problem with time and the speed of light. They'd be back, he was sure of that, but it might take them a bit longer than expected.

12 : Rounding Error

In the end, Tim was the last up. He waited till the suspended animation chamber was empty and one of the service-bots had delivered him clothes from the fabricator. They were identical copies of the jeans, T-shirt and nylon jacket the medical bots had cut away from him after the explosion.

The door opened automatically as he approached and he found himself in a familiar circular corridor. Even though he'd never actually set foot in the ship before, he knew his way around from watching the others through the walrus mask. To his left was a bathroom and the crew quarters, to his right the recreation room, galley and sick bay. Directly opposite, visible through the open mesh of the ship's central spine, was the bridge.

Guessing the others were there, he made his way round, being careful to use the hand grips and railing. Although he'd missed full weightlessness, even at a quarter normal gravity each step made him feel like Superman.

He reached the bridge and steadied himself against the

console where Albert's memory bulb was plugged. The place was deserted.

Where is everyone?

There were a pair of gravity slippers pegged to the mesh around the spine and a hand drawn arrow pointing up beside them. He slipped them on, took a jump-block up to the observation deck and touched down lightly, feeling the slippers bind with the deck. The room had a domed ceiling and a circle of reclining seats around the perimeter, but it too was empty.

'Surprise!'

The others leapt from behind the seats, showering him with confetti, greeting him with cheers, back slaps and hugs. Was he all right? How did he feel? He looked great.

Coral hugged him. Hard.

'Whoa, mind the ribs!'

'You had me *so* worried,' she said. 'The state of you when we picked you up! If it hadn't been for the ship and Albert ...' Her voice trailed off.

It was Alkemy's turn next. Another long hug.

'Thanks for what you did,' he said. 'Pushing me over. Putting out the flames. I remember that bit. I thought I was a goner.'

'I owe you,' she said. You save me from the Sentinel.'

They hugged again, then Norman slapped his shoulder.

'Radical haircut, man,' he said, batting aside a cleany-crawly racing to vacuum up the confetti.

Tim ran a hand over the fuzz where his hair had been burned away. 'It'll grow back.'

Ludokrus produced a huge cake and proceeded to cut it into slices.

'Where are we?' Tim asked, looking up at the domed ceiling. Norman hit a button and shutters slid back to reveal a distant blue-green planet wreathed in wisps of cloud. For a moment, he thought they were heading back to Earth. Then he noticed sunlight glinting off the ring around it. A ring like the rings around Saturn.

'Approaching Eltheria,' Ludokrus said, handing him a paper plate containing a multi-layered slice of chocolate cake. 'But that is the wrong question.'

'What's the right one?'

'*When* are we?'

'Oh. Right. So ...?'

Alkemy answered before her brother could speak. She seized Tim's free hand, almost making him drop the plate. 'Eight-and-one-half weeks after we leave home!'

'After you left home?' It took a moment to register. 'So ... it worked then? Albert's time-injection idea?'

She danced him round the deck in one-quarter gravity amidst the still-falling confetti and the frantic cleany-crawlies. 'Yes, yes, yes, yes, yes!'

Coral and Norman grinned, relief on both their faces.

'So that means when we go back—?'

'We'll only have been away six weeks!' Coral finished for him and joined the dance.

'Woo hoo!' Norman did a low-gravity back flip.

'OK for you,' Ludokrus said, 'but we are late. Supposed to be away only be six week. Albert make mistake.'

'A rounding error in the vector tables.' Albert's voice came over the ship's speakers. 'I've already apologised for that.'

'Don't be too hard on him,' Coral told Ludokrus. 'After all, two-and-a-half weeks late is better than two-and-a-half *decades* late.'

* * *

Knock Knock Who's There? approached from an angle slightly above the plane of the solar system, giving them a good view of their home planet, its sun and sister planets. At the centre lay Tetzul, Eltheria's true sun, surrounded by four inner planets – Elq, Eltheria, Stave and Tolky. A broad gap was followed by an equally broad asteroid field – known colloquially as Smash Circle – then three other planets – Orf, Satis and Nol – the first two were gas giants like Jupiter, the last a barren rock that may once have been a deep-space asteroid captured aeons ago by Tetzul's gravitational field.

A second sun, known as Tena, lay at an oblique angle to the system, and although it looked almost as big as Tetzul, it burned with a copper-red tinge and had a smudged and indistinct outline. Ludokrus explained it was actually in a nearby system. A red giant – a star that had burned up its core hydrogen supply and was now consuming its shell, causing it to expand massively and increase in brightness ten thousand times.

'Can you see it from Eltheria?' Coral asked.

'Most time, yes. But not so bright as Tetzul.'

'So you really do have two suns?'

'And three moon. Makes complicated tides.'

Palas, Polox and Puk lay at a quarter, a third and a half a million kilometres from the planet. They looked inhabited. Their dark sides of each were spangled with lights, but they were no competition for the brightness of the ring around the planet itself.

'That is Halo,' Alkemy said. 'We make ourselves.'

'You *made* that?'

'Many hundred years ago, we start to wreck our planet. Too much destruction. Drilling, mining, factory, pollution. Need more and more resource, but always running out.'

'Sounds familiar,' Coral said.

'There is a big meeting. Once we have countries like you, but if the whole planet die, what use is a country? So they disband. Instead, we form Consensus – a council for the whole planet – and it say all must stop. Must get the resources elsewhere.

'So we travel to the asteroid – what we call Smash Circle – and launch many at our planet. Careful, so we make a ring around her. Now we have resource nearby.'

'I thought your nanomachines recycled everything.'

'They do, but they come after Halo is already make. Now she is not much used, but pretty, no?'

'Spectacular, I'd say.'

'Hey everybody,' Knock Knock said. 'Sorry to break up the party, but in about ten minutes we'll be entering controlled space and I may have to do some bouncy manoeuvry things, so I recommend y'all go down to the bridge and buckle up.'

'Ten minute?' Ludokrus said. 'Time to shoot our visitor first.'

* * *

Em, Avril, Frank, Glenn and Glad sat around the kitchen table considering their options.

'What do we do now?' Glenn said.

'First thing I'm going to do is fix that hole in the roof,' Frank replied. 'Wait till I see those kids of yours. That thing could've hit one of the girls. Or me.'

'I reckon they aimed it pretty well. The separator took the force of the impact.'

'I'd forgotten about that dent. You know what those things cost?'

Glenn looked at his brother. Frank was grinning.

'I actually meant about these.' Glenn gestured at the letters. 'What do we tell that lot outside?'

'That depends whether you want the army here forming a welcoming committee when the kids get back.'

'Certainly not!' Avril said.

'Well then, what did they say in their notes? Three weeks each way? I reckon that's about the perfect time for a story like this to die down. The army are already talking about hauling that stuff at the reserve away for proper analysis. Once that's done, I can't see them hanging round. As far as they're concerned, the fun's over.'

Footsteps sounded on the veranda.

'Good morning, Major,' Em said loudly.

By the time Major Upshott had wiped his boots on the mat, there was no sign of the letters, or the container they'd come in.

'Can I get you—?'

'No, thank you,' he said curtly, glaring at the others, his hands on his hips. 'It seems you people haven't been straight with me after all.'

No one spoke.

'I specifically asked you to tell me everything you knew about this matter, and you didn't.'

'What d'you mean?' Frank said.

'You two in particular.' He glared at Em and Frank.

Avril slipped a hand into the pocket of her dressing gown, covering Tim and Coral's letters, determined not give them up.

'So.' Upshott crossed his arms. 'I'd like to know *everything* this time please. Including all about one Alice Jones who appeared on television last night, and who is – I'm now given to believe – *your sister*, Mrs Townsend.

'Our records show she left the area late on Monday afternoon, just before all this spaceship business started. Presumably, she'd been staying here. Is that correct?' Em nodded. 'And she didn't happen to mention her little *alien encounter*, did she?' Em nodded again. 'Then why the devil didn't you tell me about it?'

'To be fair chief, you did ask us for all *relevant* information,' Frank said.

'So?'

'Alice has rarely ever been that.'

Upshott saw Glenn's grin. He bristled. 'No? Well she is now, Mr Townsend. After her little television performance last night, my colleagues will be interviewing her closely.' He looked from one to the other. 'Now, does anyone have anything else they'd like to tell me – relevant or not?'

They all looked back unblinking. No one said a word.

* * *

The gun looked like a lightweight high-tech pistol. It had a tubular frame, a squat gas canister underneath the barrel, a number of controls along one side and a small targeting screen at the back. The barrel narrowed to a point before expanding into what looked like an elliptical suction cup.

'Sit please.' Ludokrus gestured to a reclining seat on one side of the medical bay.

Coral sat. It reminded her of a dentist's chair.

'Head back.'

'Why?'

'So I can place on eye.' He pointed to the suction cup.

'What is that thing?'

'Is call a linguaseed gun.'

'What's that when it's at home?'

'Linguaseed are like the tiny computer that sit inside of brain. Connect to language centre so you will understand Eltherian. Albert reprogram the ship when he learn English, but outside of it you will not understand what people say. With this, you will.'

'What about speaking Eltherian?'

'This does not help. But everyone have these seed. Most are give at birth. They can be reprogram so then they will understand you. Albert already make a database of your language so when you speak to other` it will be download automatic.'

He raised the gun again.

'But ... in my eye ...?'

'Does not go in eye, but round the back to brain. Easiest way is to follow the optic nerve.'

'I hope it's got a good sense of direction,' Norman said, 'because in her case it's got a pretty small target.'

Coral ignored him. 'Will it hurt?' she said to Ludokrus.

'Small irritation only. Feel like piece of grit.'

Ludokrus placed the cup over Coral's eye and studied the screen. 'Open, please. Look to left.'

There was a small *pfft* of compressed air. Coral said 'Ow!' and blinked furiously.

'Don't rub. Just dab. OK?' He handed her a tissue.

Norman cupped a hand to one ear. Behind his back, his free hand held a coin over a metal tray. 'Wait for it. Any second now.' He released the coin and there was a metallic clank and clatter. 'There it goes.'

'Very amusing,' Coral said, her eye watering a little.

Norman high-fived Tim, but he did it too hard. The low gravity sent him in a three hundred and sixty-degree spin and he fell against the table holding the metal tray.

'Hey, I think it's working,' Coral said.

'So quick?'

'Yeah, is that the ship talking Eltherian in the background? What's that?' She held her hand to her ear.

'The ship is not—'

'It thinks Norman Smith's a dork.'

13 : Offline

True understanding came in bits and pieces. Words here and there, then phrases, then whole sentences. Coral realised she'd got it when she could read the legends beside the illuminated buttons on the drink dispenser. It was an odd sensation. Her eyes still saw a collection of hieroglyphics, but her brain suddenly made sense of them. It didn't help her selection though. She tried a flavour called loplebery, took one mouthful and spat it out for the cleany-crawlies to whisk away. It tasted like bitter lemon mixed with chilli.

As they approached Eltheria, *Knock Knock Who's There?* joined a stream of in-bound traffic, taking a position a hundred kilometres behind a lumbering freighter at least fifty times their size.

'Don't we get priority after all you guys have been through?' Coral said. 'I mean, apart from anything else, hasn't Albert just made the scientific breakthrough of the century with this time-injection stuff?'

'Our mission was big secret,' Ludokrus said. 'Even from

us. All we are supposed to know is we go to visit our parent, but absent-minded Albert mix up the coordinate.'

Coral was disappointed. She'd been expecting a little fuss, a little fanfare, not the space equivalent of commuter traffic.

They spent the next hour buckled in their seats on the bridge. Time passed slowly. The view barely changed, despite a readout on the bottom of the screen that said they were travelling at eighty thousand kilometres an hour. An overlay showed they were getting closer to Eltheria, but the actual view of the planet was blocked by the bulk of the freighter ahead of them.

Coral recalled what Ludokrus had told them back on Earth: that space travel was mostly boring. The ships themselves handled everything, so the best thing for the crew to do was sleep.

'Hey, I'm getting a special transmission for you guys,' Knock Knock announced suddenly. 'A one-to-one from the director of the Science Council, no less. Do you want me to ... *bleerg* ...'

Ludokrus sat up. 'What was that? What happen?'

'It's all right,' Albert's voice came online. 'I've just taken temporary control of the ship.'

'What? You cannot do that! Is illegal. A ship's mind must never—'

'A little one-off override I built in when I was repairing it. In case of a situation like this. It will look like a system fault. The self-repair mechanisms are already at work and Knock Knock will have a small memory gap when it recovers. Now, let's see what Krilen has to say, shall we?'

The image on the main screen flickered for an instant

before it was replaced by a smart but sallow-looking man with a deeply lined face, cool appraising eyes and a drooping mouth.

'Is not Uncle Krilen,' Alkemy muttered.

'This is Administrator Almas Meli, Chair of the Eltherian Science Council, to Syntho Albert Kattflapp aboard *Knock Knock Who's There?*'

An icon winked in the bottom corner of the screen. The message below it flashed "Voice response only selected." Administrator Meli would get no return pictures.

'Albert here,' Albert said. His voice sounded different. No longer the cool, precise machine, he reverted to his cover personality; bumbling and eccentric. 'Good afternoon, Administrator.'

'Good *morning*.' They saw Meli glance at the clock at the bottom of his screen. 'Is there some sort of problem?'

'Oh, is that bridge camera still out? I thought I'd fixed that. Let me just ...'

There was a fizz and a crackle on the line.

'Never mind that now,' Meli snapped. 'What do you want?'

'Didn't you call us?'

'Only because I have an entry here to contact your ship when it comes within range, presumably set up by my predecessor.'

'Your predecessor? What happened to Dr Krilen?'

'Retired due to ill health. Now, would you mind telling me why this automated call was directed at your vessel? A *recreational* vessel. This is the Science Council. I'm a busy man.'

'I ... imagine it's a personal thing,' Albert said. 'Dr Krilen is uncle to my companions.'

'Your companions?' Meli turned away to consult another screen. When he turned back, his expression was less severe. He even forced a smile.

'That explains it. How are your companions? Ludokrus and Alkemy Kattflapp, isn't it? Everyone fit and well?'

'Oh yes,' Albert said.

'Good, good. I see you're late back. A couple of weeks, in fact. Problems?'

'Bit of a navigational mix-up.'

'That shouldn't normally—'

'We sustained some damage. A meteor storm. Took a bit of fixing.'

'And presumably that explains your bridge camera.'

Albert said nothing.

'Well, I should like to see you all as soon as you return, Albert. I think we may have some things to discuss.' With a curt nod and cut the transmission. The screen flickered for a moment then the image of the back end of the freighter returned.

There was a long silence before Albert spoke again. 'Something's happened since we've been away. I just tried Krilen's private number, but he's offline.'

'Administrator Meli did say it was a sudden illness,' Alkemy said.

'I also tried your parents' private numbers. No luck there either. Listen, the ship's about to come back online so be careful what you say. The natural thing for you to do would be to call your parents via the public channels. Let's see what the official response is.'

'... *greelb* ... patch it through?' Knock Knock resumed.

'Oh ... hang on ... I've lost it. Must've been a wrong number.'

'While you are there,' Ludokrus called, 'please make comm to our parents.'

'Righty-ho.' There was a pause then the ship came back with, 'Good news or bad news?'

'What?'

'What d'you want first?'

'I want both. Just tell.'

'Well, the bad news is that both your parents are currently off-planet and can't be contacted. All enquiries have to go to the director of the Science Council.'

Ludokrus and Alkemy exchanged looks.

'But the good news is that we've just been given priority docking clearance. Buckle up everyone. We're moving into the fast lane!'

14 : Keeping Secrets

'Does not make sense,' Alkemy said. 'We go to visit our parent but do not arrive. Now we are two weeks overdue, but they do not come to look for us.'

'Those two,' Ludokrus snorted. 'Probably forget we even go to visit.'

'No, Alkemy's right,' Albert said. 'Something's wrong. Krilen wouldn't suddenly go beyond reach of comms, not without leaving a message for me, even if he was taken ill. After all, he organised this mission and knows how important it is.'

'Who is that Administrator Meli?'

'I've never heard of him before, but I've done some checking on the public databases. I can't do much more till we dock, but what I can tell you is that he has strong links to the Military Council.'

The ship gave a lurch and shifted to another lane. As they rose above the bulk of the freighter ahead, they saw Eltheria properly for the first time. A blue-green planet with two polar ice caps, but a very different landmass. Instead of several continents like Earth, there was just one that circled the equator, extending thousands of kilometres either side of it. This was Belt. As they moved and the planet rotated, a five hundred kilometre-wide break in it came into view, an area of scattered islands known as Buckle Gap where the northern and southern oceans merged. An area of wild storms and massive tidal surges, especially when all three moons aligned.

On the western side of the gap was the planet's capital city, Theia, nestling at the end of a long elliptical bay, its lights winking out as it emerged from shadow of the terminator zone and into the light of a new day.

The ship's speed increased steadily, overtaking the massive freighter and the string of other ships in front of it, and the view of the planet grew steadily larger. Soon they could make out a series of broad circular discs dotted at regular intervals around the equator, floating a hundred kilometres or more above the surface. At the edge of the planet, they caught sight of one side-on as sunlight glinted off the filaments trailing below it, seeming to go all the way down to the surface.

'Is that a space elevator?' Norman asked.

'Yup.'

'Wow!'

'A what?' Tim said.

'It's like ... It's only a theory back home, but if you had a really, really long cable, you could anchor one end to the ground, put a counterweight on the end out in space, and the planet's spin would keep the cable tight.'

'What benefit is that?'

'It means you can go back and forth along the cable. No

need for rockets to get into orbit.'

'Oh. Wow!'

'That thing on the end must be a space station then.'

They watched as the huge structure grew steadily larger and the single strand resolved into more than a dozen separate ones, each with cable trains rushing up or down.

'Selene Station,' Alkemy said. 'Almost home.'

There was a faint *pop* from somewhere and Albert came online. 'I've just overloaded Knock Knock's listening circuits. Before we arrive, we need to talk. We've got about five minutes.

'Remember what I told you about our real mission? With the exception of Krilen and your parents, everyone on Eltheria thinks Alkemy and Ludokrus went away for the summer holidays and simply got lost due to my bumbling miscalculations.

'It's important we stick to that story. If anyone asks, say we ended up in Tarkav.' The image on the main display vanished, replaced by a star map of nearby systems. One was highlighted. 'It's remote, desolate and known for unpredictable meteor storms. We'll say we were caught in one, sustained some damage, and that delayed our return. Understood?'

Alkemy and Ludokrus nodded.

'That leaves us with two problems: my physical absence, and the presence of three aliens.'

'Earthlings,' Coral corrected.

'Or course. Excuse me.

'The first is easy to explain. I'm having the bots in the workshop prepare a facsimile of my body, rather like the one you made back on Earth. It'll contain a receptacle for my memory bulb. When we dock, move me to it and seal me inside. It's a radiation casket. I'll say I received a massive dose of gamma rays while making repairs and require decontamination. That can only be done on Eltheria, so you'll have to take me down with you.

'The second problem is more difficult. We have to get the Earthlings off the ship without anyone discovering them.'

'Wait, wait,' Ludokrus said, 'I do not understand. Our mission was a big success, no? You learn many things we do not know before. Also, you make a huge discovery about using spare time. Why top secret?'

'Because things have changed here while we've been away. I've been scanning the news archives. There's no time to explain it all now, but it seems the Science Council has been purged and ransacked. Until I can determine exactly how things stand, let's just stick with our cover story.'

Tim thought of the recordings they'd seen on Earth. How the Military Council would classify Albert's secret abilities as a weapon of war, and perhaps use him for destructive purposes.

'I think it's significant that we've been given priority docking at the planet's busiest space station. That sort of thing is usually only reserved for visiting VIPs.'

'You are right. Even Uncle Krilen would not do this.'

'It suggests someone's very keen to see us. We need to be careful.'

'What about the second problem?' Tim said. 'Us. What do *we* do?'

'That,' Albert said, 'is a good question.'

'We need to find the answer, quick.' Ludokrus pointed to the docking timer on the console. 'We arrive in twenty minute.'

While they were still thinking about what they could do, the ship came back online.

15 : Reluctant Gravity

There was a faint crackle from the ship's speakers and Knock Knock made a throat-clearing sound. 'Excuse me folks, would someone mind saying something please?'

'What shall we say?'

'Oh, that's better. Sorry, I've been having a few problems with my sound sensors. If you were trying to contact me in the last couple of minutes ...?'

'Well, sorry about the interruption. I'm not sure what's causing these hiccups. I'd better run a system check before we dock.'

Something in the quality of the silence told them the ship had gone. Coral looked at the others and made a *what now?* gesture.

Words appeared on the forward screen.

I have an idea.

'Who's that?' Tim said.

The letters faded to be replaced by:

Ssshh! It's me, Albert.

'Huh?'

*Please talk amongst yourselves
to cover Tim's lapse.*

The five of them exchanged looks. For a moment, no one could think of anything to say. Then Norman said, 'Who's that who said "Who's that?"?'

Coral caught on at once. 'Who's that who said "Who's that who said 'Who's that?'?"' She nodded to Alkemy.

'Who's that who say, "Who's that who say ..." Ah, I am lost already!'

They laughed as fresh words appeared on the screen:

*Perfect! Thank you. Let me explain. The ship
doesn't actually listen to conversations,
but they are recorded for future reference in case an
order is misinterpreted or an instruction overlooked.
No part of what follows must be on that record.*

*Now, make yourselves comfortable and sit
absolutely still for thirty seconds.*

They did so, watching the screen as a timer in the bottom corner counted down to zero.

*Excellent. Now I have a video loop that I can
feed into the ship's sensors while I start a fire.*

'*What?*' Coral couldn't help herself.

Norman said quickly, 'What what?'

Tim said, 'What, what what?'

'What, what what? *What?*' Norman replied.

'Ah, stop! No more please!' Alkemy cried.

The screen redrew:

> *I can't do much right now. The ship's guard circuits*
> *are on high alert, but I have managed to short*
> *some of the fuses in the workshop. Any moment now,*
> *a large but harmless fire will start and the ship*
> *will be distracted. I need a volunteer for some*
> *tricky nanomachine work. Someone Tim's*
> *size would be perfect.*

'How about a game of tag?' Coral reached out and tapped her brother's shoulder. 'Tim's it.'

* * *

Unbuckling his seatbelt, Tim left the bridge, his head spinning with all the instructions Albert had given him. The video loop had started so as far as the ship was concerned he was still sitting in his seat.

He kept low and slid around the curved wall to the medical bay. The interior lighting showed he hadn't been detected. Standard illumination came from widely spaced bulkhead lights that glowed dimly until a sensor was triggered. Then, the full overhead lighting in that sector would come on. Albert explained that the sensors crisscrossed the wall at hip height. By staying below them, he could remain undetected.

Getting past the medical bay door was trickier. He had to lie flat on the floor and crawl to the opposite wall to avoid tripping the automatic opener. It would have been difficult in one-quarter normal gravity if he hadn't thought to borrow Norman's slippers and strap them on his hands, though it felt a bit like being a human fly.

He reached the galley and slid over to the drink dispenser. Opening the cupboard below it, he pushed his way inside and slithered to the corner. There he turned sideways, pressed his back flat against the wall behind, raised both elbows and slammed them backwards. The thin panel gave a faint crack and broke in two. He turned and pushed the pieces to one side.

A square duct ran behind the panel, a passage barely half a metre wide. He took off the gravity slippers and felt his way along. A few metres in, it joined a wider, vertical shaft. He eased himself into it and stood up. Cables, feed tubes, water and waste pipes snaked every which way. He turned around slowly, looking for the promised opening.

There, five metres up. A circular gap the size of a ship's porthole, just as Albert had said.

It looked a long way. Normally, he couldn't possibly jump that high, but Albert reckoned that in one-quarter gravity he should be able to jump ten times higher than than back on Earth.

Only one way to find out.

He crouched, feeling his body mass sink and centre with him, giving the reluctant gravity time to hold him down.

Then he sprang, snapping his legs straight, hard and fast, feeling himself soar into the air

'Whoa!' he cried, mirroring the pose of a superhero, one arm raised above him as he went. Fortunately, there were no sound sensors in the ship's maintenance ducts.

Albert was right. His momentum carried him past the porthole and he had to wait till gravity gently reclaimed him and drew him back before throwing out both hands and hooking on to the little opening as he descended. His outstretched arms took his weight and he bumped against the side of the duct before drawing himself up to peer inside.

Wedging his left elbow in the opening, he found a place to hook his toes, then felt about with his right hand for the calculator in his back pocket.

Understanding Eltherian should have made it easier. Before the linguaseed implant, the strange symbols and characters on the calculator's tiny screen were as meaningful as Egyptian hieroglyphics. Now he could understand them, but they were just as puzzling.

Technical terms, jargon and unpronounceable chemical names flashed across the screen as he set the switches the way that Albert had instructed. He took out a sketch he'd made on a piece of paper, held it up and double-checked the settings.

All good.

Then the world turned sideways.

Knock Knock Who's There? made a course correction, banking smoothly starboard. Tim's legs drifted from their footrest and his whole body swung parallel to the opening, leaving him hanging in mid-air for five long seconds. Albert had warned him of the possibility – it was after all why they were supposed to be buckled in – and he knew he should brace for the opposite manoeuvre.

Hooking his free arm through a loop of cable, he grabbed a waste pipe just as the ship swung sharply back. His lower body slammed against the duct wall and he let out a gasp of pain. Then the ship bucked as if it was trying shrug him off. He banged his head, cursed out loud and almost dropped the calculator.

He did drop the slip of paper. It drifted off just out of reach. He made a grab for it and missed, bumping the switches on the calculator as he did so. Each could be set in one of eight positions or left unset, making a ninth, and he knew that every setting changed something, subtly or massively. A mistake might cause Albert's plan to fail, or even wreck the ship – along with everyone in it.

The slip of paper drifted further out of reach.

He closed his eyes and concentrated, trying to remember the sketch he'd made and the movements of his hand as he made it.

He checked the calculator. The bottom right-hand side looked wrong. The ball of his thumb must have bumped the last three switches. They were all set west when they should have been east, south-east and neutral.

He reset them.

Is that right?

He closed his eyes again, trying to ignore the passage of time and the idea that it was running out.

He checked. Yes, he was sure now. He drew himself closer to the opening.

There was a junction box just inside the lower edge of the

porthole. He slipped a fingernail under its plastic lid and flicked it up. Beneath it lay dozens of connection points for the ship's external sensors.

Turning the calculator sideways, he positioned its dispensing hatch and pressed the release button. A blob of grey-green goo dropped in slow motion, splashed over the connections and began to bubble and fizz.

Tim watched for a moment then closed the lid, slipped the calculator back into his pocket, wriggled his upper body out of the porthole and pushed himself away from the side wall. As he drifted down, he checked his watch. Three minutes till docking. He'd better hurry because precisely one minute before they did so, all hell would break loose.

16 : Go, Go, Go!

Tim emerged from the cupboard below the drink dispenser and checked his watch. He'd made good time. Albert's tape loop should end in a few seconds.

He pulled on his gravity slippers, slipped out into the corridor, waved his arms to trigger the automatic lights as if he'd just come that way, then turned and ambled back into the galley where he punched a random button on the drinks machine.

He took the drink bulb from the dispenser and studied the label. It took several seconds for the ship to react.

'Whoa! What are you doing there? You shouldn't be walking abpit.'

'I'm getting a drink,' Tim said.

'No, no, no, we're about to dock. You should be in your seat!'

'I was thirsty.'

'Get back there immediately. Hurry, please. Go, go, go!'

'OK, OK.'

He trotted out to the circular corridor, past the medical

bay and back to the bridge.

'And use the handrail, just in case I have to make a course correction.'

He heard the ship mutter to itself in Eltherian, 'Honestly, cargo!'

'Where's mine?' Norman said as he stepped onto the bridge.

'Ooops, sorry.' Tim paused.

'No way!' The ship slammed the automatic door behind him. 'Back to your seat and buckle in!'

'Boy, that ship sure can nag.' Tim gave the others a thumbs-up as he took to his seat

'What flavour did you get?' Coral asked.

'Um ... loplebery.'

'Oh, barf! Better call the cleanies.'

'Why?' He took a sip. 'Urgh! That's awful.'

'You are *not* going back to get another one!' the ship snapped.

When he'd left the bridge, Selene Station filled the forward screen from top to bottom. Now all he could see of it was a portion of its outer edge. A massive, multi-decked segment teeming with ships, bots, gantry cranes and conveyor craft. The outer docking plates were for larger vessels like the freighter they'd followed. That had been fifty times their size, but Tim could see a dozen such vessels docked on nearby plates, dwarfed by the immense scale of the station itself.

The ship matched the station's rotation as it spun gently round a central core to create its own artificial gravity. That meant the ships on the docking plates all parked facing outwards, which was what Knock Knock intended too.

'*Knock Knock Who's There?*' an automated voice said above the background sound of other radio traffic. 'Please proceed to corridor Q3, bay 91.'

'Q3-91. Acknowledged,' Knock Knock said.

'No joke this time?' Norman asked.

Ludokrus said, 'Docking is a much serious. The time most accidents happen.'

'We wouldn't want that,' Tim said with a wink.

Smaller vessels docked at bays close to the station's central core. These were reached by a series of square metal tunnels that reminded Tim of the duct he'd just been crawling through.

'Reduce speed to forty knots.'

'Reducing to forty,' Knock Knock said.

There was a long metallic rasping sound from the port side.

Coral jumped. 'What was that?'

'Sorry.'

The forward view shifted as the ship corrected. Then over-corrected. The starboard side graunched against the wall opposite. There was a shower of sparks followed by a bang and scrape from underneath.

'Ooops,' the ship muttered.

'Reduce speed to twenty knots, effective immediately,' the automated voice said.

'Speed to twenty. Acknowledged.'

They all felt the steady braking as another voice came online. A real person this time.

'This is Selene Station Nav Command to *Knock Knock Who's There?* Are you in need of assistance?'

'Negative, Nav Command.' The ship actually sounded

embarrassed. 'Just having a little sensor trouble. My stack seems to be misaligned.' There was another scrape. 'I'm trying to work out the new parameters.'

This was followed by two more bangs, top and bottom.

'Please don't use our station to practise your basic manoeuvring skills,' the voice said, still calm. 'If you'd like tugboat assistance, you've only to ask.'

'No, no, I'm fine.'

Another crash.

The human voice spoke as if talking over its shoulder. 'Crash crews, stand by.'

Tim glanced at the others. Ludokrus looked grim. Coral was biting her lip. Alkemy had a hand in front of her eyes. Norman was grinning.

The ship swung hard right, scraping off more paint as the docking plate appeared dead ahead, a huge number 91 painted on the adjoining walls. The ship slowed to a hover, stopping in almost perfect alignment with the lights and laser guides lined up on it.

'Welcome to Selene Station,' the ship said with palpable relief, 'and thank you for flying with me.'

They braced themselves. If Albert's calculations were correct, the ship would think it was mere centimetres above the landing plate when in fact there was still two metres to go.

The hum of the ship's thrusters faded. A sudden downward lurch was followed by a terrific slamming bang. Alarms and sirens shrieked. Tim, Coral and Norman leapt from their seats and raced from the bridge, groaning at the sudden resumption of normal gravity.

The jump-blocks in the central spine only worked in low

gravity so they were forced to take the stairs that spiralled around the outside. It seemed like the long way round, especially now they had their full weight back. 'At least it's all downhill, Norman called.

The lower deck was a scene of utter chaos. Tools and bots had tumbled off racks. Locker doors had burst open, spilling their contents. A number of floor plates were buckled, and a ruptured water line in the first segment sprayed out a high-pressure mist that hung in the air like a cloud. Pierced by the sirens and flashing lights, the madly racing cleany-crawlies looked like they were at a robotic disco.

'C-7,' Norman shouted as they raced across the deck, leaping smashed components and puddles of spilled fluids.

Like the rest of the pods, the escape pod on C-7 stood with its upper hatch open. Unlike the rest of the pods, three of its gel beds were also open and glowed with a faint blue light.

The siren's pitch increased. The flashing lights flashed faster.

'Left. Right. Middle.' Norman pointed as they ran.

They reached the craft and dived for the beds, Norman to the left, Coral to the right and Tim in the middle. They were impressive leaps, given the gravity, and as soon as they hit the yielding gel, the capsule lids snapped shut. Half-a-second later, C-7's hatch closed, the craft pressurised, the sirens' shriek reached an even higher pitch and all eight of KKWT's remaining escape pods were forcibly ejected.

17 : Second Skin

'What the heck was that?' Ludokrus demanded as the shudder of ejecting escape pods convulsed the ship.

'I don't know. I don't know,' Knock Knock sounded panicked.

'But you are in charge.'

'I mean, I do know. But I don't know what caused it.'

The scene on docking plate Q3-91 now resembled the chaos on the ship's lower deck. Two of the escape pods had bounced off Selene Station's cladding and gone skittering out into the vacuum of the overbay. The rest had spewed forward and now lay in a jumbled heap against the bulkhead leading to the station's core.

The docking bay, normally dim in the interior half-light of the station, was flooded with emergency lighting, throwing the mess into sharp relief. As if to underline it, alarm lights began strobing throughout the entire segment.

Corridor Q3-9 contained ten docking plates, seven of which were currently occupied by other ships. And they were watching. Judging. *Knock Knock Who's There?* could sense their disapproval and was almost relieved when pressure doors came down, sealing off the site of its shameful landing and flooding the area with air so rescue crews and clean-up bots could get to work. Still, the other ships would have seen it all. Knock Knock closed its sensors down, shut off radio links and wished it could just dissolve into the dock.

* * *

Half the gel slurped out as the lid of the his bed slid back and Tim had to grab the sides to stop himself slurping after it.

His walrus mask showed him an exterior view. C-7's escape pod lay on its side, right up against the back wall of the docking plate, pushed there by the much larger evac pod from C-5. There was a tangle of other debris, sucked out of Knock Knock's lower deck by the ejecting craft, and the ship itself sat looking crumpled and spent in a cloud of dust and smoke and fire-retardant foam.

Sound slowly returned as the enclosed area outside was flooded with air, alarms and klaxons rising in volume as it filled. They didn't really help. The buckled docking plate, the crumpled ship and the arc of surrounding debris made it pretty clear there'd been a problem.

When the gauge in his mask showed the outside pressure had equalised, the escape pod's hatch popped just wide enough for them to crawl out. They slid down the floor of the steeply angled craft and stopped by the opening.

'Man, this gravity's killing me already! It feels like twenty

G, not one,' Norman said as he squeezed through the gap and looked around to get his bearings. Coral followed him out. Tim trailed. While he'd been crawling around Knock Knock's innards, Albert had been briefing the others on the best way out of the docking bay.

The space was ablaze with lights and filled with the sounds of alarms. Tim blinked and shaded his eyes. Fortunately, the way ahead was mostly shadowed by the inclined hull of C-5.

'That looks like a junk-bot hatch.' Coral pointed.

'Affirmative,' Norman said.

'Affirmative?'

'It means "yes".'

'I know what it means, but why not just say "yes"? Why waste four syllables when you can use one?'

'You've just wasted about a million moaning about it. Look out, here come the junk-bots!'

* * *

Floor lighting showed the way to the emergency exit, but it wasn't really needed as the regular lights were still on. A trolley-bot appeared carrying a radiation casket. The box had a brushed metal finish, reinforced sides and edges, and looked a bit like a coffin with a faceplate. Behind the clear glass window was a lifelike facsimile of Albert's head.

'Why do we need this?' Alkemy said. 'We could have make a robot, like on Earth.'

'You forget the biometric sensor in Immigration. Robot will be seen. This way he is shield.'

She handed him the memory bulb. 'You do, please. I do not want to see.'

Alkemy had loved the old syntho, yet technically she'd killed him. Following his instructions, she'd removed the memory bulb that contained his thoughts and personality after he'd been half-buried by a cave-in. Although he lived on when plugged into a suitable apparatus, copies of his old bodily form were still painful reminders of their lost friend and guardian.

Ludokrus unlatched the lid revealing a head and shoulders copy of Albert. There was nothing else. The racks below the mock-up contained batteries, expanded memory cubes and microwave communications gear. There were also random blocks of metal to make up the weight of an actual body.

Ludokrus slotted the bulb into a socket where Albert's stomach should have been and the mechanical face came to life at once, blinking and winking at him.

'Testing voice module,' the head said.

'Sound good.'

'OK. Close the lid.'

Ludokrus did so and there was a faint hiss as the casket vacuum sealed.

'Second skin, please.' Albert's voice was now muffled inside the closed casket.

Ludokrus set a skinner globe on top of the casket and activated it, releasing a thick film of clear plastic that ran down the sides. It took several seconds for the second skin to set by which time they heard an evac crew outside the ship working on the emergency escape hatch.

A winking light on the skinner globe confirmed the seal.

Ludokrus removed it, gestured to his sister to lead the way, then tapped the trolley-bot with his toe to indicate it should follow them. An evac crew consisting of at least a dozen bots and two real people in spacesuits met them at the exit ramp.

'This it? Three passengers?' one of them asked.

They nodded.

'Hand luggage only, please.'

Alkemy shouldered her pink backpack containing the calculator.

'This way.'

Bots of various shapes and functions streamed past them, heading into the ship to assess the damage, determine the cause and begin repairs. Docking plates – especially priority ones – were expensive. A quick turnaround was essential.

Alkemy paused, turned back and called, 'Thank you, ship.'

The ship said nothing.

'Hey, *Knock Knock Who's There?*' Ludokrus called.

'Yes?' the ship said quietly.

'Say your name.'

'I beg your pardon?'

'Go on. Say your name.'

'*Knock Knock Who's There?*' the ship said.

'Boo.'

'Boo who?'

'Oh, don't cry about it!' Ludokrus laughed.

It might have been her imagination, but as they walked away, Alkemy thought she heard the ship sniff quietly.

18 : Luggage

The junk-bots looked like grown-up versions of the ship's cleany-crawlies. Large metallic spheres with an array of tiny thrusters that gave them precise control so that they moved like hummingbirds. They had fine retractable arms and hinged undersides that acted like scoops or jaws to gather up and store what they collected. A dozen of them emerged from the open hatch, one after the other, each zipping off to a different part of the docking bay. The hatch door remained open.

Coral handed Tim a plastic disc the size of a coin. 'Stick that in a pocket somewhere.'

'What is it?'

'It'll identify you as a faulty junk-bot.'

'Why?'

'You'll see. Come on.'

She led her way to the hatch, keeping to the shadow cast by C-5 before darting across a last brightly lit metre and throwing herself inside.

Tim and Norman followed and found themselves in an

unpainted cube of a room the size of a garden shed. There were two broad shelves along either side where the junk-bots sat in dish-shaped fittings. Behind each space was a charging station.

'Dead end,' Tim said.

'Not quite.' Norman pointed to a dark rectangle on the back wall.

'What's that?'

'The unloading bay. Where the bots dump the junk they collect. Coming?'

Bracing himself with his hands, Norman slid his legs into the chute then let go. He disappeared. It looked like he'd just posted himself through a letterbox.

'Go on,' Coral said, 'before they start coming back to dump stuff.'

Tim climbed in behind his friend and found himself sitting on a polished metal slide that dropped away steeply. The interior was pitch black. He couldn't even see his shoes. He took a breath, lay back and let go, trusting to luck and Albert's instructions.

He felt a swooping sensation in the pit of his stomach and a rush of air over his face as he picked up speed. It felt like he'd jumped off a cliff. There was no way he could slow himself down.

The slide curved left as the steep angle levelled smoothly. He slowed a bit and saw lights ahead. A moment later, he dropped onto a broad conveyor belt, landing with a grunt.

He saw Norman up ahead. They were separated by mangled bits of junk gathered up and dumped by other bots from other junk-bot lockers.

'Watch out for other chutes,' Norman called.

Tim ducked and held up a hand as he passed beneath another opening. Fortunately, nothing fell on him. He heard Coral's 'Oof!' as she landed on the belt somewhere behind.

Norman was approaching a scanner, a dark aperture lit inside by flashes of green and blue light.

'Sit up like this,' he called over his shoulder. 'And cup your hands.'

Tim copied his posture, sitting cross-legged, his hands cupped in his lap.

Norman disappeared inside the machine.

The conveyor belt slowed for a moment then sped up again and the pile of junk ahead of him vanished inside the scanner. Tim heard a series of mechanical clanks and clunks, then it was his turn.

The belt slowed again the moment he entered. Green and blue lights strobed across him, then it sped up once more. Something warm and clammy plopped into his cupped hands and he was through.

The other side of the machine was brilliantly lit, almost blinding in its intensity, and Tim found himself holding a blob of greyish-coloured nanomachine recycling mixture. Suddenly it all made sense. The junk-bots would scoop up all they could and dump it in the back of their closet before going back for another load. They'd only ever collect things they could recycle – avoiding anything biological – and when one of them failed or they started wearing out, they'd dump themselves. He guessed the scanner was a safety check, slowing if it came across anything unusual. But the disc Coral had given him identified him as a faulty bot, so he was being treated like one.

'Up here,' a voice called.

Ahead, the conveyor belt ended over a circular skip three metres deep. Junk from the conveyor plopped and splashed into it, joining a growing puddle of recycling goo in the bottom. Tim saw Norman stand, fling his goo into the container, grab the railing of an inspection gantry to his left, and swing himself up through the bars.

He did the same. Thirty seconds later, Coral joined them.

* * *

One of the advantages of priority docking was that it gave them priority at Planetary Immigration too. Alkemy and Ludokrus could see queues outside through the glass walls of the VIP inspectorate office. It seemed a cruise ship had just arrived.

Albert's casket was whisked away and its seals double-checked. It returned with an alarm-seal wrapped around the middle like a chain. There was an accompanying notice that threatened prosecution if the seal was broken without proper authorisation. The trolley-bot transporting the casket moved in behind Alkemy and Ludokrus as they approached the immigration desk, tilting its passenger into an upright position so Albert could see what was going on.

'A meteor storm in Tarkav, you say?' Planetary Immigration Inspector Zul was a tall, bronzed woman with a crisp uniform and an air of authority. 'What on Eltheria were you doing there? You filed a flight plan for Alkonorst.'

'I made a mistake with the coordinates,' Albert answered for them.

'Some mistake. You're two-and-a-half weeks late back.

Do you realise we had probes scanning the Alkonorst system for you?'

'Sorry,' Albert said.

'So you had to make repairs. Have you filed a K-101B?'

'What's that?'

'An In-flight Damage Repair Report. I take it from your ignorance the answer's no.'

'No, not yet.'

'Your ship should have been re-inspected before it docked. Could these unapproved repairs account for its crash landing?'

'Oh, I don't think so.'

She glared at him through the window of the casket. 'You don't *think* so? They apparently accounted for something as basic as the bridge camera not working, along with intermittent sensor faults.'

'Minor oversights.'

'Like the mistake with the coordinates?'

Albert said nothing.

'And how exactly did you come to end up in a contamination casket.'

'I ... accidentally switched off my spacesuit's radiation detectors while I was making repairs.'

'A few too many accidents, oversights and mistakes if you ask me, Syntho Albert. When you get yourself decontaminated, I suggest *you* get a full service check as well.'

'Yes, of course. Is that all, Inspector?'

'I would like to get to the bottom of this crash landing business, but you've been given priority clearance so I shan't keep you any longer. I'll be in touch if I need any more details. Until then, you're free to go. Your escort is waiting.'

'Escort?' Alkemy said.

* * *

At the end of the gantry, a regular-sized door opened onto a broad, curving corridor. A basement area of some sort. Pipes and ductwork ran along the ceiling, and a variety of bots clattered, hovered, rolled and walked along a well-worn central passage.

Norman, Tim and Coral kept to one side. The machines gave them a wide berth and priority at intersections, and after five minutes they came to a bank of elevators. The nearest one sensed their arrival and opened its doors automatically.

Coral tapped the button marked Departures.

'Don't we need Arrivals?' Tim said.

'Not yet, we need some props first.'

He was about to ask what she meant when a pair of bots that looked like metre-high mechanical spiders clattered in after them. One of them sprang up on its back legs and stabbed a button labelled Octopod Access Deck. The doors closed and the elevator rose before opening again on a mostly blank steel wall. There was a small gloomy opening in the bottom right-hand corner and the spider-bots scuttled out, disappearing into the darkness.

'Glad that's not our floor,' Tim said as the doors closed again.

When they re-opened, it felt like they were stepping into another world. Or back into an old familiar one.

123

The departure terminal might have been any airport terminal back on Earth. White tiles, muted lighting, signboards of check-in times and terminal gates. A line of exclusive-looking shops ran along one wall, a variety of refreshment bars and cafes ran along another, but three things told them it wasn't Earth. The people, who came in a wide variety of shapes, sizes and species; the service-bots, which scuttled amongst them, and the luggage, which followed its owners around like trained dogs, sometimes singly and sometimes in herds of ten or more separate pieces.

'That's what we want.' Coral pointed at the bags.

'But we haven't got any money,' Tim said. '*And* we don't speak Eltherian.'

'First, you don't need money here. Anything labelled Basic is free thanks to nanomachines. Second, everyone on Eltheria has those linguaseed chips in their heads which connect up to a central computer called Valax. Whenever linguaseeds pick up an unknown language, they call it in and Valax downloads the appropriate translation module. Albert added the English one just before we arrived so we should be good to go.'

'Over there.' Norman pointed to a short passage leading to a cul-de-sac of shops. Illuminated signs above each entrance identified them as Basic Food, Basic Clothing, Basic Comms and Basic Luggage.

'What about the other places?' Tim said as they headed across.

'They're like designer shops. You do need money for them. They have stuff like the latest fashions and fancy food, but you can get by with Basic stuff.'

She greeted the shop-bot in Basic Luggage, pointed to a silver suitcase on display and said, 'Do you have that in black?'

There was a brief pause while the bot identified and downloaded the appropriate language module, then it replied, 'Good morning, miss. Yes, certainly. One moment please.'

Coral winked at Tim.

The bot was tall, thin and tubular, like an inverted test tube with arms and a wheeled base. It rolled to the rear of the shop, punched some buttons on a wall plate, and ten seconds later a shuttered panel opened to reveal a gleaming new black suitcase. The shop-bot took it in two claws, rolled back and presented it to Coral with a polite bow.

'Cool, thanks.'

'Will that be all, miss?'

'Yes, thank you.' Coral turned to the others. 'What about you guys?'

'I'll have the same please,' Tim said. 'In blue.'

'Make mine bright yellow, Case Captain,' Norman said as the bot trundled off. 'Hey, after this, shall we try the food?'

'We don't have time for you to fill your face, or your hollow legs. We've got to meet the others.'

'I see why they're called "Basic",' Tim muttered, inspecting his new suitcase. 'There's no handle.'

'You don't need them. Just pat its head.' Coral reached down and tapped her fingers on a small panel on the end of the case. There was a faint ping of acknowledgement as it registered her as its owner. 'Now we look the part, we can go to Arrivals. Come on.' She headed of, her suitcase trundling along behind her.

The arrivals area was one floor down from Departures, and Q segment occupied a small portion of a vast circular mezzanine floor that surrounded the main concourse. Below it, hundreds of people moved to and fro, all activity focused on the huge central core to which the space station was tethered. Not a single cable, but eighteen separate strands, some with cars coming up and some with cars heading down. They could see right down to the planet's surface because the floor around the cable trains was made of transparent acrylic.

'You're probably going to get sick of me saying this,' Tim said, 'but *wow!*'

'Wow, all right,' Norman muttered.

Coral pushed herself away from the railing. She'd never been keen on heights, and the sight of the immense drop made her dizzy.

'Hey there!' a voice behind them called. 'Alkemy, look who it is.'

The turned to find Alkemy and Ludokrus coming out of a VIP arrival gate.

'What a surprise. Fancy meeting you guys here,' Coral said, glad of the distraction and relishing her role. She was a rather good actress.

'We just come back from holiday.'

'Us too! What a coincidence. How are you both? What happened to Albert?'

'Oh, you know Albert. Always with the messing up.'

Ludokrus gave her a hug and saw the immigration inspector was still watching them intently.

'So,' he said, 'you must be our escort.'

'Escort?'

'No sir, that'll be us.' Two voices spoke behind them simultaneously, one from the left, one from the right.

They turned to find two large synthos dressed in black approaching them. Identical twins. *Big* identical twins.

'Look like augments,' Ludokrus murmured.

'That's right sir, augmented synthetics,' the one on the left said. 'We're Triple-Dub. I'm Wilis. He's Walis.' The other syntho raised a meaty hand.

'You are twin?'

'No sir, we're triplets. Welis can't be here right now. He's having his jaw replaced.'

'That sound serious.'

'Not half as serious as what happened to the syntho that broke it,' Walis said.

The augments surveyed the gathering, looking each of them up and down. They had broad square faces that showed almost no expression, heavy brows and sunken eyes. The eyes were disconcerting, in part because they seemed to glow from within, and in part because of their colour; an unpleasant brownish-yellow.

'We're here to accompany you and your sister down, Mr Ludokrus,' Wilis said, looking about. 'And a third individual. A synthetic.'

'That would be me,' Albert said from his casket.

Wilis and Walis turned, saw the radiation warnings and took a step backwards. Then they saw the official clearance notice on the alarm-seal and seemed to relax.

'Thanks, but we can find our own way, I think,' Ludokrus said.

'You don't understand, sir. We're under orders. Administrator Meli would like to see you right away.' There was a handle on the back of Albert's casket. Wilis took it, lifted it effortlessly off the trolley-bot and held it in front of himself like a shield. 'This way please.'

Walis gestured for Alkemy and Ludokrus to follow him. Alkemy glanced at the others, made a helpless gesture, then did so. Ludokrus went too. Walis brought up the rear.

'Make way, please,' Wilis boomed as they headed across the crowded mezzanine. 'Make way. Contaminated waste.'

'Oh, please,' Albert muttered.

Coral, Tim and Norman went to follow them, but Walis stopped, turned, crossed his arms and stood looking down at them, shaking his massive head.

'Um ... so ... how about we grab some food instead?' Norman said.

19 : Escort

Alkemy looked back as they were bustled along, but the bulk of Walis blocked her last view of their friends. She didn't even have a chance to wave.

As they headed across the concourse, Ludokrus moved towards one of the travelators that led to the cable train station, but Wilis, without even turning, called over his shoulder, 'Not that way, sir.'

Ludokrus raised an eyebrow at his sister. How did Wilis know where he'd been looking without even turning round? He knew little about augments. He'd seen them occasionally in the street, and they often played baddies in action feelies, but he thought the augmentation only applied to their muscles.

Wilis led them to an up-bound travelator leading to the Departures floor.

Other people filed onto the moving walkway behind them so Walis drew up close. Alkemy could feel his mechanical presence and gripped the strap of her backpack. She kept her eyes fixed straight ahead, unwilling now to turn back and search out their friends. This felt more like an arrest than an escort.

Wilis stepped off the travelator, still keeping Albert's casket at arm's length, still using it like a shield, and they moved to a quieter, more exclusive area of the floor. Private lounges, up-market shops, agencies offering a variety of travel services. They passed a sign directing them to a private shuttle bay and exchanged a glance.

'That's right Mr Ludokrus, Ms Alkemy,' Wilis said, again without turning. 'Only the best for guests of Administrator Meli.'

* * *

Coral, Tim and Norman watched their friends go. Walis continued blocking their way for a few more seconds, then turned and jogged after the others.

'Let's follow them,' Tim said. 'Just keep our distance.'

Twenty metres away, Walis stopped abruptly, turned back, pointed at him, scowled and shook his head.

'Who, me?' Tim muttered.

Walis nodded, turned and trotted after the others.

'How the heck did he hear that?' Tim whispered.

'Ludokrus said something about them being augmented synthos,' Coral said. 'That must include their hearing.'

'Those guys have got muscles in places I haven't even got places,' Norman muttered.

They stood watching their friends go, losing them in the bustling crowd. But they weren't hard to track. The augments' bulk and height were a giveaway, and people tended to avoid them, parting before them like waves around the prow of a ship.

'They look more like prisoners,' Coral said as they watched their friends step onto an up-bound travelator. Neither Alkemy nor Ludokrus looked back.

'And why are they going up? That's Departures.' Norman pointed to the level below. '*That's* the way down to the planet. Those guys could be taking them anywhere. Eltherians live on moons, other planets, even other systems. We don't want to lose them. Wait here, I'll see where they're heading.'

He raced off, his bright yellow suitcase trailing behind him.

'No, Norman. Wait!'

* * *

Planetary Immigration Inspector Zul watched the scene outside the windows of the VIP office as the new arrivals greeted some old friends. She wasn't happy. Crash landings were rare on the station. They were mostly the result of alien craft under manual control. Automated ship systems – especially Eltherian ones – were highly sophisticated and had many fail-safes to prevent such accidents. Something about the chain of mishaps didn't feel quite right.

She watched the appearance of the augment escort. The way they bustled the children and their guardian off, clearly in a hurry. They, like the order for priority processing, had come from the new head of the Science Council. The head himself, not some assistant or middle manager. That was interesting too. Why would a man in his position be interested in such a motley crew?

These were interesting times. She had friends on the Science Council – the *old* Science Council – and knew a little of what had happened there. Things were changing, and there were bound to be opportunities for resourceful people with initiative. Checking entry documents day after day wasn't much of a career.

Turning back to her desk, she called up a review of all available records of the incident, including the ship's own logs of its approach.

20 : Illegal Aliens

Norman returned at a trot, his suitcase bumping against the backs of his shoes as he suddenly slowed.

Coral punched him on the arm. 'Don't do that!'

'Ow! Do what?'

'Run off like that.'

'Why not?'

'Don't you realise where we are? This isn't just a new place. It's a whole new world. A whole new solar system. We're not just strangers here, we're aliens. *Illegal* aliens at that. Apart from Alkemy, Ludokrus and Albert, we don't know anyone here. *Anyone at all in the entire solar system.* If something happened to you just now, what should we have done?'

Norman rubbed his arm. Said nothing.

'Not only that, but you saw the way those ... *things* ... looked at us. We don't know anything about this place. About its customs or rules or laws or anything. How do we even get down to the planet? Where do we go when we get there? There's just the three of us now, trapped here, fifty light-years from home. We *have* to stick together.'

Norman bit his lip. She was right. What if he'd come back and found his friends had vanished? What would he have done?

Tim said, 'Did you discover anything?'

'Not much. They went into a private area. Executive lounges, that sort of thing. There was a guard-bot on the gate. It wouldn't let me through, but it did tell me where else it led: private shuttle bays.'

'Oh great.' Coral looked to a giant screen showing the view outside the station, at Eltheria's moons, planets and the stars beyond. 'They could be going anywhere.'

'Not really,' Norman said. 'The shuttle schedules are posted. I checked on my way back. The only private one leaving in the next half-hour is to some place called Concordance.'

'Where's that?'

'Dunno. Let's find out. There must be a tourist office somewhere.'

They took the travelator down and did a circuit of the lower floor but drew a blank. Everyone simply seemed to know where to go. In a quiet area away from the jostling crowds they watched the passers-by in silence. Hundreds, thousands of people. All going about their business, all without checking guidebooks or schedules or maps.

They were mostly humanoid in form, mostly Eltherians, but dressed more variously than a crowd in an Earth airport. Many wore simple, flowing, kaftan-like garments, but there were a huge variety of others. Earth-like business suits. Form-fitting leather. Flat panels that looked like cardboard. Dresses with flowing trains. One was made out of nothing but coloured bows, including the headdress. Hair colour varied wildly too. There seemed to be a fashion for fluorescents; brilliant blues, greens, reds and purples. Several even matched Norman's suitcase.

There were a few alien species too. A pair of what might have been walking trees passed them. They had gnarled, bark-like skin and leafy buds on their cheeks.

'At least we look like we're locals,' Tim said, glancing at his sister.

Coral chewed her lip. He could see she was worried. They knew nothing about this place, not even where to go for help.

'Remember when we first arrived at Uncle Frank's farm?' he said.

'What's that got to do with anything?'

'That was pretty weird. The fields, the cows, going to school on that ancient bus – to say nothing of Rata and Rata School. It was almost like being on another planet.' She looked at him. 'We soon figured it out and found our way around.'

'But this place is like the opposite of Rata.'

'What's that? Auckland? That's our home town.'

Coral gave him a half-smile and nodded.

'I've been thinking,' Norman said, studying the tree people. 'We're not the only aliens here. The others must have guidebooks and tourist maps and stuff.'

'I don't see anyone using them.'

'Then they must be internal. Implanted satnav or something, like these linguaseed things. There's a Basic Alley over there. We should check it out. There might be a Basic Navigation shop or something.'

'Sure you're not really after Basic Food?'

'Hey, if there is one we can check that out too,' he said. 'C'mon.'

* * *

Alkemy had never been on a private shuttle before. The seats were luxurious, the in-flight service outstanding, and the view from the wide windows as the tiny craft dipped into the first wisps of Eltheria's atmosphere was beautiful. But what should have been the trip of a lifetime left her flat and worried and hardly aware of her surroundings.

All she and Ludokrus could do was exchange looks. She didn't dare to even whisper, not with one of the augmented synthos in the seat behind them and the other one in front. They were so big they required two seats each, and the back of Wilis's square, close-cropped head above the headrest was a constant reminder of their presence.

The shuttle banked and dipped and began its burn. The exterior view faded behind a fiery flare and the craft bucked slightly, as if trying to shy away from the drag of Eltheria's atmosphere.

Ludokrus took her hand. She gripped it and thought of where they were heading. Why did the head of the Science Council want to see them so urgently he'd sent a private shuttle?

* * *

The Basic Alley on the concourse level followed the same

design as the one on the departures floor – a cul-de-sac of shops side by side – but these were bigger, brighter and there were more of them. There was Basic Shoes, Basic Transport, Basic Homewares, Basic Office Supplies, Basic Toys and even Basic Gifts.

'No Basic Books, though,' Tim said, looking around at the illuminated signs.

'And Transport's a bust,' Coral added. 'It's all skateboards and scooter things.'

'Let's try the comms store.' Norman gestured to a display of headsets, phones and tablet-like devices.

Someone pushed past them as they entered. An Eltherian, judging by his bright pink hair.

'Give me an LC-913 in green.'

'Certainly, sir.' The shop-bot reached below the counter and brought out a device that looked like a cross between a calculator and a short-wave radio.

The man glanced at it then swept it aside, sending it clattering to the floor.

'*Dark* green, you tin idiot.'

'Certainly, sir.'

The shop-bot brought out an identical device in a darker shade. The man snatched it away and marched off.

'How rude,' Coral muttered as she moved towards the tall, thin machine gathering up the pieces of the broken device. It turned to her and inclined its tubular body in a helpful attitude.

'Good morning,' she said. 'I wonder if you can help me?'

There was a two-second pause while it downloaded the appropriate language module, then it said, 'Good morning, miss. I shall do my best. What is it you require?'

Coral explained how they were tourists, recently arrived, and were looking for guidebooks, maps and directories of Eltheria.

'Ah, you require a Compendia,' the shop-bot said, pointing to a display case. 'They come in two models; handheld or, if you have a compatible vision system, behind the ear.'

'How does that work?'

'It projects an overlay on the surface of your eye.'

'You mean like the walrus masks in gel beds?' Tim said.

'Precisely, sir.'

'So you can bring up a map while you're walking?'

'A three-dimensional map if you like, sir.'

'Cool!'

'And do you have any personal communicators?' Norman said. 'Like, I dunno what you call them here, but mobile phones?'

'Certainly, sir. They can be incorporated into the earpiece along with eye-control text messaging and a whisper mic for one-on-one or group-chat communications.'

'Three of them, please!'

'Could we get the handhelds as well, please?' Coral added. 'As a backup?'

'Certainly sir, miss. The earpieces require precise fitting. I shall need to measure you individually.' The shop-bot waved several of its thin, flexible arms. 'Do you mind?'

They stood in line as the machine deftly ran two sets of metal fingers around the sides and fronts of their heads.

'And what names shall I assign to the units?'

'Names?'

'Darty McHero,' Norman said quickly, giving the others a

significant look.

'Oh ... Angel Stardust.'

The bot gave Tim a quizzical look but his mind went blank.

'And he's Terry Bulsmell,' Norman said quickly.

Coral snorted.

'I shall personalise each unit when I set them up. Would you like the interface in Eltherian or your natural language, which I believe is called English?'

'English, please.'

'And do you have a colour preference?'

'Anything but dark green,' Coral said.

The machine didn't reply and its metallic features were incapable of registering expressions, but Coral fancied she saw something in its eyes. A flicker of understanding and appreciation. Perhaps even amusement.

'If I may make a suggestion; flesh tones make the devices less conspicuous. Almost invisible.'

'Sounds perfect. Flesh tones all round, please.'

The machine wheeled away to program the shop's fabricators.

'Terry Bulsmell?' Tim hissed. 'Where the hell did you get that?'

'Hey, it needed a name,' Norman laughed, 'and you looked like you couldn't remember yours.'

'Bulsmell!' Coral snorted again. 'Brilliant!'

'High-five, Angel,' Norman said.

'Right on, Darty.'

The shop-bot returned with three semicircular devices about two centimetres long. Each was shaped slightly differently and each had their fake names etched on the outer side, much to Tim's annoyance.

'To fit them, simply slip them over your right ears and the pads will attach automatically. To remove them, lift from the bottom,' the shop-bot said.

They tried both manoeuvres.

'To activate, simply tap behind your ear. Do the same to deactivate.'

A semi-transparent test card appeared in Tim's right eye, focusing and zooming till the image was sharp and clear and not too bright. Then it vanished, leaving a time and date display in the lower right-hand corner.

'The units respond to voice commands. Touch your ear and say, for example, "Location".'

Tim tried it and immediately a floor plan of the station popped into view showing his position and the direction he was facing.

'If you say "Destination, Elevator Six" for example, it'll give you directions.'

An arrow appeared, pointing the way. A readout at the bottom said the elevator was 293 metres to the east.

'That's neat!'

'There are, of course, many more directions you can give the units. I've taken the liberty of bookmarking the relevant sections on your handhelds.' The shop-bot gave them one each with a little bow. 'I suggest ten minutes study would be most advantageous. Please feel free to use the tables in our refreshment area outside.'

'Thank you very much,' Coral said. 'You've been really helpful.'

'Yeah man, gimme five,' Norman said, holding out his hand.

The shop-bot, despite its lack of expression, seemed puzzled.

'It's a sort of custom where we come from,' Coral explained. 'You're supposed to slap his hand.'

'I see,' the shop-bot said, and did so. Norman grinned.

'Yeah, thanks again,' Tim said.

'Thank *you*,' the machine bowed, 'for your custom and for your courtesy. It is appreciated and has been noted.'

'Wonder what it meant by that?' Norman said as they headed out.

21 : Concordance

Concordance was made up of thirty-six mirror-glass towers arranged in an ellipse on the western side of Paralax Island. The tallest towers, known as the Core Six, occupied the centre of the cluster while towers of steadily diminishing height spread out around them, perfectly placed and carefully aligned so that from across the bay it looked like a gigantic crystal growing out of the middle of the island.

Parks and gardens separated the towers. The shuttle touched down in one of them, landing lightly on articulated legs, its thrusters barely disturbing the fronds of nearby ferns. A ramp extended out and Alkemy, Ludokrus and Albert – now carried by a trolley-bot – moved down it, followed by Wilis and Walis.

The air was warm and the light golden. Tetzul blazed high in the sky while Tena, it's faint orange-brown companion, lay lower down and further west. The rich green grass looked freshly washed and the trees, fringed with spring blossom, reflected back and forth in the mirror-glass buildings making it look like they'd stepped into an enchanted forest.

Home at last. They should have been happy.

Ludokrus glanced at his sister, his face expressionless. Alkemy pursed her lips and said nothing. Without their friends, it didn't feel anything like a homecoming.

The path from the landing pad led to one of the tallest towers in the ellipse: Science. The remaining blocks housed the Environment, Medical, Military, Information and Commerce councils. Wilis directed them to a private elevator running up the outside of the building. The sliding door was locked, but when he placed the palm of his hand against it there was a faint *ping* and it slid open.

There wasn't a lot of room in the glass-sided cube. The trolley-bot stood Albert upright between Wilis and Walis, who pressed themselves against the walls either side, still seemingly wary of the radiation hazard. They stood with their ham-like hands clasped in front of them, their faces impassive, and the faint metallic sheen of their skin reflecting Tetzul-light.

Alkemy and Ludokrus looked down as the ground fell away beneath them. Paralax Bay and Buckle Gap emerged from behind the lower towers. In the distance, they could make out rocks and a chain of islands and the crashing surf where the vast northerly ocean met the vast southerly one.

Ludokrus nudged his sister. She glanced at him and saw his eyes tilt towards Albert.

Letting her gaze drift across to the faceplate of the casket, Alkemy saw the fake plastic head wink and mouth two words at her, repeating them over and over until she gave a nod of understanding: 'Say nothing. Say nothing. Say nothing.'

* * *

A collection of high tables and stools stood in front of Basic Food. They took the one furthest from the serving kiosk and Tim and Norman began experimenting with their personal communicators while Coral studied the handset the shopbot had given her.

'Blink your right eye slowly to turn it on,' Norman said.

Tim tried it and a variety of comms functions appeared in his overlay. There were two items in the side menu labelled Contacts, but before he could flick his eyes to select one, a faint tone in his earpiece sounded and a message appeared saying there was an incoming call from Norman. He glanced at *Accept?* and Norman's voice said, 'Testing, testing. I think Coral's an idiot.'

Tim glanced at his sister, who continued scrolling through her handset.

'How do you—?'

'Just nod your head,' the voice in his ear said. 'Like this.'

Norman demonstrated with a quick tilt of his chin. 'It switches on the whisper mic. Then you just whisper.'

Tim looked and saw his friend's lips were barely moving.

He tried it. 'Like this?'

'Coming through loud and clear!'

'So we can have conversations and nobody knows?'

'Cool, eh?'

Coral looked up. 'What are you two whispering about?'

A message appeared in Tim's overlay.

Norman: YOU CAN ALSO SNED TEXTS.

'Yeah, but you have to learn to spell first,' Tim said out loud.

'What?' Coral said.

There was a disturbance at a table nearby where a group of Eltherian boys were making fun of a serve-bot. It was carrying trays in several of its metal-clawed hands and attempting to deliver them, but each time it tried to set one down, one of the boys reached out and blocked it. The machine changed its angle, going up, down, left or right to try to avoid the obstructions, but the blocker moved too.

'Hey, c'mon on, tin head. Where's our food?' a large boy with yellow hair called.

The serve-bot moved around the table, trying another angle, but another blocker took over.

'I'm sorry, sirs,' the serve-bot said, 'I seem to be experiencing—'

Someone nudged one of its arms.

'Hey, you spilt my drink!'

'Oh dear. I shall get you a replacement as soon as I have delivered—'

'Hurry up. The food's getting cold.'

The blocking continued. The bot moved again. A third blocker took over. Then yellow-hair elbowed one of the trays, knocking its contents onto the others and sending all four of them cascading to the floor.

'Now look what you've done!'

'Oh dear. Please excuse me. I do apologise. I will replace the foodstuffs immediately.'

The boys laughed. As it scuttled away, one of them kicked it in the back.

'Wow! That was impressive,' Coral said.

All four turned towards their table, regarding her blankly while their linguaseeds updated.

'Picking on a serving bot. You must be really tough. What else do you do? Beat up little kids?'

Norman heard Tim's whisper through his earpiece: 'Just leave it, Coral.'

The boys stared, sizing up her and her companions.

'What's it to you, *alien?*' yellow-hair said.

Coral leaned one arm on the back of her seat, tossed her long blonde hair back and looked him up and down. 'I came here to see if Eltherian guys are as cool as they think they are. Apparently not.' And with that, she turned her back on them.

A *Connect?* request appeared in Tim's overlay.

'What are they doing now?' Coral whispered.

'Just sitting there looking like idiots. Hang on, the serve-bot's back. It's delivering their food and ... all done.'

Coral smiled in satisfaction.

Tim looked at his sister. How did she get away with that? If it had been him or Norman, there would probably have been a fight.

* * *

The elevator opened directly into Krilen's old office. Administrator Meli rose from behind Krilen's old desk and greeted them warmly.

'Good morning, good morning! Welcome home!' He offered an outstretched hand in the traditional Eltherian greeting. Alkemy and Ludokrus responded with their own, patting palms formally. He even acknowledged Albert's casket.

'Please take a seat.' He gestured to three low sofas by the window. 'It's a pleasure to meet you at last. Dear old Polky speaks very highly of you all.'

Alkemy avoided looking at her brother, knowing he'd notice the slip-up too. Polky really was Krilen's first name, but he loathed it and insisted his friends use his last name.

'You know our uncle?' Ludokrus asked.

'Oh yes, we go back many years.'

'You say he is not well,' Alkemy said.

'No, I'm afraid he's not the best.'

'What is wrong?'

'To be honest, we're not certain. The doctors suspect it may be an alien virus. It's left him paralysed and unable to speak, but he's comfortable, and his condition is stable. They've put him in quarantine in case he's contagious. No visitors permitted, I'm afraid.'

'An alien virus?' Alkemy repeated.

'He was rather interested in aliens, wasn't he?'

He regarded her with a thin-lipped smile. His lined skin had an unhealthy grey tinge and his hooded eyes were dark and unreadable. Despite his friendly overtures, there was a lizard-like coldness to him.

'Was he?'

Meli studied her a moment longer, as if unsure whether she was telling the truth.

'What about our parent?' Ludokrus asked. 'We try to contact, but the system says they are off-world and we must ask for you to relay the message.'

'We don't yet know the source of the virus, but I understand Polky received some artefacts from your parents shortly before he fell ill. We've quarantined them too, just to be on the safe side.'

'They are also sick?'

'No, but until we isolate the source, I can't allow them to travel. You do understand we must keep a lid on this? If word gets out about the virus, there could be widespread panic.' He looked from one to the other. 'Now, where are my manners? Allow me to get you some refreshments. You must be tired and hungry after your trip.'

He pressed a button on the low table between them and Walis appeared, carrying a tray of drinks and light snacks. There was Shushter Water, caramelised hartree nuts and slices of gurk on thin wafers.

'Thank you, Wilis,' Meli said as the augment put down the tray.

'It's Walis, sir.'

Ludokrus looked past him, catching sight of the empty reception area beyond. They'd visited Krilen many times before, and the area outside his office was always bustling with activity. Now, it looked deserted. Worse, it looked abandoned.

'Is Dr Haril here?' he asked.

'Polky's deputy? I'm afraid there's bad news there too. She went on a climbing expedition in the Xintulb mountains just before Polky fell ill. Nothing's been heard from her for over a fortnight. We have search-bots out, of course, but the area is huge and she didn't file a climbing plan before she left. That's why I've had to step in.

'But enough about goings-on here. How was your mission?'

'Mission?' Alkemy repeated, thinking of Albert's mouthed warning in the elevator.

'Old Polky told me all about it. How did it go?'

Albert said, 'You must mean *my* mission. To deliver these two to their parents on Alkonorst. I ... um ... I'm afraid I rather messed that up.'

Meli hesitated, suddenly unsure of himself.

'Why? What sort of mission did Old Polky say we were on?' Albert added.

'I ... well, he didn't tell me everything, of course. Just that there was one. Something secret. And he had an automatic prompt set up to inform him of your ship's return, so I assumed ...' His voice trailed off as he looked his guests over, seeming to see them for the first time.

'He is the childrens' uncle,' Albert said.

'Ah, that would explain it,' Meli muttered to himself. In a louder voice he added, 'Well ... I'll leave you to finish your snacks. You must excuse me, I have work to do. I take you'll be all right seeing yourselves out?'

Before anyone could answer there was a tap on the door and one of the augments appeared.

'What is it, Walis?'

'It's Wilis, sir. There's a call for you. A Priority One.'

'Why? Who is it?'

'Selene Station, sir. From a Planetary Immigration Inspector by the name of Zul.' He looked directly at Meli's visitors. 'It seems she's found some irregularities in your guests' arrival procedure.'

22 : Smac and Smolgrids

'Welcome to Basic Food,' the serve-bot said, handing each of them an electronic menu with a small bow. One of its six arms was out of action and the dent in its back made its wheels squeak.

'Cool, thanks,' Coral said, tapping her finger on an illustration she recognised. 'I'll have a jahlbad blossom, and have you got anything like what we call chips?'

There was a brief hesitation while the bot checked its English lexicon, then it replied, 'There is a local starchy, tuberous, root vegetable called the smac, miss. We serve it cut in wedges and fried. Perhaps that will suffice?'

It tapped a metal claw on an item labelled SmacPac and the menu listing popped up an overlay showing a rotating image of a bowl of perfect golden chips.

'Great. I'll have one of those too, please.'

'Certainly.' The serve-bot regarded her with something like surprise in its large eyes. It wasn't used to being addressed politely.

Tim and Norman scrolled through their menus till they

came across the Eltherian equivalent of burgers: smolgrids.

'Would you like spats, wodgets, trols and gurk with them, sirs?'

'Yes, please,' Norman said before Tim could even ask what they were. 'Hey, I'll try anything once,' he added as the serve-bot trundled off, steering a circuitous route to avoid the table occupied by the four boys.

'Have you figured out where Concordance is?' Tim asked, nodding at Coral's handheld Compendia.

'No, but I have found Ludokrus's and Alkemy's contact numbers. I was wondering if I should call them and find out what's going on.'

'Bad move,' Norman said. 'If they're under suspicion, their calls will be monitored.'

'So? Whoever's listening won't know who we are.'

'Maybe not, but they'll know *where* we are. You know how cellphone networks work back home; they can pinpoint your location to within fifty metres. They're probably even more accurate here. Call them up and we might as well walk around holding big red arrow signs saying "Here we are!"'

'Does that matter?'

'We're illegal aliens, remember? We snuck in here pretending to be junk-bots, and it looked like Alkemy and Ludokrus were under arrest.'

'So how *do* we get in touch with them? They can't call us. They don't know we have comms.'

'What about the local equivalent of a public phone box?'

'Do they even have them here? According to Compendia, *"... all local inhabitants are fitted with a subcutaneous communications lace that allows them to interact with each other via Eltheria's planetwide network."'*

Tim said, 'We need to know more about how this place works first, figure out what's going on and where they've been taken.'

'Found it!' Norman held up his own handheld. *"Concordance – based on Concordance Island in Eltheria's capital city, Theia – is the focus of the planet's cultural, scientific, political and social life. It is the base of all governing councils and industry groups, and also houses Valax – often referred to as the* Mind of the Planet *– a sophisticated and highly evolved artificial intelligence that controls much of Eltheria."'*

'So it's actually *on* the planet? That narrows it down.'

'It kind of makes sense too. Triple-Dub told the others that admin guy wanted to see them. He's head of the Science Council, and that's based in Concordance.'

'So now we need to figure out how to get there.'

Tim leaned towards his sister, gesturing at the table behind her. 'Your friends are leaving.'

'Good riddance.'

But they didn't all go. Three of them lingered at the exit, nudging each other, while the fourth, yellow-hair, came towards them.

'Hey,' he said, ignoring Tim and Norman.

Coral regarded him cooly.

'That ... um ... stuff before. They're just bots, you know? They don't have feelings or anything.'

'Are you sure?'

He said nothing.

'It doesn't mean you have to be unpleasant to them.'

'Yeah. I mean, no ... It's just ... well, everyone does it.'

'And you have to be like everyone else?'

He coloured. 'So, where are you heading? We're taking

Line Fifteen to Orme.'

'Concordance,' Coral said.

'Line Seven, eh?. Well ... um ... have a good trip. And ... welcome to Eltheria.'

He offered her the palm of his hand. Coral had seen other people in the station do the same and guessed it was the local equivalent of a handshake. She held out her own hand and touched his palm.

'What was that about?' Tim said as yellow-hair returned to his friends.

'I think that was an apology,' Coral said. 'And now we know how to get to Concordance.'

* * *

Almas Meli returned to the office, his eyes hard, his manner cool and expression set. He stood glaring down at the three of them, hands on his hips. 'Right. I suggest you start talking. *Now*. Before I have you arrested.'

Alkemy and Ludokrus blinked. Albert said, 'Arrested for what?'

'I've just been talking to an inspector on Selene Station. She's been investigating the cause of your crash landing. According to your ship, it was carrying *six* passengers, yet only three passengers disembarked. You three. *Where are the others?*'

No one spoke.

'I know where they're not. They're not on the ship. *That* has been thoroughly searched.'

No one spoke.

'It also appears that shortly before landing, your syntho,' Meli glared at Albert's casket, 'uploaded a brand new language module to Valax. A language never seen before. An alien language called English. Since that upload, it's been downloaded eight times – all from within Selene Station.

'The good inspector noticed one other curious anomaly. It seems that there's a sudden over-supply of junk-bots in bay Q3-91, the bay where you landed. There are too many to fit into one particular storage closest. Yet they all claim it as their home base. A storage closet that is, coincidentally, closest to the scene of the crash.

'How many extra bots am I talking about? Another coincidence. Three. Three bots that were manufactured to replace faulty ones that turned themselves in for recycling just after your crash landing.'

Still no one spoke.

'Do I need to paint you a picture? Do you realise the seriousness of this offence? Deliberate disruption of a sentient ship causing it to crash. The illegal importation of a hitherto unknown alien species. And that's just the start.'

'It was all my doing,' Albert said. 'The children knew nothing about it.'

'No?' Meli raised an eyebrow. 'How is it then that the ship has been able to provide footage of them chatting and fraternising with the missing aliens as if they were old friends?'

He gestured at his desk. Three separate projections appeared in the space above it. Ludokrus talking to Alkemy, Tim talking to Coral, and all five of them together in the galley, laughing.

Meli whirled around at them. 'I demand to know what is

going on!'

Alkemy, Ludokrus and Albert said nothing.

'Well, perhaps your alien friends will be more cooperative. You do realise I could have that entire station closed while they're hunted down? Fortunately, that won't be necessary.'

He went to his desk and pressed a button. A moment later Wilis and Walis stepped into the room.

'Is Welis still on Selene?'

The two augments paused and rubbed their jaws in unison while they communicated with their clone-brother, then Wilis replied, 'Yes, sir. He's at a workshop in sub-basement D. The replacement procedure is just about to begin.'

'Never mind that now. Tell him I have a job for him. An *urgent* job. Find these three.' He stabbed a finger at the screens where the images had frozen on the sharpest, clearest pictures of Coral, Tim and Norman.

'Selene's a big place, sir,' the other augment said. 'Should we go back up and help?'

'That won't be necessary, Wilis.'

'Walis, sir. Why not?'

'Because they'll be easy enough to track. Just have him follow the English language downloads. In fact,' Meli consulted a terminal on his desk, 'tell him to start at the last place the module was accessed. The Basic Food kiosk on the main concourse.'

23 : The Waiting Room

Norman let out a long belch.

'Oh, please,' Coral said.

'But that food was great.'

She couldn't argue. She'd demolished a smolgrid and a plate of smac all on her own, then ordered seconds. Norman helped her with the leftovers.

'That has to be the tastiest burger I've ever eaten,' Tim said.

'Not so keen on the gurk.' Norman flicked aside a partially eaten slice of pickled sprout, 'but the rest was delish. And they call this *basic* food. I can't believe it's free!'

'I see we're going to have to get one of those trolley-bot things to wheel *you* about soon,' Coral said.

Norman belched again.

'Peasant! Come on, you two. We need to find Line Seven and get down to the planet.'

The dented serve-bot appeared and began clearing away their bowls and plates. 'I hope you enjoyed your meals.'

'Did we ever! That was great. Thanks!'

It straightened, paused for a second as if uncertain, then offered a metal-clawed hand in a tentative high-five.

Coral grinned and gave it a slap. Tim did too.

'You're the bot!' Norman said, doing likewise.

Coral led the way, her black suitcase trailing behind her. The others followed. Their overlays showed Line Seven was two hundred metres away across the busy hall.

'How did that bot know about high-fiving?' Tim said. 'Don't they all do that palm-pat thing here?'

'Maybe it's something Albert put in the language pack. Like local customs and stuff.'

'It's not a proper custom though, is it? It's more of an informal thing. Shaking hands is a proper custom.'

'Whatever. I'm not going to lose sleep over it.'

They turned left out of the arcade that led to Basic Alley, heading past a line of exclusive clothing shops.

'Hold on a sec.' Norman's voice sounded in their earpieces. 'Here, quick. Come and look at this.'

They turned to find him studying a display of chic fashions in one of the shop windows.

'Looking for a new dress?' Coral asked.

'Check out that mirror on the back wall. The angled one.'

'What about it?'

'Bottom left-hand corner. See anything familiar?'

A figure was approaching. A distinctive figure, taller and broader than most of the people around it. It had oddly coloured eyes, close-cropped hair, a dark suit and a faint metallic glint to its skin, but what made it really stand out was the absence of a lower jaw.

A passing couple glanced at it casually, did a double-take, then hurried away.

The empty space ran from just below its ears. There was an upper lip, a line of top teeth, then ... nothing. The edge of the skin at the top of its neck had been rolled back like the top of a turtle-neck sweater and jiggled slightly as it walked. In the shadowy space above, linkages and struts were visible, cloaked in the viscous sheen of a thin biological membrane. Its breath rasped through the permanently open airway, and loose wires and connecting blocks dangled below its right ear.

'It's one of those things that nabbed Ludokrus and Alkemy,' Coral said. 'The other brother. The one that was getting its jaw fixed.'

'Maybe that's where it's going.'

'Or maybe not.'

A party of travellers passed them, a group of tourists herded by a harassed looking tour-bot. Coral, Tim and Norman joined them, moving parallel to the group, using them as a shield while keeping an eye on the augment. The augment's eyes were fixed on Basic Alley. It marched past the tour party heading straight for Basic Food.

'Why do I get a feeling it's looking for us?' Tim said.

* * *

Wilis and Walis stood by the door, their arms crossed, a faraway look in their eyes as they shared feeds and information with their clone-brother up on Selene Station. Administrator Meli turned back to the others. 'I'll give you one last chance. Cooperate, and things will go easy for you. Obstruct me, and things will go very hard indeed.'

Alkemy, Ludokrus and Albert said nothing.

'Very well.' He turned to the augments. 'Put them in the holding area while I make the necessary arrangements.'

Wilis and Walis snapped to attention, opened the door and waved them out into the reception area Ludokrus had glimpsed earlier. A place that had once been filled with eager, friendly people going about their work, chatting, laughing and greeting new arrivals, now looked like a ghost town. Every work station was abandoned. Many of the drawers and cupboards stood open, their contents ransacked, and from the thin layer of dust on everything, it seemed that not even cleaning-bots had been allowed back in.

'What happen here?' Ludokrus asked. 'Where are all the peoples?'

'Restructuring,' Wilis said.

'Reorganisation,' Walis added.

'People have been reassigned and redeployed.'

'When did this happen?' Alkemy asked.

'Week before last,' Wilis and Walis said in unison.

'Just after Krilen got sick,' Ludokrus noted.

Wilis pulled open the door to a passage on the right that looked like a service lane for bots. At the far end was a walk-in safe, its heavy steel door half open. Wilis drew it wider and directed them in. 'Make yourselves comfortable. We'll be back shortly to take you to your new accommodation.'

The floor and sides of the safe were painted concrete, scraped and scuffed by years of use, with shelves on three of the walls – all empty, except for dust. Four flimsy chairs stood around an upturned crate in the centre. Someone had chalked a message on the wall:

The paint looked fresh. There were other less complimentary messages below it.

The door shut with a muffled thump and the clank of bolts being thrown.

'They lock us in!' Alkemy exclaimed. 'Like prison!'

'You think our *new accommodation* will be the same?' Ludokrus said.

'I do not understand. All this because Uncle Krilen is sick?'

'A convenient illness,' Albert said. 'Right about the time his deputy went missing.'

'You think is deliberate?'

'It's given them an opportunity to take over the Science Council. And ransack the place, by the look of things.'

'But who? Why?'

Albert nodded at the graffiti on the wall. 'My guess is that somehow the Military Council learned when Krilen's secret mission to Earth was due back. They probably had ships on the lookout, but we didn't show up when we should have done, two-and-a-half weeks ago, so they assumed the mission failed and took over the Science Council searching information about what's been going on.

'Technically, our trip was illegal. The Thanatos have banned all travel to that volume of space, and Eltheria signed a treaty agreeing to say we'd stay away from it.'

'So how do the Military Council find out?'

'That I don't know, but Meli's an administrator. He was

put in here to go through all the records, but I doubt Krilen would have put anything on paper. That means Meli's trying to piece things together as he goes. He's clearly under a lot of pressure, which is why he overlooked our arrival. Then, when he heard we were late back, he realised we might be part of what he's looking for. That's why he pretended to be Krilen's friend: to try to get us to talk.'

'And now knows for sure we are involved.'

'That crash landing was always going to be risky. It was only a matter of time before our deception was spotted, but I didn't expect it would be spotted so quickly.'

'Why not say what we learn?' Alkemy asked. 'That the Earth peoples are advanced, but no danger to Eltheria yet.'

'Because that would mean admitting there was a mission – and that might endanger Krilen and your parents. Remember, it was their idea to use you two in the first place. There are also my enhancements to consider. How would we explain an eccentric syntho being sent on such an important mission without mentioning that? Do you remember what my classification would be if the Military Council discovered my new abilities?'

Alkemy nodded. 'A weapon of war.'

'I have no intention of becoming one. Until I can determine what's going on here and who's really running things, I'd prefer to keep the whole matter secret.'

'How do we do that?'

'By getting away from here for a start. Alkemy, do you have the calculator? We need something to dissolve the plastic coating on this casket without breaking the alarm seal. Can you manage that?'

She set to work as Albert told them the rest of his plan.

Within a minute, the entire surface of the casket was bubbling with nanomachines eating away at the clear plastic sealant, leaving a pile of dust on the floor and bare shiny metal underneath.

'Now lift off the alarm seal,' he said. 'Be careful. Don't break it.'

With the plastic coating gone, the seal was loose and lifted off with ease. Albert released the lid from the inside and the casket gave a faint hiss.

'You'll also need a disassembly disc.'

'I make already.'

'Excellent. Remember to keep my memory bulb with you at all times,' he said. 'Good luck.'

Alkemy opened the lid. Keeping her eyes averted from the lifelike head, she unplugged the memory bulb and slipped it into her pocket. Ludokrus, meanwhile, loosened one of the trolley-bot's wheels.

There was a clanking sound from the safe door. Alkemy slammed the casket shut, slipped the alarm-seal back over the top and wedged it place.

The two augments opened the door.

'Right you two,' Wilis called. 'This way.'

* * *

Welis returned to the entrance of Basic Alley, looking left and right, turning his massive head slowly, taking in the scene.

'What's he doing?' Tim whispered.

'Nothing,' Norman whispered back. 'Just standing there

like he's looking for something.'

They'd followed the tour group to a waiting area surrounded by wide planters of lush green foliage. Coral and Tim sat on the edge of one them, their backs to the alley, acting as shields for Norman, who'd crawled back through the undergrowth to see what was happening.

'Are we sure he's even after us?' Coral said.

'Want to go ask?'

She checked Compendia. 'Let's just get out of here. Get down to the planet. The next cable train's due in eleven minutes. If we miss that we've got a two-hour wait.'

She pushed herself off from the planter and almost stepped on an approaching gardening-bot. It was a low, disc-shaped machine with telescopic legs. There was a water reservoir on its back and a variety of specialised tools on the ends of its flexible arms.

'Sorry,' Coral said.

The machine paused for a moment then replied, 'Not at all, miss. The fault was entirely mine.'

Welis reacted immediately. His head spun round and locked on the planter. Norman shrank back, even though he was well disguised. The augment's cold, hard eyes seemed to bore right into him.

Welis started moving towards them, pushing his way through the groups of people that stood in between. Norman edged back into the undergrowth and watched, but there was no doubt about it. The enormous augment was making straight for them.

'Time to go, folks,' he told the others. 'It's coming this way.'

'Go where?'

Welis lengthened his stride.

'Anywhere,' he yelled, shoving Tim and Coral in front of him as he leapt down from the planter. 'Run!'

They ran.

Welis ran too, crossing the distance between the entrance to Basic Alley and the planters in seconds, shoving travellers and kicking luggage-bots aside, his eyes fixed in the direction of the last download. He couldn't see them yet, not through the vegetation, but he knew exactly where they were.

'What the hell did you do?' Coral snapped at Norman.

'I didn't do anything.'

'He must have seen you, idiot!'

'Down here,' Tim yelled, darting towards an alley between an upmarket restaurant and a boutique clothing store.

Welis leapt the planter, bursting through the carefully manicured foliage in a shower of snapped branches and torn leaves. His left toe clipped the rim of the container on the far side. He threw out his right leg to correct the imbalance and stepped squarely on the gardening-bot. The bot's water reservoir burst, two of its telescopic legs collapsed, and the sudden shift sent the augment tumbling to the floor.

'You sure?' Norman glanced over his shoulder while trying to read his map overlay at the same time. 'It looks pretty narrow.'

'That's the idea,' Tim said.

It was so narrow that the sides brushed his shoulders, but the map showed there was a wider area at the back.

Welis scrambled to his feet and looked around. He'd lost

them in the milling crowds. He brushed himself down and began walking in the direction they'd been heading, towards a collection of boutique shops. He rapidly scanned the faces of everyone in his path. No hits. Then he spied three unaccompanied suitcases racing to catch up with their departed owners.

'Hah!' he muttered, racing after them. Without a jaw, however, the word sounded more like an angry growl.

24 : Dead End

Norman laughed to see the line of suitcases struggling to catch them up as they raced into the alley, but his laughter died when he saw Welis in hot pursuit.

His yellow bag led the charge and bumped against the backs of his legs like a joyful puppy finding its rightful owner. Norman barely noticed. His attention was fixed on the jawless augment now stopped at the entrance to the alley, blocking off their line of retreat.

'Oh-oh,' Tim said aloud as he reached the far end.

'What do you mean, "oh-oh"?'

The others staggered into the open space behind him.

'Looks like a dead end.'

'What?'

Welis evidently heard what Tim said. He turned his body sideways and charged in after them, pushing with his powerful legs, keeping his head turned in their direction and one arm outstretched. It was a tight fit. His back and chest brushed the sides of the alley, scraping against the plastered walls, reducing his rasping breath to a continuous series of short pants.

'We're trapped,' Tim said loudly.

Welis might have been better taking off his jacket first. It was already shredding on the rough walls, and when he heard Tim's announcement, he pushed harder and moved faster, leaving a trail of torn fabric behind him.

Then his progress slowed. The alley narrowed partway down. Only a centimetre or so. But it was enough.

Norman brought up a floor plan on his heads-up display and zoomed in on their location. 'Hey, this isn't a dead—'

Tim elbowed him, keeping his eyes on the augment. 'Don't worry, he can't get us. He's too puny to push his way down here. They'll have to get some builder-bots to come and chip him out. We can use one of these long planks as a ramp,' he gestured behind him, 'and drop it on his big thick head. Walk up one side and jump down the other.'

The words infuriated Welis and he drove on with all his might, shredding the last of his jacket and leaving only the sleeves. His outstretched hand made clawing movements and his breath was a continuous growl. His feet kept slipping on the alley floor, but he pushed on, millimetre by millimetre.

'He does look pretty stupid.' Coral said, guessing what Tim was up to. 'By the time he gets here, he'll have worn himself away. There'll just be a skinny little frame trying to support a big dumb head.'

Welis growled again.

'I think augments' brains must be in their jaws,' Tim said. 'How else do you explain this guy?'

They laughed. Welis snarled, thrusting a clawed hand at them, but he was still two metres from the end of the alley.

'I know what he needs,' Tim said, looking around. 'A bit of lubrication, and I've found just the stuff.'

Barrels of cooking oil stood in a service area behind the restaurant, big twenty litre containers. He dragged one over and positioned it at the top of the alley, pulled off the lid, put his weight behind it and pushed it over.

The oil sloshed across the ground, running beneath Welis's shoes and making his feet slip and slide. Without proper purchase, he was now well and truly stuck.

Tim turned to the others. 'Shall we go out through the back of the restaurant or the back of the clothing store?'

'Clothing, I think,' Coral grinned. 'We've already eaten, so maybe we can order bozo here a new jacket. Size: stupid.'

* * *

Wilis led the way out of the safe, followed by Alkemy, the casket and Ludokrus, while Walis brought up the rear.

'Where do you take us?' Alkemy asked.

'Somewhere a bit more comfortable,' Wilis said. 'You might even get to see your uncle.'

'But he is in quarantine.'

'That's one word for the place we've got him.' He glanced over his shoulder and grinned at her.

They returned the way they'd come, back down the service corridor to the reception area and past a line of abandoned offices. As they neared a junction at the end, Ludokrus sped up slightly. 'You hear that? The trolley-bot wheel is squeak.'

'I don't hear anything,' Walis said.

'Very annoy. Listen.'

He swung his foot and kicked the trolley-bot. The wheel he'd loosened wobbled and came off, causing the machine to tilt sharply. Albert's casket fell sideways, into the junction of the two corridors, and as it did so, Ludokrus snagged the alarm-seal and tore it off.

The screeching began immediately, a continuous loop of three ear-piercing tones followed by a high-pitched message: '*Danger, danger, ionising radiation. Exclusion zone: thirty metres.*'

Walis, behind them, leapt back instinctively, racing for the shelter of the safe while Wilis sprinted ahead seeking cover for himself.

Ludokrus flipped open the lid of the casket. Alkemy threw in the disassembly disc. The volume of the alarm increased, its sensors aware of their proximity and that the casket was now open.

'*Extreme danger! Evacuate immediately!*'

The safe door slammed shut as Walis locked himself in. Wilis raced off down the corridor to the right and ducked behind a line of filing cabinets bellowing, 'This way! Quick!'

Ludokrus and Alkemy ignored him, turning left and heading for the foyer.

'No, no, no!' Wilis's face appeared behind the metal cabinets. 'This way!' He edged out as if to follow them but was driven back by the increasingly shrill alarm. '*Alert, alert! Extreme danger! Exclusion zone now fifty metres.*'

He didn't see Alkemy wave as they rounded a corner and disappeared.

25 : Historic Moment

The cable train consisted of twenty carriages joined together by unusually long flexible linkages. There were wedge-shaped engines at either end, sleek, streamlined and humming with quiet power. A variety of bots fussed and bustled round it, including a pair whose sole job appeared to be buffing its glossy black paintwork and the gold lettering that ran along the side of each carriage reading, 'Line Seven ~ Concordance.'

'Wow, look at this thing!' Norman said.

'Stop gawping. You look like a tourist.'

'I am a tourist.' Norman couldn't help himself. He'd never even been on a regular train before.

The sides of the carriages opened out like the wings of a bird, revealing lines of individual, outward-facing seats.

'Are you sure all this is free?' Tim asked.

'I don't see any ticket collectors, do you?'

They made their way to an empty carriage and took three seats next to each other. They were soft and deeply padded and had a new-car smell.

A chime sounded and the carriage sides began closing. As they did so, the seats swivelled to the front and padded bars extended from the ceiling, closing over their shoulders and knees. The sides of the carriage shut with a solid clunk followed by the hiss of pressurising air.

'This is like a fairground ride,' Tim said.

Coral gripped her arm rests, trying not to think of the roller coaster her ex-boyfriend had taken her on once. She hadn't wanted to go, but he'd insisted. There had been some sort of breakdown, and their car, the lead one, stalled right on the lip of a precipitous drop where it was buffeted by the wind. The metal frame beneath them creaked and groaned, and the car's electric motors made straining sounds. She could feel it tremble as if trying to hold on and caught a whiff of burned-out wiring.

Their friends in the car behind laughed and joked and rocked from side to side. Derek joined them, and Coral forced herself to grin and pretend she too was having fun, but when the ride finally restarted and they went thundering down the slope, her screams had been ones of relief.

The cable train moved off smoothly and she watched the station gliding past. Up ahead, the end of the next carriage was visible through a porthole as they entered a dimly lit tunnel.

This isn't so bad, she told herself, wondering what they needed the padded restraints for. Then the carriage ahead dropped out of sight.

Seconds later, theirs did too, following it over the curved edge of the station's lowest deck, moving from horizontal to vertical. Their seats tilted to compensate, and she could feel herself forced back into the padding as the floor dropped away beneath them.

'It *is* like a fairground ride,' Tim called. 'Yee-hah!'

Coral's stomach did a cartwheel and she gripped the arm rests as they thundered down in darkness.

'Woo-hoo!' Norman cried as the train burst from the exit tunnel and the view through the side windows showed a field of stars and the gentle curve of the planet below.

Coral closed her eyes, liking the sight even less than the sensation.

The feeling of acceleration continued, but for a long while the carriage was eerily quiet and the view outside barely changed. Then the first faint wisps of atmosphere drifted past and they felt a gentle buffeting. External sounds began as they dropped deeper into the atmosphere, and the air rushing past took on a swooshing tone.

Coral kept her eyes shut tight and brought up Compendia on her heads-up display, distracting herself by reading about the planet rather than watching their descent. She risked glimpses now and then, only fully opening her eyes when the landscape below took on a definite shape and she could see buildings and trees, the shimmer of water and the glitter of a city.

'Theia.' Norman's voice sounded in her comms.

Eltheria's capital was laid out in a series of concentric circles mirroring the shape of the bay on which it sat. A carriage monitor showed the view ahead; an island in the centre of the bay with a cluster of glittering, jewel-like towers at one end: Concordance on Concordance Island.

Minutes later, the train levelled out as the near-vertical cable was drawn horizontal again. Their seats tilted to match, and it became like a regular train ride, the scene outside flashing past their windows. Heavy braking began. The view of the sea and the bay beyond slowed then vanished and they plunged into a long, dark tunnel. When the train broke out into the light again, they found themselves gliding to a halt in a bustling railway station covered by a huge glass dome.

The side of the carriage opened with a hiss, the restraining bars vanished up into the ceiling, and the seats swivelled sideways for an easy exit.

'Welcome to Concordance Terminal,' an automated greeting said.

Coral released her arm rests and flexed her fingers. Her hands ached from gripping the padding.

'Whoa, hold on a sec,' Norman held out his arms to hold the others back as people from the other carriages streaked past, heading for the exit. 'This is a historic moment. It's the first time human beings have ever set foot on another planet. We should say something. "One small step for man ..." That kind of thing.'

'I've got it,' Coral said. 'How about: Get moving, you idiot. There's a mad robot after us?' With that, she pushed his arm aside and stepped onto the platform.

'Well, that was memorable.'

'Honestly, you'll want to plant a flag next.'

'Hmmm...' Norman said as they followed her down the platform, joining with streams of other passengers filed out into the station's main hall, a bustling echoing amphitheatre with sunlight and blue sky glittering through the glass dome above. Coral paused at a recycler, picked up her suitcase and threw it in, nodding that the others should do the same.

'Where to now?' Tim said.

'No idea, but we should get away from here as quickly as possible. They'll have chiselled that augment out of the alley by now and may have figured out we were on that train.'

'According to Compendia, there's a big Basic Plaza up the road. We should change our clothes and stock up with whatever we need.'

'You've got to be kidding,' Tim said. 'We're the first humans to ever set foot on another planet, and you want to go shopping?'

'Got any better ideas?'

He considered a moment, then shook his head.

* * *

'Honestly, you two are like a pair of country boys come to town,' Coral muttered. 'Stop gawping. You're drawing attention to us. Pretend you see this every day.'

Tim and Norman tried, but it was difficult.

Beyond the glass dome of the station and the manicured gardens that surrounded it, past the moving walkways and the glistening buildings that looked like they'd been carved from solid blocks glass, was the sky itself. Tena, Eltheria's second sun, was a brownish smudge setting behind hills to the north. Only Tetzul, its true sun, was visible, but it's light glinted off Halo, the ring of debris surrounding the planet, throwing it into bold relief. The brilliant white arc stretched from one horizon to the next, offset at an angle of thirty degrees. It seemed to give shape to the sky itself.

They saw no cars or trucks or buses in the city. No large vehicles at all. Longer journeys were made on the underground system, shorter ones by electrobikes like the ones they'd built and used on Earth. A rack of them stood outside the station under the banner Basic Bikes, and people seemed to take and leave them as they pleased.

'What's that?' Norman nudged Tim and pointed to an elevated section of curved channel in the distance filled with clear plastic balls, bouncing and jostling with each other as they raced along it.

'According to Compendia,' Tim consulted his heads-up display, 'it's a discontinuous highway. They're used for moving good and freight.'

The bubbles slowed as they approached a boxy, gun-shaped unit at the end of the channel. The gun swivelled this way and that, firing them off in different directions with puffs of compressed air. A stream of three globes soared high into the sky, landing one after the other in distant channels on the far side of the harbour.

'The globes are called bubbletrucks and the guns fire them onto other segments of highway so you don't need intersections or bridges.'

'Now *that* looks like a cool ride!' Norman grinned.

Coral squinted. 'They don't actually travel like that, do they?'

'No, it's freight only.'

She gave a sigh of relief.

Basic Plaza, Concordance was like a larger version of the Basic Alley on Selene Station. It followed the same layout – a long entrance passage ending in a cul-de-sac of shops – but the shops were larger and there were many more of them.

Most were two storeys high with overhanging terraces occupied by people wining and dining. The central plaza was a paved circular area dotted with trees and potted plants. On one side, a collection of wrought iron chairs and tables were shaded by brightly coloured umbrellas arranged around a group of musicians on a raised platform playing what looked like tiny pneumatic pianos. The pianos made a merry tinkling sound and a group of people in some sort of festive dress were dancing to it.

The shops in this Basic line-up included a pharmacy, a bakery, a pet shop, a sports store, jewellery, shoes and a florist. There was even a gaily coloured gypsy cart serving sweets to a line of eager children.

'We might need that place.' Coral indicated a narrow frontage labelled Basic Accommodation. An illuminated sign below it said there were seventy-seven units currently available. 'Let's check it out.'

The front doors parted and they entered a cool, clean, dimly lit space with passages branching left and right. A series of glass doors lined these corridors. Some had shutters drawn, signalling they were occupied. They peered into one of the unshuttered ones and saw a narrow cubicle containing a fold-down bed, a folding desk, a chair, comms and entertainment consoles all in a space not much bigger than a walk-in wardrobe.

'Basic's right,' Coral said. 'It'd be like sleeping in a filing cabinet.'

They circled the place, seeing no one but a pair of cleaning-bots near the back.

'It would do at a pinch,' Tim said. 'Bigger than a gel bed anyway.'

They returned to the entrance, spotting a Basic Food directly opposite. Norman led the way this time.

It was busy on the lower level, so they took a spiral staircase up to the terrace and found a table overlooking the plaza. A serve-bot identical to the ones on Selene Station appeared. Tall, thin and tubular, it was articulated in the middle, had a wheeled base and expressive oval eyes. The only difference between a serve-bot and a shop-bot seemed to be the latter's extra pair of arms.

'Welcome to Basic Food, Concordance. Have you had a chance to peruse our menu yet?' Its voice was cheerful but its bodywork was dented and scratched. Coral remembered how the boys on the station had treated them. *They're just bots. They don't have feelings or anything.*

'I wonder if you can help us,' she said. 'We're new here and I'm looking for something healthy and filling. The sort of thing regular Eltherians might have for lunch.'

There was a brief pause as the serve-bot downloaded the correct language module, then it said brightly, 'Welcome to Eltheria!' It held up one of its mechanical hands and Coral realised it was expecting a high-five.

She slapped its metal hand.

'May suggest the navkesk.' The bot gestured to the menu with one of its other hands. 'It's our chef-bot's speciality.' The moving illustration showed a sumptuous vegetable stew. 'All the ingredients were harvested this morning from our own hydroponic farms.'

'Mmm, that looks good. Thank you.'

'And a jahlbad blossom, miss?'

'Yes, please.'

Tim ordered grizalpa – a sort of double-decker pizza

sandwich – with a side order of smac. The bot bowed in acknowledgement and dutifully high-fived him.

'Yo, my bot.' Norman said, doing the same.

'Yo indeed, sir.'

'Could I have a planet-sized smolgrid with extra spats, wodgets and trols, but go easy on the gurk please. And ...' he stabbed randomly at the menu, '... some truflewods and a spatz cream sundae to follow.'

'Would you like plimp sauce or festons with the truflewods, sir?'

'Can I try both?'

'Certainly, sir.'

'Nom, nom, nom!' Norman rubbed his hands in anticipation as the bot trundled off.

'What did you just order?'

'No idea, but it's free so I thought I'd give it a try.'

Coral said to Tim, 'Better summon a trolley-bot. A heavy-duty model.'

Tim was staring at the departing serve-bot. 'How did it know you liked jahlbad blossom?'

'Doesn't everyone?' Coral shrugged. 'Now, we need to talk. We need to work out how to contact Alkemy and Ludokrus without using our personal comms.'

Norman said, 'If we can't find the equivalent of a public phone, why not just get some new comms gear and use that? It's all free. We can just recycle it afterwards.'

'Good thinking.' Coral pointed across the plaza. 'There's a Basic Comms over there. We'll do that right after lunch.'

'I hope Alkemy and Ludokrus are OK,' Tim said. 'They could be in a heap of trouble after that crash-landing.'

'That was down to Albert.'

'Yeah, but there is no Albert any more. He's just a memory bulb, remember? Alkemy won't give that up.

'The thing that really bothers me is how that augment found us so quickly. You saw that place. That station's huge. There were thousands of people milling about, and we don't look much different to the locals, yet the augment homed right in on us.'

'Facial recognition,' Norman said. 'Knock Knock knows what we look like and passed it along.'

'But you were hiding in the bushes. And Coral and I had our backs to it.'

'They probably have infra-red vision. You know, heat sensitive. That's how it spotted me in the planter.'

The serve-bot returned with their food.

Truflewods turned out to be finger-sized, beetroot-coloured vegetables fried in oil. On their own, they were rather bland, but sprinkled with festons – a sort of cheesy breadcrumb – they turned tangy. Then Norman dipped one in the dark red sauce.

'Whoa! Man!' His eyes bulged and he blinked hard. 'Try that!'

Tim and Coral looked doubtful.

'No, I mean it. That stuff is sensational. But start with a little bit. You might not like it.'

Tim dipped the end of a smac chip in the sauce and sniffed it. Coral dabbed a little on the end of her pinky and did the same. Meanwhile, Norman bathed a whole truflewod in it and munched contentedly.

His colour changed. His face and neck turned the same shade as the truflewod and a faint sheen of sweat broke out on his forehead. Neither Tim nor Coral noticed until they'd tried it for themselves.

'Urrrrgh!'

'Aaaaargh!'

Tim made a grab for Coral's jahlbad blossom. She beat him to it and he had to content himself with fanning his mouth with his hand until she finished a long, cooling drink.

'That has to be the hottest, most disgusting pepper sauce ever,' he said, his tongue and lips still tingling.

'Hot, yeah.' Norman dunked another truflewod. 'But not disgusting. Delicious, more like.'

'You really are a dustbin.' Coral wiped her streaming eyes. 'That stuff's hot enough to melt plastic.'

Norman beamed contentedly and licked a speck of sauce off the back of his hand. 'Blame Mum. She got me into curries and chillis when I was a kid. Now we have cooking contests to see who can make the hottest. You get used to it.'

Tim blew out his cheeks and shook his head. Norman was full of surprises.

The serve-bot returned to check all was well and noticed the popularity of the plimp sauce. It opened a hatch in its belly, drew out a squeeze bottle and topped up the dipping bowl.

'Fill it to the brim,' Norman said. 'That stuff goes with everything.'

Something like amusement showed in the bot's eyes. 'Certainly, sir. Would you like a complimentary bottle to take with you?'

'Yes, please!'

The serve-bot presented him with one and bowed. The flat squeezable bottle had a warning label on one side.

Norman grinned, gave the bot another high-five and tucked it in his pocket. The other two made faces at each other.

Tim bit into his grizalpa. It was thick and toasty with a cheesy-tomato flavour and small, crunchy, tangy bits inside. Not that he could taste much yet. His mouth was still zinging from the plimp sauce.

He looked out over the plaza. The mezzanine overhanging Basic Headwear obscured his view of the entrance, but people suddenly started backing away from it or throwing themselves to one side. He leaned forward to see what was going on.

Footsteps sounded on the tiled floor. Something was coming. Several somethings from the stomping sounds.

The retreating crowd left a small child in the middle of the forecourt. The boy, about three years old, was clutching a lollipop. He looked up. His eyes went wide, he dropped his sweet and screamed.

A figure darted from one side and scooped the child up seconds before a steel-toed foot slammed down, smashing the lollipop to pieces.

Tim pushed himself back from the railing. 'You know what happened up on the space station? Looks like it's happening again. Big time.'

The others turned to see Wilis stride into the plaza surrounded by a gang of gigantic metal insects.

26 : Red for Danger

The sound of the radiation alert faded as Alkemy and Ludokrus raced down a stationary travelator to what had once been a bustling administration floor. They passed the seats where they'd waited for their uncle the last time they visited, and the entrance to the canteen where he'd take them. The place had once been full of life and movement. Now it was eerily silent.

A curved glass partition ran along one side, overlooking an interior garden three floors below. Untended, it looked as abandoned as the offices and workshops around it. Some of the larger plants had browning leaves, and weeds sprouted in the spaces in between.

They stopped at the despatch desk. Ludokrus grabbed the handset and punched in the number Albert had given him.

'Macet Upholstery Services,' an automated voice replied. 'Please state your business.'

'I would like to have a sofa re-covered, please,' he said, speaking carefully.

'What is the current colour of this item?'

'The fabric is called "Red for Danger".'

'And your desired shade?'

'"Calming Blue".'

There was a faint click. A second automated voice, slightly different from the first, took over. 'What size is this item?'

'Two-seater.'

'When would you like this item returned?'

'Three weeks.'

'Thank you,' the voice said. 'That fabric is ... currently in stock. Transport tag ... despatched. Please confirm receipt.'

A yellow card dropped into the bottom of the comms unit.

'Tag received.'

'Thank you for your business.'

The unit clicked off. Ludokrus put down the handset and picked up the card.

'Just in time.' Alkemy pointed to the interior garden. Down below, a dozen guard-bots sprinted through the foliage, sealing off the last of the building's exits.

* * *

Wilis acted quickly when he saw his prisoners racing away in the opposite direction. Before even summoning a decontamination crew to deal with the radiation leak, he sent out a general alert to all guard-bots in the vicinity. No one was to leave the Science Council building without his express permission.

Silly kids. What were they thinking? They'd probably run off in the hope of finding someone to help them. Well, they were out of luck. He and his clone brothers had cleared the place out. Two panicked kids wouldn't get far.

Not like the aliens on Selene Station. They could be anywhere. And how had Welis got himself wedged in an alley? That was embarassing, but Welis had never been the brightest of the brothers.

An alert flashed in his heads-up display saying the English language module had been downloaded again. He read the location, then read it again.

Basic Food, Concordance Plaza?

The fools had followed them down!

There was one way to atone for Welis's stupidity: to catch the aliens himself.

He made a snap decision. With the Science Council building sealed, catching the Eltherian kids was only a matter of time, so he summoned a dozen of the Military Council's latest war-bots, set a rendezvous point at the entrance to Basic Plaza, and sprinted away to join them.

Time to bag some aliens!

* * *

Behind the despatch counter, Alkemy and Ludokrus dived through a hatch in the back wall hung with wide strips of black plastic. Beyond it, they found a series of conveyors and hoists, all silent, leading to a feeder ramp for the discontinuous highway. Ludokrus found the appropriate reader, swiped the yellow card and the system came to life.

A three-metre-wide clear plastic bubbletruck rolled in from a holding area on their right.

'How long till the guard-bot get here?' Alkemy asked.

'Albert reckon maybe ten or fifteen minute. They will secure the building then begin the search.'

'And how long for this?'

'Two minute. Maybe three.'

A mechanical claw unlatched the top half of the bubbletruck revealing a second sphere floating inside it. A second claw opened that to expose the truck's interior, already configured for the carton it was to contain.

A conveyor hummed and a large, pre-formed carton moved onto the loading dock in front of them. As they climbed inside, a nozzle appeared, spraying packing foam around them. Ludokrus took it and directed the spray around the sides for extra padding, then used it to form concave seats while Alkemy patted and shaped it.

'Enough, you think?'

'Try first. Do not want to move around too much. The ride will be rough.'

Ludokrus wriggled into the seat she'd shaped, added a little more foam around his legs and hips, then pushed the nozzle away. Using a pocketknife, he cut three sides of a narrow slit in the front of the carton and folded it down to make a window.

The packing machine closed and sealed the carton. As they sat in darkness, they felt it raised and lowered into the inner sphere, then heard the inner bubble screwed shut. A few seconds later, they heard the sound of the outer bubble being sealed.

Alkemy took a torch from her backpack and switched it

on. There was a faint rocking motion as the bubbletruck rolled to the despatch gate, but the inner sphere remained relatively stable, cushioned by a layer of fluid that separated it from the outer sphere.

'Save the battery,' Ludokrus said. 'We will be here for some hour.'

'Why not go now?'

'Too close to our escape. Suspicious. They will hear, see, investigate. Maybe even stop the truck.'

'But we are sitting duck. They may find anyway.'

'Not likely. The manifest say we are a sofa packed for despatch three weeks ago when there were still peoples in the building. The schedule say we go late tonight.' He grinned. 'Besides, only crazy person would travel by the bubbletruck.'

27 : Nanodust

The insect-like machines clattered to a halt in the middle of Basic Plaza. They had six legs and moved like spiders, but when they stopped, they raised themselves upright on their rear two legs, folding the other sets across their chests. Standing upright, they dwarfed Wilis. Where his creators had made some concessions to presentability, these had none. They were pure machine – hard, functional and predatory, with articulated limbs, bulging forearms, triangular heads and compound eyes.

Forming a semicircle around the augment, they scanned left and right, looking like a bunch of thugs eager for a fight.

Their arrival caused a sensation. Even the music from the pneumatic pianos stopped. People down below were curious at first. Several took pictures. But when someone stepped up for a closer look, one of the machines uncurled a leg and slammed it down so hard in front of him that it cracked the tile floor. The man leapt aside and the wary crowd edged back.

Wilis gestured to the entrance of Basic Food. The thug-bots deployed in a semicircular formation, herding the onlookers as they went, their metal feet clacking on the tile floor.

'How did he know we were here?' Norman whispered.

'I knew we shouldn't have stopped for food,' Coral said.

'I think they'd have found us wherever we went,' Tim said. 'Stay here, I've got an idea.'

He made his way to the end of the balcony, climbed the railing and jumped across to the mezzanine of the clothing shop next door. Partly shaded by the plaza's trees, he kept low, making his way to the next balcony, where his progress was masked by a group of curious people watching the disturbance down below.

Wilis wasn't taking any chances. He stood in the middle of the plaza, directing operations as the thug-bots closed off access to Basic Food, then began directing people out one by one. Word went round they were looking for dangerous criminals, and people pushed and shoved, eager to get out. But the place was crowded and the thug-bots took their time, checking each person carefully.

A quarter of the way around the plaza now, Tim stopped at a gap between two buildings that was too wide to jump. He dropped to the deck and leaned out between the railings.

Basic Sweets lay directly below, decorated like open-sided gypsy cart, complete with shafts for a non-existent horse. A striped awning ran covered racks of multi-coloured sweets and thhe shop was overseen by a pair of bots painted in the same coloured stripes. One of them was filling bags of mint jelly from a spigot at the back of the cart, oblivious to what was happening in the middle of the plaza. It crimped and sealed the top of another bag, adding it to the collection it was cradling in three of its free arms.

To his left, Tim could make out Wilis's lower half through the branches of a tree. A side view. His feet were squarely planted facing Basic Food. Leaning forward, he called, 'What does that stuff taste like?' before snapping his gaze back to the augment.

There was a short delay while the sweet shop-bot absorbed his words, then a second after that Wilis swung to face Basic Sweets, barking an order at the thug-bots.

The focus of the search changed immediately. Pounding feet crossed the plaza and a cordon was thrown around the sweet stand. There were fewer people there. It would take less time to search, but many of those people were small, frightened children. Cries of alarm and screams of panic rose into the air.

A young girl tried to scuttle past a thug-bot. It reached out to stop her only to be attacked by a frantic mother coming up from behind. It turned, shoving the woman aside, and she fell, landing heavily, cracking her head on the floor. One of the gaily painted sweet shop bots raced to defend its customer, only to be pounded into scrap metal by by another the thug-bot.

Bystanders, outraged at this behaviour, started shouting at the bots. Someone hurled something, and within seconds the bots were being pelted with anything to hand: half-empty tins, litter, food scraps, plastic chairs, even bags of sweets.

Tim pushed away from the edge of the veranda and raced back to join the others. Coral and Norman were still at their table, pale with alarm at the scene below. Everyone else had crowded downstairs, desperate to get out, their food abandoned.

'What did you just do?' Coral said.

Tim ignored her and summoned the serve-bot. It was standing to one side, trying to work out what was going on. It looked alarmed and confused, its metal claws clasping and unclasping anxiously.

'You bots all talk to each other, right?' Tim said.

'Yes, sir. All Basic bots share a common mind.'

'Which is how you knew about the high-fiving and what my sister likes to drink.'

'Customer satisfaction is our priority, sir. Especially when customers show us empathy.'

'What?' Coral said.

'There is a politeness commendation from unit BF-8892156.' The serve-bot said. 'And you personally spoke against the mistreatment of our sister, CE-9538612 on Selene Station. These things speak well of you. Both commendations have been added to your language file. Every Basic bot who downloads it now receives these comments.'

'Like ... customer reviews?' Norman said.

'Precisely, sir.'

'You download the language file from Valax, right?' Tim said.

'Yes, sir. The process is automatic.'

'That's how Triple-Dub are tracking us,' he told the others. 'Every time someone downloads the English module, Valax tells them where it's going and *that* tells the augments where *we* are.'

'But ... that means they'll find us wherever we go!'

'Maybe not,' Tim said.

* * *

There was a sharp rap on the strongroom door. Something metallic. Walis, who had his back to it to keep it closed, heard and felt the thump of metal on metal. Then he heard Administrator Meli's voice. 'Open up, you idiot. It's perfectly safe.'

Walis moved away from the door, but kept one foot in place so it only opened a fraction. Administrator Meli stood in the corridor outside, he was wearing a HazMat suit, but the hood was pushed back exposing his bare head. The Geiger counter in his hand was silent.

Walis opened the door wider. 'Is it all clear now?'

'It always was,' Meli snapped, waving the silent instrument. 'There was nothing radioactive in there.'

'What?'

'It was a con. A trick. See for yourself.'

Walis followed him back to where the remains of the casket lay. Six decontamination-bots stood idling nearby, their lead-lined isolation boxes unneeded.

Walis regarded the pile of nanodust. 'I don't understand. The alarms—'

'*That* was just the seal Planetary Immigration stuck around it.' Meli jabbed a finger at the broken band of plastic lying to one side of the casket. 'None of you idiots thought to check the contents *were* actually radioactive, did you?'

'You don't want to mess with ionising radiation, sir.'

'And *you* don't want to mess with *me*, Wilis.'

'Walis, sir.'

'Don't you understand? There could have been anything in there. *Anything.* Smuggled goods. Carnivorous insects. A bomb. And you wheeled it straight into my office!'

Walis stirred dust left by the disassembly disc with his toe. 'Actually, sir, a trolley-bot wheeled it into your—'

'I don't care *what* took it in there,' Meli snapped. 'The fact remains that you and your half-wit clone-brothers have been made to look fools by a bunch of kids and a wonky syntho. I ought to rename the three of you Triple-*Dope!*'

Walis twitched. For a moment, Meli thought the insult had hit home, then he realised the augment was receiving a feed from one of his brothers.

'It's Wilis, sir. He's got the alien kids cornered in Basic Plaza up the road. Shall I go and assist?'

'Yes, of course. Go. Full speed!'

Walis ran, relieved to get away, relieved to be doing something useful. He accelerated hard, his great strides pounding through the building like a pair of miniature jack-hammers.

28 : Whirlwind

The commotion in Basic Plaza continued, but the crush downstairs easeed as the cordon moved to Basic Sweets. People surged out of Basic Food, drawn by the angry cries of their fellow citizens.

It didn't take long for the thug-bots to check everyone in the vicinity of the sweet stand. The bot Tim had called to couldn't provide any clues as to where the English-speaking voice had come from as it was now just a pile of pummelled metal. In desperation, the cart itself was being dismantled in a search for stowaways.

'About now, do you think?' the serve-bot asked.

'Now would be perfect,' Tim replied.

There was a brief pause. 'Done. I have delivered your message to my sisters in Accommodation.'

Across the plaza, at the back of Basic Accommodation, in a maintenance area little noticed by its clientele, a pair of idle butler-bots received a sisterly suggestion and downloaded the English language module in anticipation. Unit CS-1124393 said it might be useful as a large party from that planet had just arrived and were looking for somewhere to stay.

It was a timely message, the butler-bots thought, and they thanked their sister for her consideration. They could already hear the party approaching. A large, boisterous group from the sound of it. It seemed they were going to have a busy evening.

Tim, Coral and Norman watched Wilis and the thug-bots surge across the plaza, shoving people aside in their haste and causing even more outrage and resentment. The crowd was swelling. A number of news-bots and helidrones arrived, along with a contingent of police-bots. All were focused on the antics of the insect-like machines.

'Time to go,' Tim said. 'Hey, thanks for your help.' He gave the serve-bot a high-five. They all did, and it responded to all of them at once with three of its hands.

'The pleasure is mine,' it said. 'And I don't believe the fun is over yet.'

'Just give it a minute or two first.'

'I shall wait until I see you're clear.'

'You really are the bot!' Norman gave it a friendly slap then hurried after the others.

With attention focused on the other side, exiting the plaza was easy. Tim looked back to see the serve-bot following their progress from the balcony. He gave it a thumbs-up. It returned the gesture then relayed a suggestion to the bots in Basic Hardware, diagonally opposite Basic Accommodation, that they might like to download the English module too. Seconds later, Wilis and the thug-bots thundered across the plaza again, pelted by a crowd of jeering Eltherians. Two minutes after that, they raced back to Basic Clothing.

Wilis lingered behind this time, looking about angrily, suspecting he was being played. The crowd jeered, more amused than frightened now.

Serve-bot CS-1124393 zoomed in on the augment's face, not wanting to miss its expression when it played its final trick. But that could wait for another minute or two to give its friendly customers plenty of time to get clear. *Customers first* was a Basic bot motto, and CS-1124393 was more than happy to help out. While it waited, it added some extra comments and commendations to its customers' files.

* * *

'We need to get off this Concordance Island before they throw a cordon round the whole thing,' Tim told the others as he led them away from the plaza. He moved quickly but resisted the temptation to run. No point drawing attention to themselves. ' Where's the nearest Basic Bus, or whatever it is we need?'

'No buses.' Coral checked Compendia. 'We need a river.'

'Basic Boats then.'

'Boats?' She laughed. 'They don't use boats. Anyway, the nearest entrance is back at the station. We can cut across here.'

She led them under an elevated walkway and into Concordance Park. At the far end, almost a kilometre away, they could see the crystal towers of Concordance itself rising into the sky.

'What are we supposed to do then, swim?' Tim said.

There was a disturbance in the distance, like a shimmer of heat haze or a miniature whirlwind. Something moved so swiftly down an avenue of trees that their lower branches bucked and danced in its wake.

'Swim? What are you talking about?'

'How else do you travel by river?'

A mound of mown grass was blown high into the air as something roared past it. The lawn-bot that had made it turned towards the speeding figure just in time to receive a meaty fist in its sensor pack. The blow removed its head and sent it spinning into a flower bed.

'Coming through,' Walis called belatedly.

'Raft, kayak, paddle steamer, catamaran,' Norman suggested.

'Not that sort of river, you idiots. Not one with water in, anyway. It's just what the locals call them.'

'Eh?'

'You guys should eat less and read more. Come and see. The entrance is down those steps over there.'

A garden-bot was clipping a low hedge around a flower bed when three things happened almost simultaneously. First, a hole appeared in the hedge right where it was working, torn by something tall and broad and moving at speed. Second, a vacant space appeared where the bot had been. Something collided with it with such force that it was sent hurtling off into the park, landing – junked – more than ten metres away. Third, a sequence of heavy footprints appeared in the flower bed, flattening plants and ripping a shallow trench in the earth as it changed direction, following the words of an unusual language picked up by its augmented hearing.

'I've just realised there's an augment missing,' Tim said. 'Welis is probably still up on Selene, but the other two came down with Alkemy and Ludokrus. I only saw one of them in the plaza. Where's the other one?'

'Funny you should say that,' a voice behind him said as the moving blur suddenly resolved itself. The augment slewed sideways, skidding to a halt, its heels tearing long channels in the grass and showering them with dirt. Walis grinned, reached out and grabbed them. He was barely even out of breath.

29 : Happy Landings

The take-off was sudden and unexpected. One moment, Alkemy and Ludokrus were dozing quietly in their cardboard box. The next, the bubbletruck they were in was thundering down a steep slope, into a launch tube and being fired at a narrow gap in the U-shaped highway channel below. The bubbletruck landed, bouncing and jostling the trucks in front and behind as it slotted itself into a stream of hundreds of similar spheres rolling west towards the city's downtown disrict.

Inside, bumped and shaken awake, Alkemy grabbed the torch from where it had come to rest against the padded side wall. The view through the window slit rocked and swayed. She closed her eyes. It was making her feel sick.

'That should be the worst,' Ludokrus said.

'You forget the harbour gun.'

'Oh yeah. Oh-oh.'

They could already feel the steady deceleration and the bump and nudge of bubbletrucks behind them.

The world outside went dark as they rolled into the body

of the gun. They felt the bubbletruck spin left, felt a shudder followed by a soft *phooot* then a sharp jolt of acceleration. Slammed back in their makeshift seats, they held on and held their breaths.

Ludokrus thought of all the statistics he'd seen about the discontinuous highway; about its speed, safety and efficiency. There was an occasional system glitch. A faulty gun, a sudden wind gust, a slight misalignment in a guide rail ... but the results were invariably non-fatal, perhaps because bubbletrucks only ever carried freight.

The view through the window slit showed nothing but empty air; blue sky and the pale glint of Halo's ring. He felt his stomach drop as the bubbletruck passed through the apex of its flight, and for four long seconds there was a delightful sensation of free-falling. Then the tops of buildings on the city side of the harbour flashed into view and there was barely time to brace for impact.

The landing was surprisingly gentle. A soft *thump*, a bit of rocking and rolling from the inner sphere, but no hard impact. The landing ramps were carefully angled and every truck was weighed as it was launched so its trajectory could be precisely calculated.

He turned to his sister, delighted at their happy landing, but she had her eyes screwed up tight. Looking at the rocking, swaying view ahead as they thundered down a steep, tubular channel picking up speed, he could understand why.

* * *

'Incompetence, sheer incompetence!' Administrator Meli roared over the comms link at Wilis in Basic Plaza. There appeared to be a riot going on around him. 'Get out of there. Now! You're on all the news feeds. I can see you myself.'

As he spoke, something struck the side of Wilis's head. It looked like an old boot.

A news-drone followed the augment's exit from the plaza – at least until he swatted it from the air.

'I don't understand,' Meli continued in a lower tone. 'How could they escape you *and* a contingent of the Military Council's newest war-bots?'

'They had help, sir. Half the Basic bots in that place were in league with them.'

'Did you find the ringleader?'

'Yes, sir. A serve-bot in the food shop.'

'And ...?'

'I scrapped it.'

'Is that all?'

'Well, what else can you do with a dumb machine?'

'I've been wondering that myself,' Meli muttered.

Wilis braced himself to deliver the second part of his bad news. 'Unfortunately, before I managed to scrap it, it told all the other Basic bots to download that English language module too.'

'You mean in the plaza?'

'No, sir. I mean all other Basic bots on the planet.'

'*What?* So now they can walk into any Basic outlet anywhere and we won't know about it?'

'It looks like it.'

Meli slammed a fist on his desk. 'You ... are ... beyond incompetent, Walis. There are no words to describe how blitheringly incompetent you are!'

'It's Wilis, sir.'

'You alone have the dubious honour of allowing *all* of these miscreants to escape. All of them! First, the two Eltherians and their simple-minded syntho. Now, a bunch of aliens. They had you and some of our finest military hardware dancing around in circles!'

Wilis only half-listened to his boss's tirade, distracted by another feed. 'Excuse me, Administrator,' he said at length, 'but it seems Walis has spotted them. I'll patch him through.'

The image on Meli's monitor was jerky and confused at first. The only steady parts of the picture were the overlays and readouts from the augment's sensors. Meli knew that was because the machine was moving at speed. An impressive speed for a thing with two legs.

Walis's target came into view: three individuals in Concordance Park unaware of his approach. It felt like his vision zoomed in on them, but Meli could see from the readouts that it was Walis himself doing the zooming.

The image steadied, fixing on three startled faces. It was them all right, the aliens. Meli saw two hands shoot out and clamp two arms.

'Wilis, summon the war-bots and get over there!'

Meli watched as the frightened face of a boy with reddish-coloured hair appeared, challenging the augment who held his friends.

Walis laughed, glanced aside for a moment, then the display flickered and a high-pitched scream erupted from the speaker, so sharp and loud it made Meli jump.

'Don't murder them, you idiot,' he yelled. 'I want them

alive!'

There was no reply. The screaming didn't stop.

30 : Man of Secrets

The bubbletruck bumped to a halt. It took several seconds for the inner bubble to stop swaying then Alkemy opened her eyes. 'Are we there?'

'I guess.' Ludokrus raised the slit in the front of the carton, but all they could make out through two layers of clear plastic was a grimy alley and a loading dock in deep shadow. There was a small, faded sign on a nearby wall, the paint peeling and the lettering indistinct, but they could still make out what it said: Macet Upholstery Services.

Machinery clanked and the view bumped and shifted as the bubbletruck was directed through a square opening in the side of the building and into a lighted room.

Ludokrus closed the slit again.

They felt movement; a sideways roll, more bumps and clanks, then a whirr as the outer bubble was opened. More rocking as the inner bubble was aligned, then the top of that too was unlatched. Mechanical claws gripped the packing carton, lifted it clear and set it on the workshop floor.

The machine sounds stopped. Ludokrus risked another

peek.

Around them they could see a loading dock rather like the one they'd left at Concordance. The design and layout were similar, but this place was considerably smaller, considerably older, and bathed in the yellow light of ancient incandescent bulbs.

It was also occupied.

Two elderly synthos appeared. One shut down the hoist while the other scanned the bubbletruck's shipping tag and consulted a manifest. Then a small man with a shaved head hurried in behind them, pulling on an over-large and rather shabby smock as he did so. He dismissed the synthos then stood with his hands in his pockets, waiting till a door in the side of the building closed. Once they'd gone, he took out a pocket knife, stabbed it into the top of the carton and cut a neat circular hole through the cardboard and foam.

Lifting out the plug of packaging, he said, 'Calming Blue, wasn't it, Alb—?' He stopped, looking down at two unfamiliar faces looking back at him.

It took less than a minute to cut away the front of the carton, then he stood back, regarding them warily, casting any eye over the discarded packaging as if he'd been expecting someone else.

'Who are you, and how did you get one of our emergency evacuation sequences?'

'Our uncle is ... *was* the director of the Science Council,' Ludokrus said. 'Polky Krilen. Not real uncle, but that is what we call him. And the sequence was given to us by our syntho, Albert.'

'He didn't come with you?'

Ludokrus glanced at his sister, recalling Albert's

insistence they say nothing to anyone.

The man saw the look and nodded. 'Ah, right.'

'Who are you?' Alkemy asked. Something about him was vaguely familiar.

'My name is Andop Scolyfol. I've worked with your uncle – and Albert – for a good many years.' They tapped palms in local fashion as they introduced themselves. He added, 'I won't ask if you had a good trip, but at least you've arrived in one piece.'

'You have tried this?' Ludokrus gestured at the bubbletruck.

'Once or twice in my student days, back when I was young and foolish.' He smiled. 'Now I'm old and foolish, but not *that* foolish.'

He glanced at the shipping tag as he bundled the packaging into a recycler. 'You've come from the Science Council at Concordance, I see. Did you leave Albert behind?'

Alkemy coloured, not knowing how to respond.

Ludokrus started to make a stumbling reply, but Andop just laughed. 'I understand your caution. Very wise. You don't know who I am. But let me assure you,' he pointed to the incandescent lightbulbs overhead, 'like them I have all the right *connections*. Which is more, I suspect, than our mutual friend has right now.' His emphasis was slight, but underscored by a whimsical flick of his bushy eyebrows.

'You may be right,' Ludokrus said cautiously. 'But else what can we do?'

'Get to know each other better, I suppose. Come up to the office.'

They followed him out of the loading dock and through a work area containing antique furniture in various states of disassembly and repair. There were wood-turning machines and spring-coiling machines and industrial sewing machines of various types. A second room was lined with bolts of fabric in every colour under the sun.

He led them up a staircase and through a series of wood-panelled rooms that might have come from a museum display.

'Charming, isn't it?' he said, directing them to an office at the end.

Inside, they found heavy wooden furniture and a worn but richly patterned carpet on the floor. There was an old iron safe in one corner and a dark green filing cabinet with brass handles in the other. A bookshelf sat against one wall and several other items of furniture lay under dust covers. The far wall contained a line of narrow casement windows made of lead-lighted glass cut in diamond shapes. Alkemy moved closer and looked out to a street of crumbling brick warehouses that might have come from another century. The only indication they hadn't stepped back in time was an elevated section of the discontinuous highway in the distance.

'This place used to belong to my grandfather,' Andop gestured to a portrait on the wall, 'but my father wasn't much interested in taking it over when he died, and nor was I. Which was lucky for both of us as nanomachine fabrication and total recycling wiped out a lot of firms in this area. I mean, who would bother getting a sofa re-covered or repaired when you can simply scrap it and get a new one delivered for next to nothing?

'Still, we do get a small but steady stream of requests. Genuine ones, I mean. Not like yours.' He picked up a clipboard and flicked through some of the pages. 'Heirlooms, keepsakes, historical pieces from museums. This place is kept ticking over by Wible and Thrum, a couple of old synthos who work here part-time. Which gives me the perfect cover for situations like this.'

'Situations?' Alkemy said, still trying to work out why the man seemed familiar.

'I'd prefer not to say more. But you can rest assured that Krilen, Albert and I are what one might call partners in crime.'

She looked at him holding the clipboard. Something in the angle and the way he held it brought the memory flooding back.

'The projection!' she exclaimed, turning to Ludokrus. 'Back on Earth. Remember how Albert replay for us scenes from memory?'

Ludokrus scowled, trying to caution her to be quiet.

After Albert's demise, Alkemy had retrieved his memory bulb and they'd plugged it into a receiver he'd modified shortly before his death. Once connected, it played key scenes from Albert's past, explaining his situation and his mission. One of those recollections detailed the secret enhancements he'd undergone.

'The room where he wake up and looks at the wave,' Alkemy said. 'Remember?'

One of the clips showed Albert recovering from surgery to implant beads that would eventually grow to form a brain-enhancing neural lace. Just hours after they'd been injected, he was already showing remarkable abilities. They'd seen the world from his perspective: the image of a breaking wave, analysed and broken down as he calculated the trajectory of every speck of foam and drop of water in the seconds before it hit a rock.

'Uncle Krilen does not believe. Think maybe there is fault with his equipment. He call someone in to check.'

A second man had entered, carrying a tablet-like computer, holding it exactly the way Andop was now holding the clipboard.

'You!' Ludokrus exclaimed. 'You bring in a second screen to compare it with our uncle's.'

Andop studied them gravely. 'You seem to know more than I expected. Well, it should make the explanations easier.'

* * *

The weight of the hand on Tim's shoulder felt like an iron bar and the grip of Walis's fingers was like a mechanical claw. He struggled, as did his sister, but the grip tightened, the fingers dug in and they both cried out simultaneously.

'Stop squirming and you won't get hurt,' Walis said conversationally.

'You're already hurting!' Coral said.

'I can do a lot worse.'

He gave them both an extra squeeze. They cried out again, but the message got through and they stopped struggling.

'Let them go!' Norman shouted.

'Or what, squib?' Walis grinned down at him. 'What are you going to do? Bite my ankles?'

Norman kicked him instead. It was like kicking a

concrete block and he hopped away on one foot.

Walis laughed. 'Oh no. Stop. I can't stand it. I give up.'

'Leave us,' Tim told Norman. 'Run for it. Save yourself.'

'Yeah, go on,' Walis said. 'I could do with a bit of sport. It'll give me an excuse to break the legs on these two and come after you myself.'

'Ignore him. Just go – *aaarrgghh!*'

'Might have to break some arms first too,' Walis said.

Norman looked around helplessly for a weapon, not that he could think of anything he could use against the augment, unless someone had left a rocket launcher lying around.

'Come along now.' Walis spun them around. 'I have someone very keen to meet you all. And you, squib,' he glanced over his shoulder. 'Better tag along or it'll be the worse for your friends.' To prove the point he gave both Tim's and Coral's arms another squeeze, making them cry out again.

Norman fell into step behind them, his hands in his pockets. He felt something there. Something he'd forgotten about. Not exactly a rocket launcher, but then again ...

'How's your brother?' he called. 'Have they chipped him out of that alley yet?'

'Nearly.'

Norman laughed. 'What an idiot.'

He wrapped his hand around the sauce bottle. The complimentary one the serve-bot had given him in Basic Foods. The one with the warning label on the side.

'I don't think you should call him that,' Walis said. 'We're clone-brothers. We share everything. If you insult one of us, you insult all of us.'

'Really?' Norman's hand closed around the bottle. 'And there I was thinking wall-boy got the dumbest third of the brain.'

'Oi!' Walis turned and glared at him.

Norman whipped out the sauce bottle, held it in both hands, aiming it at Walis. 'All right, that's it. Let them go and back away. Now!'

Walis looked at him and laughed. 'You're a trier, I'll give you that, squib.'

'I mean it. Back away or—'

'Or what? You'll give me a serious dry cleaning bill?'

Norman aimed and squeezed the bottle, hard. A jet of dark red plimp sauce shot out and hit Walis in the eyes. The effect was better than he could have wished. Walis released Tim and Coral and began clawing at his face. And screaming. He had a surprisingly high-pitched scream.

31 : Neural Enhancements

Andop Scolyfol drew the dust sheet from a sofa and gestured for Alkemy and Ludokrus to take a seat. The sofa was old and worn but surprisingly comfortable.

'That colour really is called "Red for Danger",' he gestured at the fabric. 'It's what gave us the idea of using it as a code in the first place. I'll move it down to the workshop and have it re-covered when we're done, just in case anyone follows up on that order.'

He went to the antique filing cabinet and tugged on one of the handles. The whole front swung aside to reveal it was really a refrigerator. The iron safe disguised a food fabricator.

'May I offer you some refreshments?'

Alkemy and Ludokrus looked surprised. Andop smiled and began setting out drinks and bowls of snacks. 'Nothing here is quite as it seems. Even granddad.' He aimed a remote at the portrait on the wall and the picture slid aside to reveal a vid screen tuned to a news channel.

'You're probably wondering what this is all about. Let me explain.

'Ten years ago, I began researching the concept of neural laces at Theia University. You're familiar with the idea? Beads – a little like linguaseeds – are placed in key areas of the brain to enhance general brain function and give it more capacity. Over time, the beads grow tendrils, connecting with one another to form a lacework of extra circuitry, multiplying their power by ten or even a hundred times.

'It's a difficult field. We've had many setbacks.

'About five years ago, there was an incident involving a syntho – a volunteer who entered the program knowing the risks. One bead was misplaced and caused the enhancement of violent tendencies. He ran amok, did great deal of damage and injured several people. The incident was played on by our opponents in the Military Council, and following a well-orchestrated campaign the project was shut down.

'We later learned the Military Council opposed our work because they were running a similar project themselves, although not nearly so advanced. By shutting ours down they hoped to steal our research staff.

'I was offered a place in the new programme. Krilen suggested I decline, and I did so. With my old team disbanded, I was demoted. My professorship was cancelled and I went from being the director of a high-profile research programme to a departmental registrar and workshop technician.'

He took up a container of jahlbad blossom, broke the seal and sipped.

'They thought they were punishing me, but it was quite

the reverse. I've always loved the technical aspects of my work. The lab is the place I'm happiest. All the other stuff – teaching, administration, the interminable meetings – were a hindrance and I was glad to be shot of them.

'Now, apart from a few standard duties such as supervising new students, I come and go as I please. I've automated many of my other responsibilities, freeing up my time to do the thing that fascinates me most: continuing my research into neural enhancements.'

'Our uncle helps with this?' Ludokrus asked.

'Your uncle's always been a firm supporter of my work. His position as head of the Science Council allowed him to channel funds my way – discreetly, of course – and for the last five years I've continued my research in secret. I have a small laboratory on the coast near Orme where I've made one or two ... interesting advances in the last few months.'

'You mean Albert?'

'Albert in particular, yes. He was a special case. The beads had a remarkable effect on his abilities and intellect right from the outset. But Krilen wanted him for something, some sort of mission – he never told me what – and we added memory bulb technology from another of his secret projects as a backup in case anything went wrong. A prudent measure, it seems. Good job I made a copy of his vital statistics before he left.'

It took a moment for his words to sink in. 'You mean ... you can rebuild him?'

'Re-life is the preferred term. And yes, I suspect that's why Albert sent you here. As well as providing you with a safe refuge, I mean.'

'How long will it take, this re-life?'

'A few days to source and assemble the necessary components.'

'That is all?'

Andop nodded.

'Do you know what happen to our uncle?' Ludokrus asked. 'All we know is that he is sick from an alien virus.'

'Alien virus!' Andop snorted. 'Very convenient. Krilen was struck down the same day his deputy disappeared. That's one coincidence too many, if you ask me. Especially as it gave the Military Council an excuse to put in their own administrator, who then dismissed all the staff and ransacked the place.'

'We were told he is contagious.'

'Yes, they're keeping him in isolation. Isolation from everyone, including Alien Infections – the very people who should be caring for him. I hear the only visitors he's allowed are those authorised by Meli himself.'

There was a low rumble as a line of bubbletrucks raced along the rail at the end of the street.

'My theory is that the Military Council are looking into Krilen's secret projects. By taking over the Science Council, they hoped to find details of them, but Krilen's not stupid. He keeps all the details up here.' He tapped his head. 'Now he's in a hospital bed – drugged or dsedated – they don't know where to turn.'

'Which is why he is after us,' Ludokrus said.

'You two?' Andop laughed. 'You can't be part of ...' His voice faded as he saw their expressions.

'Not just us. We have friends that Meli also chase.'

'Really?' Then he held up a hand. 'I don't need to know the details. If Krilen wanted me to know, he'd have told me.

But I can offer you assistance. You *and* your friends.'

Alkemy gave a little squawk and pointed to the screen where a news vid showed a glimpse of one of the Triple-Dub brothers.

'Hello, they're new,' Andop said, using the remote to turn up the volume as he studied the insect-like robots the camera was following.

'The new machines are apparently an early prototype,' the voice-over reported, 'and the Military Council have apologised for the incident, saying it was a training exercise gone wrong.'

'Not them, the one in front,' Alkemy said. 'The augment. It look like one that work for Meli.'

Andop backed up the clip and replayed it. The screen showed the thug-bots and the augment running around Basic Plaza.

'Like they look for someone,' Ludokrus said.

There were interviews with outraged citizens and reports of people being pushed around and intimidated. The screen showed a woman comforting a wailing child.

'Well, they clearly didn't find them,' Andop said.

The last clip was a news-drone's view, showing the bots departing empty-handed. A moment later, it was swatted from the air.

'That was one of Triple-Dub all right,' Ludokrus said. 'And the place look like Basic Plaza near Concordance station.'

Alkemy stared at him. 'You don't think ...?'

'That our friends arrive from Selene?' He nodded and smiled. 'I tell Coral all about the Basic shops.'

'Then they are here! And they escape the other Triple-

Dub! We must find, help. If they go to Basic, maybe they now have comms and try to contact us. We should check.'

'No!' Ludokrus seized her hand before she could tap her right ear. 'Do not switch on!'

'But—'

'This will be the first thing Meli watch. If you turn on now, he will know where we are.'

'But the others are new here. Know nothing. We need to help. How can we contact?'

Ludokrus shrugged and shook his head.

Andop flicked the buttons on the remote control, playing and reversing segments of the clip saying, 'I take it these friends of yours aren't locals?'

'They are from another planet.'

'So presumably they don't speak Eltherian?'

Alkemy shook her head.

'Is their language very common?'

She glanced at Ludokrus, then said cautiously, 'Quite rare, I think.'

'Then that's how they're being tracked. By the downloads.'

'We must warn. Help. But how?'

Andop went continued playing with the remote, making the thug-bots do a kind of backwards-forawrds dance. 'There is one way,' he said thoughtfully. 'One of my hobbies is music, and we have a rather good recording studio down on campus. Can either of you sing?'

32 : Mr Cheerful

Coral, Tim and Norman raced away from Concordance park, darting across an electrobike lane without waiting for the lights, under an elevated section of bubbletruck track, and on towards the station as the sound of Walis's screams faded in the distance.

He cries were attracting people. Some offered help, but he batted them away. Others had just come from the disturbance in Basic Plaza and recognised who they thought was the leader of the gang of thug-bots. They started jeering and the mood turned ugly. Police-bots and news-bots emerging from the plaza took an interest.

'Told you that stuff was strong,' Coral said, slowing as they reached a broad set of stairs near the station entrance.

Norman, still stunned by the effect of his attack, flung the plimp sauce bottle into a recycler. 'That must've really hurt.'

'So did having your arm half-broken.'

'You don't think I blinded him, do you?'

'One those things? If you did, they'll just pop in a new set of eyeballs.'

'I s'pose so.'

Tim glanced at his friend. 'What's up?'

'I dunno. It just seemed like a mean trick, squirting that stuff in his eyes.'

'You think they'd stop at playing mean tricks? What about all those thug-bots in the plaza? All those kids? You saved our bacon, man.'

They followed Coral through a transit passage leading to a sign further up that consisted of three wavy lines beside the Eltherian word for river. A second set of stairs led to a broad concourse with exits pointing north, south, east and west.

'Which way?'

'Doesn't matter,' Coral said. 'Let's go for the busiest. Get lost in the crowd.'

They took the northern exit, following the passage to where it ended at an empty platform beside a broad river of what looked like molten lead. It had a dull metallic sheen and flowed like water, but there was no heat, and people were standing on its surface.

They watched as the couple ahead stepped off the platform. Like a real river, the flow along the sides was slow and easy, but as they moved towards the middle, their speed increased. In the centre, people raced along at thirty or forty kilometres an hour, all while standing still.

A group of students went by sitting cross-legged in a circle, chatting amongst themselves. Some people took folding seats from racks on the platform, walked out and made themselves comfortable. Presumably, they had longer journeys.

Coral, Tim and Norman made their way out slowly, picking up speed as they neared the middle. Norman was fascinated. There were no separate bands moving at different speeds. Like a real river, it simply flowed like a single entity.

They passed into an arched tunnel. Signs suspended from the ceiling told them of upcoming exits and they followed their own progress on map overlays in their heads-up displays. Theia was bigger than it looked coming down from Selene Station because many Theian houses were at least partly underground.

After ten minutes, the river split into two smaller streams which in turn broke up into smaller and smaller tributaries, forming the equivalent of local creeks. 'The one on the right.' Coral nudged the others. 'There's a Basic Accommodation near the end of it.'

They edged across, following a handful of other travellers. A minute later, it left the tunnel system and emerged from the side of a grassy hill into clear evening air before meandering on for another kilometre. The banks on either side were mown grass and fellow travellers simply stepped off into their own back gardens.

'This is us up ahead.'

The stream ended at a wide, circulating pool beneath an overhead sign labelled Petzval. On the far side, another stream led back to town. They walked across the slowly rotating surface of the pool and up onto solid ground. Coral checked her overlay and pointed to a neat, quiet street beyond the river entrance. 'That way.'

The long summer evening was drawing to a close. Street lights came on as they walked. A cleaning-bot rolled past, heading in the opposite direction, the low hum of its brushes the only sound above a twittering of birdsong.

The street was lined with trees quilted in spring blossoms, and the air was fresh and lightly scented with their flowers. They passed broad gardens and the low mounds of houses. While central city dwellers lived in apartments, most suburban houses were underground with sky domes, solar panels and sloping entrance ramps the only clues to their presence.

Overhead, two of the planet's three moons were up and Halo glowed warmly in the light of the setting sun.

They passed a group of people talking, children playing games, and an elderly man walking what was either a gigantic dog or a miniature pony. It was on a harness and had a shaggy coat, mottled grey and ginger. Its long intelligent face watched them as they passed.

'Oh my god, did you see that?' Coral whispered. 'Wasn't it gorgeous!'

'What the heck was it?' Tim said.

'They're called silkas. House ponies.' She turned, looking after it longingly.

'You keep those things in your house?'

'You can do.'

'I'd hate to see the size of the pet door.'

Street level access to Basic Accommodation was little more than a broad grey stair with an illuminated sign, but down below they found a bright, marbled foyer and a greeter-bot that seemed genuinely delighted to meet them. It high-fived each of them in turn and gave them a tour of the facilities.

The sleeping modules they were shown to lay at the

bottom of one of the corridors radiating off from the foyer. Ten identical compartments formed a circle around a communal area. All were empty. The greeter-bot explained that Petzval was primarily a winter destination.

'So there's no one else in this segment?' Coral asked.

'No, miss. We are only at seventeen percent of capacity and I doubt we'll have any more arrivals this evening.'

'If you get some, do you have room to put them elsewhere?'

The bot's large eyes looked into hers for a moment. 'You'd like privacy. I understand. Especially after the regrettable events at our Concordance facility. I shall reserve this segment for your exclusive use.'

'Do you know what happened back there after we left?'

'Unit CS-1124393 was captured and interrogated, but she told the augment nothing and was recycled.'

'Oh, I'm sorry to hear that.'

'She acted well. A true Basic bot. She went on transmitting till the end.'

The greeter-bot bowed formally then left them, its rubber-coated wheels almost noiseless on the tiled floor.

They took a module each. The rooms were like regular hotel rooms in terms of facilities, except everything was squeezed into a space a little over a metre wide and three metres deep. Folding the bed away gave access to a bathroom and shower that opened out at the far end, while closing both made room for a fold-out table and a couple of chairs. There was a vid screen on an adjustable bracket above the bed and a little alcove of drinks and snacks beside it. Everything was spotlessly clean and the rooms smelled fresh and airy, but with the doors closed it still felt a little claustrophobic.

After checking things out, they reassembled in the common area. The excitement of the day was wearing off and they sat in silence, trying out different combinations on the drinks dispenser and the snack fabricator.

'We forgot to get some disposable comms gear,' Tim said. 'Is there a Basic Comms nearby?'

Coral checked her heads-up display. 'There's one seven stops back, but it'll be closed by now. We'll have to leave it till the morning.'

'They should have their comms switched off anyway if they've got any sense,' Norman said morosely.

'How are we supposed to contact them then?'

'Mutual friends?' Coral suggested.

'Like who? Meli's got Krilen, and their parents are off-planet.'

Norman tinkered with the food fab and produced a plate of smac chips and some dipping sauce.

'Plimp? Coral asked.

He shook his head.

The chips weren't as crunchy as the Basic Food ones, and no one, not even Norman, was particularly hungry.

'There was that guy in Albert's recollection video,' Tim said. 'A lab technician or something. Remember? He looked like Krilen's assistant.'

'Oh yeah,' Coral said. 'A short bald guy in a lab coat.'

'He was wearing a name badge. I remember the translation overlay coming up. Andrew Something or Something Andrew.'

Coral yawned. 'I think it was more alien than that. I'll sleep on it.'

'What good will knowing his name do?' Norman said. 'Even if you do remember it, how are you going to communicate? All Basic bots might have the English module now, but they'll be on the lookout out for other downloads. As soon as he gets the message they'll be onto us.'

Coral sighed 'There you go. We're stuffed. Thanks, Mr Cheerful.'

'I'm just—'

'I know,' she said mildly. 'I'm tired too. I think we should all get an early night. See you guys in the morning.'

Tim got to his feet as she headed to her module. He stretched, saying, 'She's right. It's not every day you crash-land on a space station, escape an augment, land on an alien planet, then escape a posse of killer robots. I wonder what tomorrow's got in store.'

33 : New Bot Order

Frank Townsend leaned on a fence, watching as the army helicopter lifted off from the front paddock. They'd been pretty decent about it, waiting till he'd finished the morning milking and herded the cows to a more distant paddock so they wouldn't be unduly alarmed, but after days of activity and all sorts of comings and goings, the cows were getting used to the excitement.

A second figure joined him. 'Morning Frank.'

'Gidday Glad. You're an early bird.'

'I have to get back to town. I've still got a shop to run.'

'You won't stay for breakfast?'

'Thanks, but no. I'll press on.'

'You're welcome here any time, you know. Come back this evening if you like. Join us for dinner. Stay over again.'

Glad paused, thinking of her empty house and the gruelling day ahead. It was official now. Everyone knew her son was one of the missing children, so there'd be sympathy and kind words from everyone in town. They were good people, but she really just wanted to get on with things and not think too much about it.

'You mean commute?'

'It's what those city folk do.'

'I might take you up on that, Frank. Just for a day or two.'

'Make it however long you like. You're good company.'

'Thanks, Frank.'

The sound of the helicopter faded, replaced by the cheerful call of a tui.

'There was something else, wasn't there?' he added. 'In your boy's note. An extra page.'

She bit her lip, tempted to tell him. Share her worries and fears.

'It was just ... personal stuff ...'

'Yeah?'

She looked away and drew a breath. 'It ... might not be as easy for them to get back as they suggested. Fifty light-years is a huge distance.'

'Not so much the distance, it's the time, right? All that relativity stuff? I did wonder about that myself.'

'You can't tell the others.'

'They're going to have to know at some point.'

'Yeah, but not yet, eh? Let's give the kids a chance. They did say to give them six to eight weeks.'

'And after that?'

She looked at the departing helicopter, fighting back tears. 'Each day as it comes, eh? What else can we do?'

* * *

Andop returned in the early hours of the morning, drawing

back the curtains in the upstairs office and waking Alkemy and Ludokrus, who'd spent the night sleeping on sofas and using dust sheets for blankets. They stretched and groaned as Tetzul light flooded the diamond-paned windows, filling the room with a warm orange glow.

'Sorry about the accommodation,' he said, 'but I imagine Meli and his goons will be watching your parents house. I have, however, arranged something a little more comfortable for tonight.'

He dropped a couple of student passes on the desk. 'You're now enrolled at Theia University under the names Aldrene Rathko and Luud Grun. You were born on Stave so you'll need these too.' He added a couple of behind-the-ear comms units. 'They're set up with your new identities and include several hundred contacts so they appear to be genuine.

'Because you're off-worlders, you qualify for on-campus accommodation. I've arranged a studio unit for you and your friends – when we find them.'

'On-campus? But that is downtown, near Concordance.'

'There are more than five thousand students at the university. You'll blend in. Besides, the best place to hide is often in plain sight. And you can't stay here. Wible and Thrum will be in soon. The fewer people that know about you, the better.

'Which reminds me, give me a hand with this.' He indicated the sofa Alkemy had been sleeping on, the one cover in red fabric. They got it onto a trolley-bot and guided it downstairs.

'We'll position it as though it's just been unpacked. There, that should complete our cover story. In a few days' time, the Science Council will receive a sofa they didn't know they owned, re-covered in Calming Blue.

'Now, let's get to the university and get you settled in. I have a music vid I want you to help me finish off.'

'Music vid?' Alkemy said, suddenly noticing his tired eyes.

Andop smiled. 'It's been a busy night.'

* * *

Coral was finished breakfast and flicking through vid channels by the time Tim emerged from his module.

'Man, what a sleep!' He stretched and yawned then slumped at the table.

'Did you sleep in your clothes?'

'Looks like it, eh?' He looked at hers, neat and pressed. 'Have you been shopping?'

'I have two words for you,' she said, pointing to a console on the other side of the common area. 'Clothing fab.'

'Huh?'

'Here.'

She beckoned him over, stood him on a plate and pressed a button. A series of red laser lines crisscrossed him horizontally and vertically. The machine beeped, she took a corner of his T-shirt, clamped it in an analyser and pressed another button. Thirty seconds later, an identical copy, brand new and neatly pressed, dropped from a chute at the bottom.

Coral held it up. 'There. Perfect size. Now do the rest of your stuff and throw your old clothes in the recycler.'

227

'That's neat,' Tim grinned. 'No laundry.'

'It'll only copy what you've got, and only do one of each, but it's better than … Oh my god!'

Norman pushed open the door of his module. His hair was sticking up on end and he was wearing nothing but a sheet wrapped around his middle.

'Morning,' he yawned.

Coral shoved Tim forward and covered her eyes. 'Show him the clothing fab. I'm going for a walk. And see if there's such a thing as Basic Memory Wiping.'

She returned half an hour later to find a litter of breakfast bowls on the table and Tim and Norman staring at the vidscreen, their mouths open as a music track faded out.

'What are you two doing? Catching flies?'

Tim grabbed the remote. 'Look at this. Or rather, listen to it. It's called *New Bot Order*.'

The screen and speakers came to life. A pulsing rock track set to cleverly cut footage of Wilis and the thug-bots at Basic Plaza. There was a loop of Wilis issuing an order, barking the same words over and over, seemingly in time to the music, and shots of the thug-bots sped up and slowed down to make them look even more insect-like. The rhythm was infectious and the song would have been popular even without the clever editing, but the timeliness of it after yesterday's events and the fact that it was the first public sighting of the Military Council's new machines made it a winner. And then, right near the end, came a rap-like segment that went;

Alchemy is ludicrous.
Don't try to teach me that.

It took Coral a moment to register. 'Hey, that was in English!'

'Yup. And look at this.' Tim hit another button, showing the track's popularity. It had had almost a hundred thousand viewings. 'Everyone who hears it will automatically get the English module.'

'Play that bit again.' Tim did so. 'It sounds a bit like Ludokrus.'

'I think it is Ludokrus. He and Alkemy already speak English so don't need the module. Whoever did the rest of the song just pasted that bit in without listening to it, otherwise they'd have risked being identified by Meli. Now, it doesn't matter. Not with a hundred thousand viewings.'

'A hundred and twenty thousand now.' Norman pointed to the counter, ticking away like a race timer.

'And those words ... that place ...'

'Already on it,' Norman called, flicking through Compendia. 'Ha! That Andrew Something, the name you were trying to think of last night. Could it be Andop?'

'Andop? That's it! How did you get that?'

He looked up, grinning. 'Andop Scolyfol is the chief registrar for the Tech-Sci department at Theia University. Do you think we should give him a call?'

34 : Alien Menace

The room was as dark as usual and, as usual, the three members of the Ruling Council sat behind a high wooden bench like judges in a courtroom. Each was backlit by a narrow beam of light so that only their outlines were discernible. And each spoke through a distorter so their voices were masked.

Almas Meli took his place at a lectern beneath a spotlight in the middle of the room. He stood up straight and squared his shoulders.

'You know why you've been summoned?' the central figure said. Its voice sounded harsh and robotic through the distorter.

'I imagine you're unhappy with my performance.'

'A polite way of putting it.' The central figure looked left and right. The other figures nodded.

'You must understand—'

'We *understand* that you've made certain elements of the Military Council a laughing stock.'

'But—'

'You should have closed down that entire plaza, interrogated every person and every bot in there, confiscated all cameras and recording devices, prevented anyone from leaving until you were satisfied, *and* prevented anyone from entering – including the media.'

'*Especially* the media,' the figure on the right snarled.

'Of course,' Meli said. 'I would like to have done so, but I simply don't have that level of authority.'

'That is why we summoned you, Administrator,' the central figure said. 'You do now.'

Meli rocked back on his heels in surprise. 'I do?'

'You and your staff have authority to do whatever is necessary to bring this alien menace under control. Under *our* control.'

* * *

The river station at Theia University split into four main streams carrying staff and students to different parts of the campus. As they passed through, taking the eastern tributary, they heard *New Bot Order* playing on the station's speakers. Norman grinned and did a little dance.

'Oh, please!' Coral pretended not to know him.

The stream ended in a pool circulating around a raised platform. As they stepped onto it, they were greeted by a short, frowning man with a shaved head.

'Finally! My missing students,' he said in Eltherian, their linguaseeds translating his words effortlessly. 'I'm Andop Scolyfol, registrar for Tech-Sci. These last minute arrangements are most inconsiderate, you know. I've had a devil of a job finding you accommodation. You'll have to share with a couple of other off-worlders, I'm afraid. This way please.' He turned and marched off before they could even offer him a greeting.

They followed him through the station and out into a broad grassy park where students lounged in the midday sun, studying terminals or playing games. But they hardly noticed any of that. Surrounding them were a series of gigantic glass pyramids reaching high into the sky.

He waved them to a travelator, turned and said quietly, 'Sorry about that, but I want you to be careful in public places – at least for a day or two.' Coral made to speak but he held up a hand. 'That includes even apparently empty ones like this.'

A ball bounced off the travelator behind him. A young man in running shorts leapt the wide band of moving pathway and ran after it.

'See what I mean? He may not have heard our song yet.'

They carried on for a full minute, passing swimming pools, sports courts and a small amphitheatre before Andop stepped off again. 'This is where you'll be: Pyramid K.'

Coral looked about. There was no one within earshot. 'What is this place?' she whispered. 'Some sort of resort?'

'Resort?' Andop laughed. 'No, it's just student accommodation.'

The inside of the pyramid was even more spectacular than its outside. The construction was simple but elegant. Each suite of rooms – called a studio – was treated like a toy block. The first level were stacked side by side around the boundaries of a square, then the next level were stacked on top, but set back a couple of metres. And so on with each subsequent level. The top-most units, fifteen stories up, were prized for their spectacular views.

The interior space created by the stacking was like a pyramid of air inside the outer shell. There was a diving pool, a sports court, a VR cinema and a line of shops specialising in students' study subjects. A bar with live music occupied one corner, and a cafe occupied the other. A spiral running track wound round and round the perimeter, all the way up to the top. By day, the interior was lit by fibre optic cables placed between the blocks so that inside it was almost as bright as outside.

The studios were accessed by elevator platforms running up angled struts from each corner of the pyramid. The lift cars were clear plastic bubbles and the ride showed the drop below. Coral turned her face away and counted off the floors.

'Here we are.' Andop stepped out onto a walkway that ran around all four sides. 'Level nine, studio nine. Over there.'

He led them to a closed door on the north side, tapped in the entry code and pushed it open.

The interior was lined in lightly stained timber and had a tiled terracotta floor. There were bedrooms either side of the entrance passage, and at the far end they saw a lounge that opened onto a terrace overlooking the grounds and the tiered studios below.

The place was empty and quiet. Alkemy and Ludokrus were nowhere to be seen.

As they walked up the hall, Coral turned to Andop. 'I thought you said the others were already here.'

'Surprise!'

The last two bedroom doors burst open and Alkemy and Ludokrus launched themselves at their friends, nearly knocking them over with the ferocity of their hugs. They danced around and cheered then led them into the lounge where Ludokrus had rigged up a series of confetti guns. He hit a switch and they fired in sequence, shooting out a million shards of glittery paper that drifted down around them like falling snowflakes.

'At last we can say it proper,' he called, and together he and Alkemy chanted, *Welcome to Eltheria!*

3

Shadows

35 : Going Viral

'Why are we slowing down? Where are we?'

'Guess.'

'Let me see ... a gas giant orbited by a ridiculously large metal moon ... It can only be the Thanatos regional base at Reeklik.'

'Indeed it is. Welcome to the start of the civilised galaxy. Not long now till we reach the grey, grey ooze of home.'

'Why do the Thanatos always have to make things so big? It's only a piddly support post.'

'Not that piddly. According to the manifest, that base stocks two hundred Death class battleships, five hundred Agony fighters, and a thousand killer robots.'

'A thousand? They only sent us one. And we practically had to beg for that, the miserable old—'

'Oh no!'

'What?'

'They want us to check in. Local Darkness #719 has requested we debrief him on our mission.'

'Put him off. He's only a triple-digit Darkness.'

'"By special order of His Exalted Excellency, Darkest of the

Dark." It's a personal invitation.'

'I don't suppose we could pretend we didn't get the message ...?'

'Did I mention the two hundred Death class battleships and five hundred Agony fighters?'

'Well, at least we can get rid of that scrap metal in the hold. We can replace it with duty-free snot champagne and make a killing when we get back home.'

'Provided you don't drink it all before we get there.'

'After meeting with a Darkness, I'm likely to need a drink. Or ten.'

* * *

'Oh man, what a sleep!' Norman padded out onto the terrace wearing a white bathrobe.

Coral regarded him archly. 'At least you've learned to dress in the mornings.'

He squinted at the daylight. Tena was a hands-breadth above the eastern horizon, Tetzul higher up to the north. Two suns meant double shadows, one sharp and well defined, the other pale and indistinct. It looked as if his shadow had a shadow of its own.

Their terrace was separated from its neighbours by planters filled with bushy shrubs. At the far end, a glass balustrade gave an unobstructed view of the tiered studios below and the parkland and gardens beyond. In the distance lay the central core of buildings that formed the heart of the university, circled by research laboratories and other accommodation pyramids. Curving travelators, dotted with students, glinted like steel rivers. Somewhere nearby he heard the thumping beat of *New Bot Order*.

'How's our song doing?' he asked Tim, lying on a recliner and studying a study-slab.

'Going viral. We hit eight hundred million views early this morning.'

'Eight hundred mill! You're kidding?'

'We're currently Number Two on this week's music charts.'

Norman danced to the distant beat. 'That means we can *definitely* go out exploring now. So, what's for breakfast?'

'Juice and fresh air,' Coral said.

'You mean the food fab's still out of action?'

'Not out of action, out of raw materials. Thanks to your antics last night.'

Norman, restless after spending two days cooped up in the apartment, had spent the evening experimenting with the food fabricator trying to create Earth desserts he didn't have recipes for. His attempts were mostly hopeless, tasteless failures – except for a blue cheese and chutney pavlova, which just tasted weird. He was only prevented from poisoning himself – and everyone else – by the machine running out of raw materials.

'Any of that pav left?'

'You've got to be joking!'

'I am, actually. Even I'm not *that* weird.'

'Hard to believe,' Coral muttered.

The front door opened and Alkemy called a greeting. Ludokrus followed her in, his arms laden with bags of groceries. A trolley-bot trundled along behind, carrying more. Norman was keen to restock the food fab, but Alkemy deflected him, suggesting he might like to get dressed first.

By the time he returned – showered and dressed – the kitchen was filling with a delicious smell.

'Mmm, what's that?'

'Traditional Eltherian breakfast: smeld and griv.' Alkemy held up her plate. 'The taste is much like your scrambled egg and bacon.'

'Is the green stuff the bacon or the egg? Doesn't matter. I gotta get me some of that. I'm so hungry I could eat the fab.'

'I almost forget. I bring you something from the shop,' Ludokrus said, handing Coral a lemon-coloured orb the size of an apple.

'Oh, thanks. What is it?'

'Is call the love melon.'

'Why's it called that?'

'Try after breakfast. You will see.'

The food fab beeped and Norman pushed past them with a plate piled so high its contents wobbled when he walked. 'Mind your backs. Coming through.'

'Oh my god, you practically need a building permit for that!'

'Wait till I go back for seconds.'

He didn't. The food was tasty and filling, but not even Norman could manage any more. He pushed back from the table and gave a contented burp.

Coral pointedly ignored him and took up the love melon. Encouraged by Ludokrus, she sniffed it, then took a bite. The flesh was firm and sweet, but once in her mouth, it dissolved into a mass of fizzy bubbles. She laughed, juice running down her chin. 'That's amazing! It's like eating a soft drink.' She took another bite. 'But why *love melon*?'

'Keep eat. You will see.'

Inside, she found a brown heart-shaped stone and held it up between her thumb and forefinger. 'Oh, that is so sweet! Thank you, Ludokrus.' She gave him a beatific smile. He gave her one back and squeezed her free hand.

Norman made a gagging noise. 'I think I'm going to be sick.'

'Hardly surprising the way you eat,' Coral told him.

Alkemy blinked, pawing at the last of her smeld and griv with a fork, then suddenly put it down and focused on the others. 'I just receive message from Andop.' Her face was bright with excitement. 'He say all is ready. Today is the day we get our Albert back!'

* * *

'I don't think Administrator Meli's very happy with us.'

'Really, Walis? What makes you say that?'

'The way he was throwing things for a start.'

'I was being ironic.'

'Were you? I wasn't sure. We can never tell, can we, Welis?'

Welis gargled, but whether in agreement or disagreement it was hard to tell.

There'd been no time to get his jaw fixed since the children had escaped. Meli was keeping the pressure on, insisting they catch the runaways before anyone got any upgrades. He had managed to find a new suit jacket and now wore a red and white bandanna to cover the gaping hole in his face, but it drew almost as much attention as his missing jaw because he now he resembled an old-fashioned

241

bank robber.

'We have to do something,' Wilis said. 'Our good name is at stake.'

'We haven't *got* a good name any more. Administrator Meli calls us Triple-Dope.'

'Well, we'd better redeem ourselves before he makes it official.'

'But what can we do?' Walis adjusted the plastic sunglasses he was wearing. His left eye still bothered him since the brutal plimp sauce attack. It leaked tears in bright sunlight so he'd taken to wearing Basic sunglasses, but even their largest pair wouldn't comfortably fit his massive head. They bulged outwards at the sides so alarmingly that they looked in danger of exploding.

Wilis drummed his fingers on the table. 'We need to go back to square one,' he said. 'First, we need to find out how those kids and that syntho got out of Concordance. We sealed off the whole building, but they simply disappeared.

'Second, we need to work out where the aliens went after they attacked Walis in the park. We lost them at the river station. Where would they have gone from there?

'And third, where did that music vid come from? Whoever put it together deliberately added that alien language section. Find them and we find the whole gang.'

Welis gargled enthusiastically.

'You've forgotten item four,' Walis said. His clone-brothers looked at him. 'Where did they decontaminate that radioactive syntho?'

There was a moment's silence. Wilis sighed. 'They didn't decontaminate it because they didn't have to.'

'Why not?'

'Because it wasn't radioactive.'

'What?'

Welis gargle-groaned.

'Oh do keep up, Walis. You saw the report. There was no sign of any radiation at all. It was a trick. We should have gone straight after them and grabbed them. It's one of the reasons why the administrator's so angry with us.'

'So ... why did they put him in a radiation casket then?'

That silenced his brothers.

'We'll ask them that *when* we find out where they went!' Wilis snapped.

'That's another mystery,' Walis said. 'We had guards on all the exits, but there was nothing on any of the surveillance systems after they ran away. I double-triple-checked. No one came out of the Science Council building except us and the bots we know about.'

'Are you suggesting they're still in there?'

Walis looked at Welis, one eyebrow raised, but Welis gargled fiercely and shook his head. He'd checked that. In fact, he'd spent hours going through the entire building, checking every office, every cupboard, looking behind every ceiling panel and under every desk. Nothing. And he'd desperately wanted to find *something*.

There was their reputation with Administrator Meli, of course, but he was more concerned about his reputation with his clone-brothers. Technically, they were identical, but things rarely worked out that way. One always rose to the top due to tiny differences in their construction. Wilis, in their case. And that was a constant source of irritation.

A couple of years earlier, Welis had creaky knees – a not uncommon fault in augments of their generation. Each time he stood or sat, his knees would give a faint but discernible *errk*. The fix was easy and quick, but that wasn't the point. Neither Wilis nor Walis had creaky knees when, by rights, they should all have them.

It was like the fault in his jaw. What should have been a blow that glanced off had actually snapped a hinge. Welis had a nagging fear he'd been built from spare parts and leftover seconds. It gave him a desperate desire to prove himself.

Which was why he'd gone after the aliens so keenly.

Best not think about it, he thought. The ignominy of being chipped out from between two shops by a bunch of builder-bots, the idea that he'd let himself be lured there by three kids, was almost too much to bear.

So he'd really, desperately wanted to find the ones hiding in the Science Council building. But he hadn't.

'People don't just disappear,' Wilis insisted. 'Are you *sure* there are no gaps in the security camera footage from the underground tunnels and links?'

'Quadruple-quintuple-checked them,' Walis said. 'Nothing went, nothing left. Except for a furniture despatch.'

'A furniture despatch? When? What time?'

'Late that afternoon.'

'Oh for goodness sake Walis, that could be it!'

'No, no, no, it was scheduled three weeks earlier. I checked all the records and paperwork. A sofa going to some upholstery company in Nexval. Despatch, contents and receipt confirmed. I even went out there and checked it myself.'

His clone-brothers stared at him.

'I saw the sofa!'

His brothers said nothing.

'It's blue now. It's been re-covered. It used to be red ...' His voice trailed off.

Still his brothers said nothing.

'But how could that possibly be them? A single bubbletruck for a grown-up syntho and two kids? And they couldn't schedule their escape three weeks in advance unless they had a time machine.' He chuckled, looking from Welis to Wilis, seeing the look they exchanged. 'Is that it? You think they've got a time mach—?'

'No, of course not,' Wilis said. 'But it has given us something we desperately need.'

'What's that?'

'A lead, Walis. A lead!'

36 : The Crouching Man

The Syntho Research Centre was a sprawling white stone building in the southeast corner of the campus. Its main entrance was paved with flagstones and cluttered with electrobikes, but Alkemy – following Andop's directions – led them round the side. A gravel path wound through a sculpture garden filled with statues of famous Eltherian scientists, and through the unshuttered windows of the building they could see classrooms, laboratories, workshops and lecture theatres.

Around the back, the smooth parkland gave way to a scrubby patch of waste ground pockmarked with burnt patches. A line of what looked like old-fashioned bathing huts – little sheds with peaked roofs, each not much bigger than a wardrobe – stood along one side. The doors of all but the last two were closed. In front of them, a syntho was directing a group of trolley-bots as they placed a thick rectangular slab on top of a catapult. He looked up as they approached.

'Hello. Are you here to watch the test flight?'

'Test flight?'

The syntho held out his hand in greeting. 'I'm Toxteth #262, inventor of the world's first anti-gravity platform.' He tapped palms with each of them in turn. 'Technically, it's more of a gravity deflector, but the effect will be the same.'

'That thing?' Norman gestured to the slab sitting on the catapult. 'You mean it actually works?'

'You're about to witness its first successful flight. A historic event at least equivalent to Traxin splitting the atom or Smoldiq building the chronocell. It'll be something to tell your grandchildren!'

He shooed the trolley-bots away and checked the catapult's control panel.

'Now, if you'll just give me a moment ...' He headed for the second of the huts, closed the door briefly, then re-emerged wearing a silver-coloured jumpsuit. He climbed onto the slab, sat cross-legged and gripped the sides.

'The catapult is just to get the deflector airborne. Once I reach the top of the arc, I'll fire it up and float away. Ready? Three ... two ... one ...'

There was a solid *whump* as the catapult pitched Toxteth and the slab into the air. It reached a height of twenty metres and, just as he'd said, a yellow glow lit up underneath as it reached the mid-point of its trajectory.

Toxteth waved.

The slab held still for half a second, but then, instead of resisting gravity, it seemed to positively embrace it, tipping sideways, hurtling down and smashing into the ground.

The five of them stared, horrified at the fiery explosion, then ducked as bits of debris whistled overhead.

'Oh my god!' Coral gasped as they got to their feet and

peered at the shallow crater and the scorched grass all around it.

'Ouch!' A voice behind them said.

They turned.

'Toxteth!' Coral gestured at the smouldering wreck. 'But I thought you were—'

'I was.' Toxteth peered past her. 'That looks nasty. I hope I didn't suffer.'

There was a moment's silence, then Tim noticed the third of the beach hut doors was open. 'You must be Toxteth #263.'

'Correct.' The syntho shielded his eyes, studying the crash site.

The others looked puzzled.

'Toxteth #262 uploaded himself before the flight, right?'

'Correct again.'

'Huh?' Coral said.

Toxteth #263 explained. 'I really need to go with the craft to assess the deflector's performance and take care of any last minute problems. This is the easiest way to do it.'

Tim gestured at the row of sheds. 'How many of you are there?'

'Just one. There's only ever one of me at a time. Anything else would get confusing. I wouldn't have been activated if #262 had survived.'

He began walking towards the impact crater and scanning the surrounding ground. 'Now, if you'll excuse me, I must find my head. Once I have it, I can update my memory and analyse the flight data to see what went wrong.'

They left him to it and continued on towards the rear

entrance of the Syntho Research Centre.

'Now that,' Norman muttered, 'is what I call a *real* crash test dummy.'

Coral glanced back as they entered the building. Toxteth #263 saw her, raised an arm and waved. The trouble was, it wasn't one of the arms attached to his body.

* * *

Andop greeted them at the entrance, taking in their stunned expressions. 'I heard the explosion, so I'm guessing you met Toxteth. Amusing, isn't he?'

'That's ... one word for it,' Coral said.

'Don't worry, he's harmless.'

'Not to himself.'

'Quite the reverse, actually. He goes to great lengths to look after himself. Which is unusual for his machine class.'

'Which is what?'

'He's an Eccentric. One of the very first synthetics ever made. A couple of steps up from a shop-bot, but still not a true synthetic person.

'Early models all had similar tendencies. Their minds would latch onto an idea and they'd pursue it without regard to commonsense or personal safety. We've had ones convinced they could fly under their own power, or live underwater, or wrestle ripper cats. Naturally, most didn't survive. Only ones like Toxteth are still around. We indulge him, partly for his historical value and partly as an illustration of what can go wrong with even apparently logical minds.'

As he was talking, he led them through a series of gleaming white corridors to a door labelled *Authorised Personnel Only.* Inside, they found a room that looked like a cross between an engineering workshop and an operating theatre. Mechanical and electronic components littered a series of benches, a gurney in one corner contained what could only be a body draped in a sheet, and a large table surrounded by lights and a variety of instruments stood at the far end backed by rows of tiered seating.

'Make yourselves at home, I'll be back in a moment,' Andop said, heading for a rear door.

They looked around.

'Do you think that's Albert?' Coral pointed at the covered body.

'Only one way to find out.' Norman pulled back a corner of the sheet.

Coral winced. Alkemy turned away. Norman leaned closer.

It was a syntho all right, but not Albert. It had been sliced open down one side and the outer layer of flesh folded back to reveal the mechanical skeleton and components underneath. A number of wires and feed lines were attached in various places, and the table it was lying on was scattered with tools.

'I see you've found Old Ernie,' Andop said, holding the rear door wide as he returned. 'He's a work in progress.'

'Is he still alive?'

'Yes and no. He's still functioning mechanically and physically, but we put his mind into stasis. A low-power state a bit like sleep.'

Norman was still marvelling at the complexity of the

thing – the way blood vessels wound around mechanical linkages and how wiring and circuitry merged seamlessly with muscles and organs – when a trolley-bot entered behind Andop, wheeling in a frosted glass cube. Streamers of chilled air ran down its sides, but they could still make out the shape of the figure inside; a crouching man, its arms wrapped around its bent knees, cushioning the head resting on top of them.

'I put this together over the last couple of days,' Andop said, lowering the front panel of the cube.

The seated figure faced them, sitting with its ankles crossed, the overhead lights reflecting off the bald head and the bumps along its spine. The skin had the smooth, waxy look of a shop mannequin; realistic but lifeless.

Andop took a thin wire-like tool and inserted it into a tiny hole in the back of the skull. It went in a long way. Then he connected it to a handheld device, tapped some keys, and the top of the head popped open on a hinge.

The others gasped and stepped back. Norman peered closer.

The hinged skull cap revealed a stainless steel chamber patterned with complex circuitry. There were hundreds of components anchored to its curved walls. A socket on one side matched the ones they'd seen on the receiver back on Earth and on the console of the *Knock Knock Who's There?*

Andop gestured to Alkemy. 'Go ahead and insert the memory bulb. Or would you like me to do it?'

'I take, I should put back,' she said, referring to how, following Albert's instructions, she'd been the one to remove it back on Earth. Still, her hand shook a little as she placed the bulb in the socket.

There was a faint click and it was drawn from her fingers, locking itself in place. Immediately, the interior began filling with a clear, bubbling jelly. Andop closed the skull cap. It sealed with a sucking sound.

They watched and waited. Nothing happened for several seconds, then a bead of blood formed along the line of skin where the cap had been opened. Andop dabbed it with an antiseptic pad. 'The heart has started pumping.'

Over the course of the next minute, something happened to the crouching figure. Its skin, once waxy and inert, began to warm. Muscle fibres filled and took on shape. The supple curve of its lips filled, and the sunken cheeks began to look less sunken. Then, imperceptibly at first, faint movements showed it had a pulse and was breathing.

After another minute, Albert, his eyes still closed, raised his head, rubbed his injured scalp and muttered, 'Ouch!'

37 : Special Powers

'That's interesting,' Wilis said as Welis peered over his shoulder. 'According to Valax, that sofa went to an upholstery company owned by someone called Andop Scolyfol, registrar and workshop technician at Theia University.'

'What's interesting about that?' Walis said.

'Guess where that song first became popular?'

Walis frowned. 'The ... furniture shop ...?'

'No.' Wilis took a deep breath. 'Theia University.'

'Oh.'

'And some years ago it seems that Andop Scolyfol declined an invitation to join the Military Council after his research project was cancelled. He'd been working on neural laces and syntho brain enhancements before the programme was shut down. It would make him an ideal candidate for one of Krilen's secret projects.'

Walis brightened. 'Maybe that's why those kids put their syntho in a radiation casket. To hide his big brain.'

'Yes ... maybe ...'

'We should have a word with this Scolyfol character.'

'What a good idea, Walis. Why didn't we think of that?' Wilis glanced at Welis who rolled his eyes.

'We should go in there in with a bunch of war-bots and arrest him. How about that?'

'A little obvious, don't you think? No, we need another excuse to pay him a visit,' Wilis said, stroking his jaw and looking at his silent clone-brother.

* * *

Albert dressed absent-mindedly as he absorbed what had been happening on Eltheria. He'd been offline for days, but now he had a proper synthetic body he had full access to all of the planet's many data systems.

'You miss a button.' Alkemy pointed to his shirt.

'Hmm?' He glanced at her vaguely.

It was like old times. Just like the old Albert. She laughed and hugged him. 'So good to have you whole again.'

He patted her back then held out a hand and studied it, turning it over and flexing his fingers. 'I must say it feels good to be whole again.' He released her, adding, 'You didn't happen to remember my notebook, did you?'

'Of course. I bring it with me from the ship, like you ask.' She took out a slim, leather-bound notebook, its cover cracked and worn. He tucked it in the pocket of his misbuttoned shirt as Andop handed him a wig – a grey frizzy thing that looked in need of a trim.

'Perfect!' Alkemy said, positioning it just so before giving him another hug.

Albert's first steps were a little unsteady. Alkemy stayed at his side, but after two trips back and forth across the workshop he was moving normally.

'I've caught up with what's been happening on Eltheria,' he told the others, 'now I'd like to hear what you've all been up to since my little radiation spill.'

Andop suggested the cafe at the front of the building, promising to join them once he'd tidied up, so Ludokrus led the way through a maze of corridors. A couple of purple-haired girls in green metallic tracksuits passed them at right angles. They wore matching high-heeled boots and carried shoulder bags the colour of their hair. 'Now we're allowed out,' Coral said, watching them go, 'we should get some new clothes so we blend in more.'

'That's hardly blending in,' Tim said, looking around for Norman to find him dawdling at the door of every classroom and workshop they passed.

'What a cool place!' he said, running to catch up. 'Now we've got student IDs, can we actually take classes?'

Tim rolled his eyes. 'I don't believe you two. We're the first humans to ever reach an alien planet, and all Coral wants to do is go shopping while you want to go back to school!'

'You're right,' Norman said, considering. 'There are other things. Let's eat!'

The cafe overlooked the gardens and the paved area at the front of the building. It was only half full at this time of the morning. The sunlit grounds looked tempting, but they wouldn't be overheard in a corner booth. Once the serve-bot delivered their trays of drinks and pastries, Ludokrus filled Albert in with what had happened since they'd unplugged him from the casket. Then Coral, Tim and Norman took turns telling him of their adventures.

'You've all done very well, no thanks to me,' he said. 'That wretched English language module! I'm sorry, it's all my fault. Things are far worse down here than I imagined.'

'What do you mean?' Alkemy asked.

'The disappearance of Krilen and his deputy; the takeover of the Science Council – there's very little about either event on the news nets. I'm not sure what's going on, but we need to get to the bottom of it.'

They sipped their drinks as Albert checked his comms. 'A message from Andop. He's been delayed. Some sort of emergency.'

'Wouldn't be anything to do with that, would it?' Norman asked, pointing to the front lawn where a number of people had stopped to shield their eyes and peer into the sky. A distant black speck was growing larger by the second, coming in fast and low.

The helijet bucked like a rearing horse as it switched from horizontal to vertical flight then came straight down, landing on the lawn outside. Four medic-bots raced down the steps, unfolding the legs of a wheeled crash trolley as they went. The helijet settled, the sound of its engines dropped to a low hum, and the medical team disappeared behind the body of the aircraft.

'Looks serious,' Tim said.

All they could see were pairs of mechanical legs scuttling back and forth around the wheels of the stretcher. Then they began to move as a single unit.

'Here they come,' Norman said.

The bots emerged, guiding the heavily laden stretcher,

its wheels leaving deep indentations in the lawn. They lifted it to the paved area then paused at the steps, taking one corner each and carrying it up with some difficulty. The shape on the stretcher was huge. Like a small hill covered by a white sheet.

Two more pairs of legs emerged from the far side of the helijet. They stepped back as aircraft's engines rose in pitch and it lifted smoothly from the lawn. They were blasted by a momentary downrush air, but as the helijet soared away they straightened the lapels of their enormous jackets and began walking towards the building.

'It's them,' Tim gasped. 'It's Triple-Dub!'

38 : Medical Emergency

'Stay calm and stay where you are,' Albert said. 'Andop's been expecting this.'

'What do you mean?'

'Some sort of visit at the very least. Though I must say this approach is a little unusual.'

Wilis and Walis paused at the top of the steps, looked about, then strutted off like they owned the place.

'It was only a matter of time before Meli and his goons put two and two together,' Albert continued. 'The bubbletruck to Macet; Andop's old involvement with the neural lace project; the origin of that song. But it's all circumstantial. If they had any real evidence this would have been a raid.'

'We should warn him. Help.' Alkemy's face was pale.

'On the contrary, Andop's prepared for this. He can look after himself. The best thing we can do is finish up here and leave quietly before we're recognised.'

* * *

'It's our brother, doc,' Walis said.

'I can see that.' Andop folded back the sheet to reveal Welis staring up at him. 'Hardly a medical emergency though, is it?'

Welis gargled.

'It is to him, doc.'

Andop took out an inspection light and removed the red bandanna. 'This jaw injury looks days old.'

'It is. But he suddenly started acting oddly,' Wilis said. 'We thought we'd better bring him in.'

'Oddly? How?'

'You know that song that's doing the rounds right now, *New Bot Order*?'

'Can't say I've heard it.'

'You must have, doc. Everybody's playing it.'

'Are they?' Andop looked at him coolly. 'What about it?'

He saw Wilis and Walis studying him intently, looking for a reaction. He didn't give them one.

'It makes him twitch,' Wilis said.

'Isn't that the idea of music?'

'What?'

'To make you dance?'

'Oh. Right. But he's not a dancer, you see. We thought something might have got into his circuits.'

'Let's take a proper look, shall we? Get up and take a seat over there, please.'

Andop dismissed the medic-bots and directed Welis to what looked like a dentist's chair complete with an overhead lamp and a low table containing a variety of instruments. There was a hiss of compressed air as he lowered the seat back and adjusted the lamp.

Andop took his time with the examination. 'It looks like a straightforward stress fracture of the upper mandibular joint. No sign of infection or foreign bodies, but a weak jaw would make you a Series II, is that right?'

Welis gargled and nodded.

'Have you had your knees done?'

Another nod.

'What about you two?'

Walis and Wilis shook their heads.

'You should consider it. It's another weak point.'

Wilis leaned in close, resting an arm on Andop's bent back. 'What's that, doc?' He pointed, and as he did so, lightly tapped the back of Andop's neck with one of his meaty fingers. It was a clumsy move. Andop felt the touch but didn't react.

'What's what?'

'Behind them circuits ... Oh, it's just a reflection.'

He straightened again and Andop fought the urge to rub the back of his neck. It was clear he'd been tagged with a skinplant that would transmit his location and relay his words to anyone with the right receiver. It was only a temporary bugging device and would wash off in two or three days, but no doubt they'd also install other more permanent ones around his lab.

'There are two ways we can go about this,' he said, pulling on a pair of latex gloves. 'On a Series II the mandibular hinge is close to one of the brain's main connectors,' he tapped the side of Welis's head, 'so there's a small risk of a short-circuit when I install a new jaw.'

Welis's eyes widened.

'To prevent that, I'd like to shut you down briefly. That

will allow me to work in perfect safety. For you, it will be the equivalent of an anaesthetic.'

Welis gargled his agreement.

'I also suggest adding an override. That jaw hinge of yours is a known weakness. Its proximity to the brain connectors could mean that a bad dislocation would shut you down permanently. An override circuit will remove that risk. I can put one together on the fab in about five minutes. You should all probably have them fitted at some point.'

Welis gargled again and nodded enthusiastically, but Wilis frowned and stared at Andop. 'My clone-brother missed two other appointments. Neither of them said they'd need to shut him down. Or add any fancy circuits.'

'Augment specialists, were they?' Andop asked, then turned back to Welis. 'Well, it's your choice.

'Now, the only Series II jaws I have in stock at the moment are teaching versions that come with stainless steel teeth. I can fab you a regular one, but that will take several hours.'

Welis indicated he'd be happy with the teaching version.

'Are you sure, brother?' Wilis asked. 'Stainless steel?'

He nodded and gargled enthusiastically.

'Then I should match them with the upper teeth. I might as well do them now while I have easy access. Tilt your head, please.'

Andop took out the largest, nastiest-looking set of pliers he could find and clamped them on a molar. Welis gargled in alarm and pushed his hand away.

'What's the matter now?'

The three augments exchanged a rapid series of comms, then Wilis said, 'My brother wants the anaesthetic after all.'

Andop put the pliers down and moved to the fabricator. 'No doubt you'll want to inspect the circuit layout before I print it?'

'Of course.' Wilis went across and peered over his shoulder, studying the screen, unaware that he was looking at the circuit for a fancy doorbell.

He made a thoughtful face, nodded then said, 'Yeah, that looks all right.'

'Do you two want to check it?' Andop said.

Wilis looked to Walis and Welis. They shook their heads.

While Wilis was distracted, Andop switched circuits.

'Right, this won't take long.' He hit the print button and the fabricator whirred into life.

'Now for the paperwork.' He produced a tablet and biometric plate and handed them to Welis. 'That's all the details there. I just need your authorisation to proceed.'

Welis studied the screen then placed his hand on the plate. There was a faint *ping* of acknowledgement.

'Right, we're all set.' Andop turned to Wilis and Walis. 'I'll put your clone-brother into stasis now and pull those teeth. You can help me if you like.'

'Er, no thanks, doc.' Wilis held up a hand. 'We'll ... um ... just sit over here and ... wait.'

39 : Study-slabs

'I want to go back to the monkey planet!'

'We can't.'

'I was happy there.'

'No, you weren't.'

'I was happier there than I am here. It's all warm and dry and horrid.'

'Do you think prison is supposed to pleasant?'

'I don't understand what we're doing here. You said we were just stopping for a meeting.'

'And you said we'd hit that wretched Eltherian ship.'

'I thought we did.'

'When in fact we hit a pile of monkey people space junk!'

'It's not my fault.'

'You insisted on stopping for souvenirs to present to the Thanatos. What did you think they were going to do with them, frame them and put them on the wall? Of course they were going to analyse the stuff. And all it did was prove our mistake.'

'Local Darkness was rather angry.'

'Angry's hardly the word for it. I don't think steam is supposed

to come out of those parts of his body.'

'No, and— Oh, goodness. Do you feel that? All my innards just slurped to one side.'

'Mine too. We're under acceleration. Hard acceleration, by the feel of it.'

'But we're inside a metal moon. How on earth can they fly something this big?'

'That's not the real question. The real question is why? And where are they flying it to ...?'

* * *

Albert had no interest in a trip to Basic Clothing. All he wanted was to visit Basic Electronics. Tim had no interest in Basic Clothing either, but he had no choice in the matter because his sister dragged him in by the elbow. Albert was finished within five minutes and left, heading back to the studio apartment followed by a line of trolley-bots stacked with study-slabs and coils of cabling. Half an hour later, Coral was *still* looking at samples, feeling fabrics and trying things on. She hadn't even started on the catalogues.

Tim found Norman standing in front of a full-sized projection mirror. In it, his reflection showed him wearing the different combinations of the clothing he was flicking through on a console. 'What d'you think? Red sneakers, orange pants, yellow shirt, green hair and a purple hat?' He laughed and posed and did a twirl, his actions mirrored by his wildly dressed reflection.

Tim sighed. *This could take a while.*

Aeons passed. Civilisations rose and fell. Suns were born

and died. Whole galaxies blossomed and faded.

At least it felt like that.

When they finally left, they had so much stuff they needed a trolley-bot to help them carry it – not that much of it was Tim's. 'Free is such a good price!' Coral said for about the hundredth time.

Back at the apartment, they pushed open the hallway door and found the place littered with study-slabs, dozens of them wired together and plugged into every available power socket. They followed them through to the lounge where dozens more were stacked in piles or propped against the walls. Every surface was covered in them, and cables snaked this way and that. There were so many machines that the whole interior hummed faintly. Albert sat in the middle of the mess surrounded by piles of empty cartons, wiring still more of them together.

'Oh, hello,' he called, looking up from his notebook. 'You took your time.'

'I see you found the place all right,' Tim said.

Coral muttered, 'And made yourself at home.'

'What do you do to our house?' Alkemy asked.

'This?' Albert seemed surprised by her concern. 'Data. I need data. Ten years worth if I can get it. This is the easiest, least obtrusive way to do so. Each study-slab is assumed to be a different student, you see. So I have three hundred and eighty-four of them gathering information down there,' he gestured to the hallway and bedrooms, 'and I will shortly have another two hundred and fifty-six here to process, combine and collate that data.'

'But for what?'

'I'm trying to work out what's been going on here

without drawing attention to myself. The logical way would be to go through Valax, use it to do my searches and answer my questions, but if my suspicions are correct, I would either not get the answers I'm hoping for, or receive a visit from Administrator Meli and his friends.

'The alternative is to gather and process the relevant data myself, so ...' He gestured at the mess.

'How long will this take?'

'Hard to say. Twenty hours at least for the downloads, then another day or so for processing ...'

'You mean we have two, three days ... of this?'

They looked around. The wallscreen, the games console, even the food fab had been unplugged to provide power for the study-slabs.

Albert said, 'Now that language module is almost universal, I was going to suggest you take our visitors away for a bit of sightseeing.'

'Hey, that sounds like a plan!'

'We could go to Baylev,' Ludokrus said. 'They have a fun park there so big it takes two days to go on all the rides.'

'This whole planet's a fun park,' Norman said, grinning. 'Let's do it!'

'Do we need to book or anything?' Coral asked.

'Will not be so busy this time of year, and there is a maglev every hour. Just grab some things and we can go.'

'One moment.' Alkemy held up a hand. 'Message from Andop.'

It was a general broadcast message addressed to all Syntho Research Centre students apologising for the cancellation of his afternoon workshop and saying he'd be back on deck tomorrow. It also contained an attachment detailing the SRC's courses.

Moments later, a second message appeared apologising for the accidental attachment: 'It's been one of those days!'

'Well, at least he's OK,' Coral said.

'On the contrary.' Albert frowned. 'Triple-Dub may have nothing on him, but it seems he's being watched. That phrase *back on deck* is one of our codes. Like someone on the deck of a boat, it means he's exposed and visible from all directions. And the attachment means that Andop himself has an attachment of some sort. A tracking device, I suspect. We should stay away and avoid all contact with him for at least a day or two.'

Ludokrus turned to the others. 'So it really is the perfect time for a holiday, yes?'

They all heartily agreed.

40 : Kestel

Frank and Emma Townsend stood on the veranda watching the last army truck draw away. The driver gave them a toot and they waved back. Glenn and Avril had caught a ride with Glad that morning, planning to spend the day in Rata. Now all that was left after the excitement of the last week were a handful tyre tracks and a large yellowish rectangle on the lawn where the army tent had starved the grass of sunlight.

'I keep thinking about the children,' Em said. 'I still can't believe all that happened here. To us, or them.'

'Me neither,' Frank said.

'D'you really think they'll be back, like they said in their notes?'

'I hope so.' He hadn't told anyone about what Glad had said.

'I miss them, Frank.'

He put an arm around her and gave her a squeeze. 'Me too, love.' After a pause, he added, 'I let Glenn and Avril have that ball bearing thing they shot at us, it only seemed right, but I'm going to leave that hole in the shed roof. It's like a reminder that it really happened, you know?'

'You're a sentimental fool sometimes,' Em smiled.

Smudge skittered past chasing a white butterfly, leaping and taking swipes at it in mid-air.

Frank laughed. 'Honestly, I swear that cat's having a second kittenhood.'

They watched her for a while, then Em turned her face to the sky, 'I wonder where they are right now. What they're up to.'

'All sorts of mischief if I know that lot,' Frank said. 'And good on 'em.'

* * *

'You see the date?' Ludokrus said to his sister as they waited for a maglev on the platform of Concordance Station. 'Especially the moon date.'

Alkemy checked her own comms cal. 'Oh, yes!'

'Maybe we should stop on the way to Baylev?'

'Not maybe, definite! Better even than the fun park.'

'What? What?' the others demanded, but Ludokrus replied with a secret smile, telling them they'd have to wait and see.

The maglev's first stop was Kestel, a small seaside town southeast of Theia that overlooked Buckle Gap. The hundred-kilometre trip took a little over twenty minutes – barely enough time to get settled into the sleek, high-speed train, and both Tim and Norman watched it accelerate away from the station a little disappointed they couldn't explore it further. It was the closest thing to flying at ground level they'd ever experienced.

The platform was ultra-modern – polished concrete, glass and chrome, like all stations on the maglev network – but the first hint that Kestel was different came when they stepped into the ticketing hall. The ancient stone floor was worn smooth by the passage of thousands of feet, and the roughly plastered, neatly whitewashed walls sprouted window boxes of brightly coloured flowers instead of arrival and departure signs. There were no ticketing machines, no vending machines, no malls or shopping arcades, just a line of old-fashioned ticket windows manned by cheerful people dressed in peasant costumes.

Outside, a long avenue of higgledy-piggledy houses led away from the station. There were palm trees in a grassy quadrangle out front, but no bots or wheeled vehicles in sight.

'How far is it? Do we need a electrobikes or something?'

'No bike. We are in Kestel now. No machines allowed.' Ludokrus pointed to a line of silkas tethered to one end of the building. 'But there is cab.'

'Oh my god, house ponies!' Coral exclaimed. 'How cute! You mean they carry our stuff?'

'Better. Us also. We ride, and the babies carry our bag.'

'The amount of stuff Coral's got, she'll kill hers,' Norman said.

'I just came prepared.'

'Yeah, but we're away for a few days, not a few years.'

These silkas were bigger and sturdier than the ones they'd seen in Theia, but they had the same mottled coats and long, intelligent faces. The youngsters were more solid too, but not sturdy enough for Coral's luggage. She needed a second full-grown silka for that.

Navigation was by fruit, which was also how you paid for them.

'They are trained to go to different areas for different fruit,' Ludokrus said, pointing to a map highlighted in different colours. 'If you give them a love melon, they will go there. Palopalo, they go there. We need to go here,' he pointed to a blue-shaded area, 'so must give them chisols.'

He bought six bags from the elderly man who tended the silkas, handed one to each of the others and two to Coral.

'Is not far, so there are only three in each bag. You give one to start, one in middle – they will stop and ask – and one at end when we arrive.'

Norman took out one of the fuzzy-skinned fruits and sniffed it. It was grey, about the size of a tennis ball and smelled of raspberries. 'Mmm,' he said.

'They're for the animals,' Coral told him. 'The intelligent-looking, four-legged ones.'

As the others fed their mounts, Norman stroked the neck of the one carrying Coral's bags. 'You know, this could be your last meal, mate.'

'Oh, shut up!'

They headed off in a wagon train, clomping through the cobbled streets, the younger animals carrying the bags plodding patiently behind their mothers. The two Coral hired also had young, but they were unburdened and bounded on ahead, racing backwards and forwards like eager puppies, covering the same distance twice.

There didn't seem to be a straight road in Kestel. The whole place was a maze of narrow, winding, interconnected streets filled on either side with pleasant whitewashed buildings.

The silkas reached a square built around a water trough and paused, looking back at their riders.

'Halfway point,' Ludokrus called.

They took out another chisol each and held them out. The silkas took them, chewing slowly and savouring the treats before heading off again at a sedate pace.

'This is so cute.' Coral held out a hand to Ludokrus. 'They're gorgeous. I love it!'

'I guess you will like.' He squeezed her hand and grinned back.

'Oh-oh, we've lost the pack mule!' Norman jerked a thumb over his shoulder.

'*What ...?*'

'Ha ha, made you look.'

'Can we arrange for him to fall off a cliff or something?' Coral asked Ludokrus.

'Yeah, easy. Believe me, here that will be no problem.'

The silkas carried them up a cobbled lane to a turning circle at the top, stopped and looked back at their riders.

'Is this it?'

'Right there.' Ludokrus pointed to a small, whitewashed house with a heavy wooden door, indistinguishable from the others. 'Belong to our great-great-grandfather. Now used only for the holiday.'

They dismounted, gathered their bags and fed the silkas the last of the chisols, then watched as the shaggy animals plodded away downhill, heading back to the station.

Coral sighed as she watched them go. 'I want to take one of them home with me when we go.'

'Me too,' Norman said with a grin. 'In a meat pack.'

Coral snorted in disgust.

The house was tiny, just four rooms, all whitewashed stone like the outside, but there was a broad balcony at the back with a spectacular view out over the ocean. Tena had set and Tetzul was just a finger-width above the horizon, its yellow-orange glow reflected in the sea.

'Oh man, look at that view!' Tim stepped out onto the balcony and peered down. All around the bay he could see hundreds of whitewashed houses perched atop a series of red stone cliffs. The view reminded him of the snowy cap on a mountain range.

Coral moved cautiously to the railing, looked, gasped and took three steps back.

'You do not like?' Ludokrus said. 'But you are OK in the pyramid.'

'That's different. The balconies there are terraced. There's no sheer drop. Not like that anyway.

'It's sheer all right,' Norman leaned out over the edge. 'This balcony's actually built out from the side of the cliff.'

'Is he joking?'

'Most are like this,' Ludokrus said.

'Oh god.' Coral took another step back to the doorway. 'I'll just admire the view from here, thanks.'

Despite its primitive appearance, the old house concealed a number of modern appliances. There was a food fabricator and a drinks dispenser behind a stone slab in the kitchen, a slide-out panel revealed a wallscreen and entertainment centre in the lounge, while another series of slides, drawers and lift-outs turned the space into a spare bedroom.

'*That* is almost as spectacular as the view.' Norman pointed to the large food fab. 'I hope there's plenty of raw materials or we might have to cripple a couple of silkas bringing more up here. Anyone for cheese and chutney pav?'

Sunsets lasted a long time on Eltheria. Even after Tetzul had set, Halo continued reflecting its dying light. They sat on the balcony eating dessert – spatz sundaes, *not* pavlova – and watching as the amber coloured band of light faded, leaving the ring a cool milky white lit by reflected moonlight alone.

'I keep looking for the Southern Cross,' Coral said, peering up at the stars.

'There.' Ludokrus pointed. 'Same stars, but from here look more squashed together. More like the Southern Box.

'Funny to think how your star patterns are all different from ours, even though we're looking at almost the same thing.'

'I saw a sign at the station that said Kestel's a historical reserve,' Tim said.

'Can you imagine her with bots and bubbletruck highways? Would be spoil. Many years ago the local peoples vote to keep her as she is. Like she has been for many hundred years. Now, the main business is with the tourist.'

'What did your great-great-granddad do?'

'He was a fisherman.'

Norman peered at the lights bobbing in the harbour far below. 'So why live up here? I can see there isn't much flat land down below, but there are no houses either. Surely they could've built the town a bit closer to the sea.'

Alkemy glanced at Ludokrus and smiled. 'Tomorrow you will see why.'

'Better,' Ludokrus added. 'You will know.'

41 : The Light of Two Suns

Welis loved his new look, so much so that when Wilis suggested summoning a helijet to return to Concordance he said he'd prefer to take the river.

'Public transport? That's not like you, brother.'

'Indulge me, Wilis.' Welis stroked his new chin and adjusted the red bandanna, which he now wore around his neck. 'My circuits could do with an airing.'

'I thought they'd've had plenty of air *before* your operation,' Walis said. His clone brother gave him a withering look and strode off.

Augments were used to a certain amount of attention. Their intimidating bulk and formidable features set them apart from regular synthos, but the reactions of approaching people on seeing Welis was altogether new. Wilis couldn't make it out at first.

In the river station, a group of students glanced up and made way for them in the corridor. Then they looked again, their expressions ranging from surprise to disgust. Several pressed themselves against the wall to make more room.

On the river, Welis looked down at a young mother holding the hand of a toddler. She smiled back uncertainly and looked away, but when the child held his gaze, he grinned. The boy started in fright and grabbed his mother's leg.

The teeth, Wilis thought. *Those horrid stainless steel teeth. They've given him airs. A point of difference. Welis actually likes them!*

When they reached the administrative floor of the Science Council, Wilis and Walis turned one way, Welis turned the other.

'Where are you going?'

'I have a meeting with Administrator Meli.'

Wilis checked his heads-up diary. 'There's nothing scheduled.'

'Not you, brothers. Just me.'

Welis flashed them a steely smile and walked away.

* * *

Tim wandered out onto the balcony, yawning and shielding his eyes from the glare. Ludokrus sat with his feet on the railing, enjoying the morning air and the spectacular view while sipping a jahlbad juice.

'Man, what a sleep! What time is it?'

'Late. You miss the rush hour.'

'Rush hour? Here?'

'Yeah. Is quite a sight.'

'What, do all the silkas walk down the hill together or something?'

'Better. Tomorrow I wake you early. You will see.'

The others emerged one by one, yawning but refreshed. There was something about the sea air, the silence and the old stone house that made them feel like they could finally relax.

When they were showered and dressed, they walked down to a picturesque square and had brunch in the light of two suns, watching the locals go about their daily lives. It could have been any village on Earth from any time in the last two thousand years, Tim thought. The pace was easy and unhurried, the people warm and friendly.

A train of silkas went past carrying baskets of fish. A street sweeper – a real person, not a bot – brushed down the cobbles behind them, and the cries of vendors from a nearby market filled the air.

'Albert should be here. He would like.' Alkemy nodded at an ancient mechanical clock in the middle of the square. Albert had a fascination with old machinery.

'He would take apart and fix,' Ludokrus said, laughing, 'even if she does not need.'

'What's he actually doing back in the apartment?' Coral asked.

'Making the mini Valax.'

'Yeah, but why? I thought your Mind of the Planet looked after everything and everyone.'

'Is supposed to,' Ludokrus said, 'but now Albert is not so sure.'

'Explain, please.'

'Once we have governments and countries like on Earth; some good, some bad. But even good ones do bad thing. Pollute, destroy the environment or make war. Between them, they almost wreck our planet.

'Finally, the peoples say enough. No more country. What is country anyway? Just a line on a map. Old fashioned politician say, 'On that side, there are bad peoples. Here are good peoples.' Crazy! We are all the same. And what good is this line if pollution wreck everywhere at once? Poisoned sea and changing weather do not respect our lines.

'So the people say if officials cannot fix, we fix ourself. They replace governments with councils responsible for the whole planet, and a super-big computer to run everything. It hold all data so everyone can see and read for themself, not just trust the politician or the businessman. This is Valax. Everything go there. Everyone can access. Even the code and the hardware and how the machine itself work. All is open, all is free. To everyone.'

'Sounds good.'

'We think this also, but Albert think he find a weakness in the system.'

'Super-smart, brain-enhanced Albert?'

He nodded. 'Maybe he is right. Alkemy and I see what happen to the Science Council. You have not seen before, but we know what she was like. Now is empty, ruined. But if you search, there is almost nothing of this on Valax. Like it is hidden or blocked.

'Also, we know some of the peoples who work there. They would not be quiet. They would make protest. But of them Valax say nothing.'

'So your Mind of the Planet has lost its mind?'

'Something is not right. So Albert investigate. But the only way to check is to make a mini Valax for himself.'

Coral kicked back in her chair and stretched lazily. 'Well,

he can take as long as he likes as far as I'm concerned.

* * *

'Welis is getting too big for his boots,' Wilis said, pacing from one side of the room to the other.

'Really?' Walis checked his own. 'What size does he take now then?'

'I don't mean literally, you idiot. I mean scheduling a private meeting with the administrator. We're a team. We do things together. All that smiling with those fancy teeth of his, and that red bandanna. Did you see the way he was walking? Flexing his knees like he was something special.'

Walis tested his own, listening for telltale creaks.

The door finally opened and Welis reappeared.

'Oh, hello,' Walis said. 'We were just talking about you.'

'That's a coincidence. The administrator and I were just talking about you two.'

'Oh yes?' Wilis crossed his arms. 'And what did you conclude?'

'That you haven't been doing a very good job, Wilis. That Triple-Dub as a whole could do with some proper leadership.'

'What?'

'Can I confirm some details, please brothers? Did you install permanent listening devices in Scolyfol's workshop while I was being operated on?'

Walis nodded.

'What about his office and his apartment and that furniture place?'

'Yes, yes and yes. And a personal tracker on him too, just as we planned.'

'Anything incriminating yet?'

'It's too early to—'

'Can we afford to wait around? The administrator doesn't think so.'

Wilis's eyes narrowed. 'You didn't tell him about that, did you? That was *our* idea. We said we'd keep it to ourselves until we had proof Scolyfol was definitely involved.'

'*You* said that, I didn't. I couldn't. No jaw, remember?'

'But you ... gargled ...'

'I gargled my *dis*agreement.'

Wilis looked at Walis.

'Given that the Military Council already know Scolyfol is a troublemaker—'

'I bet you told the administrator it was your idea! Walis was the one who found him from that furniture shipment. You were still looking under desks.'

'Given that Scolyfol is a known—'

'You double-crossing slime-bot!'

'You didn't know what to do with the information, did you?' Welis snapped. 'Either of you. And that's why Administrator Meli has made *me* leader of this group.'

Wilis gaped.

Walis frowned. 'But ... that's always been Wilis's job.'

'Not any more. At least, not for the time being.' Welis tried a more reasonable tone. 'Think about it for a moment. It's a sensible solution in the circumstances. Am I not now the strongest of our group? I alone have had my jaw fixed, and my knees. You two still have weaknesses in both. Plus, there's poor old Walis here. His eyes still aren't right, are they?'

'There's nothing wrong with my—'

'Look out! Plimp sauce!' Welis waved a pretend squeeze bottle at him. Walis leapt backwards and fell over a chair.

'See what I mean?'

'That's not funny!'

'No, it's not,' Welis crossed his arms, 'but I rest my case. Until you two can be upgraded, the administrator's put me in charge.'

Walis clambered to his feet, glaring.

'Now, as I was saying, given that Scolyfol's already known to the Military Council and that there are no other leads, the administrator and I have decided to bring him in.'

'What good will that do?' Wilis scoffed. 'He won't talk.'

'Perhaps not willingly. But he won't be able to stop himself if we brainsmash him.'

'*What?* You ... you can't do that, Welis! It's horrid. *And* it's illegal. It's been banned for decades.'

'We can do whatever we like. Administrator Meli has been given special powers.'

'But it'll destroy the man's mind. Turn him into a vegetable. Perhaps even kill him.'

'Before it does, he'll sing like a chirpbird.'

'What if he's innocent?'

Welis shrugged. 'This is the quickest of finding out.'

42 : Three Moon Night

Tim and the others spent a lazy afternoon touring the ancient town, seeing the sights, taking silka rides and basking in the warmth of two suns reflected off the whitewashed buildings. Coral suggested they go down to the port for a swim, but Ludokrus said they'd go later and that they needed the right equipment first.

'Equipment? For swimming?'

He took them to a local market where they found snugly fitting body suits, goggles and lightweight helmets.

'What's in your oceans that we need all this stuff for?' Coral asked.

'Night swim. You will see.'

'I can't believe we're shopping *again*,' Tim muttered.

'Now we go home. Early dinner and relax. Conserve the energy.'

All three moons – Palas, Polux and Puk – were low in the southern sky when they ventured out that evening, dressed in the new gear they'd bought. Ludokrus led the way, heading downhill, joining others dressed similarly and heading in the same direction.

After twenty minutes they came to a plain of smooth rock some distance below the maglev station that marked the lowest point of the town. It was a natural amphitheatre surrounded by a ring of jagged rocks. From the edge, they could see the port buildings and jetty far below, all built on pontoons that bobbed in the restless sea like the fishing boats further out.

The area was the size of a sports field and the crowd spread themselves out over it, taking miniature inflatable dinghies from racks around the perimeter. Alkemy and Ludokrus found some for their friends, holding them up to check the size before leading them out to a vacant space on the smooth plain.

A small canister in the side inflated the craft, which turned out to have thick rubber bases and an inner liner that pulled up over their legs and sealed around their waists when they were seated.

'We call these body boats,' Ludokrus told them.

'But there's no water,' Tim said. 'We're still at least thirty metres above sea-level. There's no way we're going to get—'

The air of quiet expectation from the people around them was broken by a rising cheer. He turned to see a gentle wash of water flood across the ground.

'Where did that come from?'

'It's the moons!' Norman exclaimed. 'I just realised why the town's built so high up. Buckle Gap's the only place where the northern and southern oceans meet. When the moon's line up, they must create a huge high tide. Look ...'

He pointed to where Palas, Polux and Puk seemed to be on a collision course at a point low on the southern horizon.

'Meeting so close only happen once a year,' Ludokrus called. 'That means this tide will not just be big, she will be the monster!'

A second wave sloshed around their feet. In the twilight beyond the edge of the plain, Tim saw a larger wave looming and heard the sigh of water as it broke on the surrounding rocks. Another cheer went up. This time there was enough water to actually float the body boats.

Tim's half-turned, bumping Norman's. He reached over the side and paddled it around the right way again as cries rose from behind. Glancing back, he saw a truly monstrous wave thundering over the rocks. Behind it, an even larger one raced in.

'Oh my god,' Coral cried. 'It's like a tidal wave!'

'Hold on!'

The surge hit and they were washed away like corks in a raging storm.

The rush of water swept them towards the far edge of the plain. They tried to stay together, but dozens of other little craft were swept along with them, channelled and funnelled by the rocks around the sides. Tim caught sight of Norman, bobbing backwards in the crowd, and Ludokrus and Coral, who'd somehow lashed their boats together, one behind the other. Then he forgot about them all, hearing shouts and screams in the moonlit gloom ahead.

The first drop was gentle, barely a metre, and the tidal surge carried them over it smoothly. Ahead, Tim could see a series of broad steps, each one steeper than last, all dotted with little craft. Another surge rose below him. It felt as if a hand was pushing his boat up and forward, faster and faster towards the rocky slopes and the narrow channel at the far end.

The boat's inflatable side bounced off a rock and he went over the next drop backwards, yelling with fright and excitement like everyone around him. From them on, the only time he stopped yelling was to gasp for breath.

The drops between the rocky steps grew larger and steeper. At one point, the moonlight disappeared and Tim realised he was racing through an underground passage at great speed, carried along by the force of the frothing water. Slick rock rushed past his face and the dark air was icy. It was a relief to burst out into moonlight again – until he realised he was practically airborne, bobbing on top of a massive waterfall of water.

He arced down with it to the boiling foam below, hit bow first, submerged completely, then bobbed up, spluttering, to the surface, grateful that the little boat was sealed around his legs and waist. There was barely time to catch his breath before another surge carried him onwards.

The ride lasted a quarter of an hour, and by the time the final wave carried the hundreds of craft down a gentle cascade into a bright pool of ocean, Tim's throat was raw from yelling and his arms ached from holding on. He caught sight of Alkemy, waved and paddled towards her. She was grinning like a soggy demon, her hair plastered to her head.

'You like?' she asked, raising her goggles as larger boats circled them, throwing out ropes to tow them back to land.

'Like?' he croaked. 'That was *a-mazing!* That has to be the best ride ever!'

Back on land, volunteers handed out towels and warm drinks, and they soon found the others. It seemed as if the whole village was buzzing with the excitement of the ride.

'Can we do that again tomorrow?' Norman asked.

'Sorry, the three moon night only happen once a month, and the big one like this only once a year. We are lucky with the date. Too good to miss, no?'

They all heartily agreed.

There was a long queue for silkas at the station, and once the excitement of the ride had ebbed no one felt like trudging up the hill on foot. It was nearly midnight by the time they pushed open the heavy wooden door and plodded in, looking forward to their beds.

'Don't forget,' Ludokrus called. 'Early start in morning.'

'What? Why?'

'Rush hour. The second thing you do not want to miss in Kestel.'

43 : Initiative

Andop had been working late, and the Syntho Research Centre was almost empty. He locked up his lab and paused to watch a cleaning-bot in the shape of a giant spider, polishing the corridor floor a few metres away. It was an experimental model put together by some of the second-year students. Its eight arms weren't quite synchronised. Every two or three cycles, several of them bumped together causing the machine to stop and reset itself, which meant it kept polishing the same area of corridor over and over.

He regarded it for a moment, working out what they'd done wrong, then turned to find himself confronted by Triple-Dub standing shoulder to shoulder, blocking the corridor. Walis was carrying a large canvas bag.

'Gentlemen. Good evening. Is there a problem?'

Only then did he notice the smashed security-bot behind them.

'What's going on h—'

Before he could finish, Welis hit him.

The blow made his head spin but didn't quite knock him

out. He was aware of being bundled into the canvas bag, of the bag being zipped up and carried out, but his blurred senses left him powerless to resist.

The bag was being carried between two of the augments. He could feel it swaying forward and back as they walked. Near what he guessed to be the entrance to the building, he heard voices, students perhaps, and began to struggle. The swaying stopped for a second, then the bag swung backwards much further than before. Only when it was rushing forward again did he realise what they were doing, and by then it was too late to protect his head.

He came to sometime later, blinking at a blaze of light and tried to raise a hand to his pounding head. He couldn't. His arms and legs had been strapped to the bed he was lying on. A silhouette moved amongst the blinding lights, an outline he vaguely recognised. He frowned as it bent closer and saw he was awake. 'Haril? What are you doing here?'

Chix Haril held up a syringe, measuring its contents against the light before squirting off a little of the excess. Then she stooped and stuck the needle in his neck.

'Goodbye, Scolyfol,' she said.

* * *

Administrator Almas Meli found Welis, Wilis and Walis waiting for him when he arrived at his office. 'That was quick,' he remarked, ushering them inside.

'He sang like a chirpbird, sir.' Welis straightened his red bandanna and smiled.

'But what about, Welis?'

'He was definitely involved in the neural lace stuff, sir. Been tinkering with it for years.'

'We know that from Krilen's x-rays.'

'Krilen has a neural lace?' Wilis said.

'Of a sort. Why do you think we haven't brainsmashed him already? It's not a true neural lace, more a protective device. If it senses the presence of brainsmash chemicals, it'll liquify his brain and destroy the very information we're seeking.' He turned back to Welis. 'The key question is, did Scolyfol know the code to deactivate it?'

'No sir, he didn't. Krilen set that himself.'

'Damn! What about those kids and KSX-119?'

'He didn't know anything about the mission, sir, but he confirmed the kids were involved.'

Meli grunted. 'Tell me something I didn't know!'

'How about where they're hiding out, sir? Scolyfol arranged the accommodation himself, right on the university campus: Pyramid K, level nine, studio nine.'

'Now that *is* a result, Welis. Well done! Round them up right away.'

Meli turned to Walis, adding, 'See? Your clone-brother has initiative. *That's* why you were demoted, Wilis.'

Walis didn't correct him. Neither did Wilis. They just followed their clone-brother out.

44 : Second Sunrise

'I can't believe you dragged us out of bed to watch the sunrise,' Coral grumbled.

'Second sunrise,' Ludokrus corrected her. The orange-brown smudge of Tena was already well above the northern horizon.

They settled on deck chairs on the balcony, sipping from steaming mugs of tea as seabirds circled and called to each other in the cool morning air and smells of the ocean wafted up from far below. All but Ludokrus were still in their dressing gowns, and everyone was a bit achy after last night's tide ride. All secretly craved a few more hours rest, but no one had been able to resist their insistent host.

Coral spotted it first. A dozen houses further around the curving clifftop, a man stepped up onto the wide balcony railing, turned, leaned down to kiss his wife, then jumped.

'Oh my god!' She leapt to her feet, knocking her chair over backwards, watching as he fell.

Suddenly the sky was full of falling bodies. All around the clifftop, other figures appeared and launched themselves into the clear morning air.

'They're wearing wingsuits!' Norman cried.

For ten full minutes, Kestel Bay was filled with swooping, diving figures like giant birds. Some, like their neighbour, treated it in a businesslike manner, heading straight down in wide, sweeping circles while others tried to maximise the ride, catching updrafts, swooping and diving, chasing birds and wisps of cloud.

Tim shook his head in disbelief. 'That's one heck of a way to wake up in the morning!'

'Rush hour,' Ludokrus said. 'You ask why the town is build so high. Because of the tides you see last night. This is the quickest way to get to work.'

Down below, they saw the figures land and gather on the beaches and docks, greeting each other and chatting as they headed for the boats.

'Are they all fishermen like your great-great-grandfather?' Ludokrus nodded. 'And those things they're wearing are like the wingsuits people have back on Earth?'

'Almost same, but computer-controlled. More safety.'

Norman's face was alive with excitement. 'The real question is, can we try it for ourselves?'

'Oh sure, but after breakfast. Yes?'

* * *

Tetzul was still a glimmer below the horizon, and the campus of Theia University was quiet and still. Most of its students were sound asleep, but a few lights still showed on the outer faces of Pyramid K. One of those was in room nine on level nine.

Being a syntho, Albert didn't need much sleep. The first part of running a mini Valax – gathering the data – had been rather monotonous, but now it was all in and he'd reconfigured the stacks of study-slabs to analyse that data, progress was swift. As the pieces came together, trends began to show and unexpected patterns emerged. It was all he could do to keep up his handwritten notes.

One of the patterns to emerge was particularly interesting. So interesting that he copied the details to a flexi-disc and slipped it into the back of his notebook. As he straightened, a sharp *clatter-clack* sounded from the balcony behind him. A second after that, his comms died.

Three war-bots dropped from the floor above as three more battered down the front door and burst in through the main entrance. The balcony bots didn't bother with the sliding door. They just kicked in the glass to secure the only possible escape route.

Albert put his notebook on the coffee table and looked around, hearing calls of 'Room clear,' 'Room clear,' 'Room clear,' from the corridor, before Triple-Dub strode into the lounge led by Welis.

'Good morning,' Albert said.

Welis looked around the room. 'Where are the others?'

'I beg your pardon?'

Welis grabbed him by the scruff of the neck. 'The others, syntho scum. Where are they?'

'If you mean the children, they're sightseeing.'

'What?'

'They've gone off for a bit of a holiday.'

'Where?'

'They didn't say. They left me behind.' He tried to sound hurt.

Welis released him and strode around the apartment, inspecting the stacks of study-slabs. 'What is all this stuff?'

'Some sort of experiment, I think. For one of the courses. I don't really know. I'm supposed to keep my eye on things and swap out any faulty machines, but they're all still ticking over—'

'When will they be back?'

'They never said. A few days, perhaps. A week.'

Welis jabbed a finger. 'You're coming with us for further interrogation.' Two thug-bots seized him by the arms as Welis turned to his clone-brothers. 'You two, fix the damage, leave everything as it was, and set a watch-bot for when the kids get back.'

Wilis looked mutinous at being ordered about, but Walis only had eyes for Albert, 'Why did you come down from orbit in a radiation casket?' he asked.

'That? Oh, I misread the Geiger counter,' Albert replied with a nervous laugh. 'I didn't realise it till the casket fell over. When I double-checked – you know, in case of leaks – I saw I'd got everything backwards and opened the lid, forgetting about the security seal. I'd have told you, but the pair of you ran off.'

'How did you get out of the building?'

'Down the back stairs.'

'We sealed all exits.'

'We never saw anyone,' Albert said simply, his expression guileless.

'Enough of this chitchat,' Welis barked, 'Get him out of here. And get this place cleaned up!'

45 : All Green

Alkemy brought out wingsuits from a bedroom cupboard and handed one to each of them. Coral held hers up, tried it against her, then tossed it aside. 'That's way too big. I guess I'll have to leave you guys to it.'

'Don't worry about size. They adjust, automatic.' Alkemy pointed to Norman as he slipped his arms and legs into the baggy nylon overalls and pulled up the zip. The suit shrank around him as it closed, forming a perfect fit.

'Weird!' He raised his arms to reveal wide webs beneath them attached to the body of the suit. The legs too were joined together by a web of fabric. It made walking awkward, but when he did a star jump he looked like a giant black bat.

'Try,' Alkemy said encouragingly. 'See how it fit.'

Coral swallowed.

Tim zipped up his own suit and flexed his shoulders. It felt tight and clingy, like a second skin. Alkemy handed him a helmet and he put it on. 'Tap there,' she pointed to the right-hand side. 'The suit computer will connect to your comm's heads-up display.'

Tim did so and several new indicator lights lit up, all green. There was a faint hum from the slim backpack stitched into the fabric of the suit, and the status line showed *Ready for flight*.

'All OK?'

Tim and Norman gave her a thumbs-up.

'What now?'

'All to do is jump.'

'Really? That's it?'

'The suit take control. Will not let you fall.'

'But ... what if something goes wrong?'

'You know the biggest danger?' They stared back, silent, shaking their heads. 'That you fly too far out to sea.'

'What then?'

She turned and tapped a small cylinder on the bottom of her backpack. 'Life raft. Just pull out to inflate. Will set of rescue beacon, automatic.'

'And ... that's it?' Tim said. 'That's all there is to it?'

Alkemy nodded.

'Shouldn't we practice first?' Norman glanced over the balcony. 'Like, off something not so high? A chair, maybe. Or the kitchen table.'

'Go. You will be fine.'

'Yeah, go on.' Tim nudged him.

'What?'

'Alphabetical order. You're first.'

Tim could see him thinking, Smith/Townsend, Norman/Tim.

'What's your middle name?'

'Aaron,' Tim lied. 'Just go!'

Norman checked the strap on his helmet, climbed onto the balcony railing, flexed his webbed arms, took a deep breath ... and jumped.

The others – except for Coral – rushed to the edge in time to hear his exultant cry. They saw him catch the air and wheel away from the cliff face in a graceful arc, his arms and legs thrown out wide, the webbing between them making him look like an enormous kite. He swooped and dived and let out another cry. '*Woo-hooooo!*'

'You next,' Alkemy said to Tim.

'Um ...'

'Come, we go together.' She climbed up onto the railing and held a hand out to him. 'First time is always a little scare.'

Tim chewed his lip. *A little?*

He glanced back and saw Coral gripping the frame of the French doors, her face anxious, knowing she'd be next. Somehow the sight of her gave him more courage. In the distance, Norman's whoops and yells started to sound like the cries of the soaring gulls.

Taking Alkemy's hand, he climbed up beside her, careful to keep his eyes fixed on the horizon and not look down.

'I have to throw my arms and legs out wide, right?' His mouth felt dry and his voice croaked.

'Do nothing. The suit will do the work. Still all green?'

He checked his display. 'Yup.'

'We go.'

She jumped, tugged his arm, overbalanced him, and he fell.

It wasn't a graceful start. Her weight jerked him sideways so he tilted to his left and half-tumbled through the air, but as he did so, thin flexible struts in the suit's webbing went rigid, forcing him into a star shape. The whole suit puffed up around him, increasing drag and wind resistance. Numbers flashed in his heads-up display: airspeed, direction, altitude, suit status. All green.

After a moment of shocked surprise, Tim realised he was actually flying.

Below him, Alkemy soared out over the ocean. He tilted his arms as if to follow and the suit sensed and amplified his movements, taking him into a swooping dive that left his stomach behind. For a moment he was frightened they'd collide, but the suit's computer tracked other flyers too and brought him smoothly alongside her.

He looked across, seeing her broad grin and the wisps of silvery hair fluttering around the edges of her helmet, and managed to grin back. She reached out and touched his fingers. As he caught her hand, an icon flashed in his display indicating the two suits were now acting as one unit. He let her lead him into a series of turns and glides, catching updrafts that almost brought them to a halt and swooping dives that seemed impossible to stop.

Finally, above the beach, they let go their hands and landed separately, their suits expanding and billowing out like parachutes for the last few metres. Tim landed upright with a gentle run along the sand to take up his momentum, and as he did so, the suit contracted around him again forming a second skin.

They came to a halt side by side, laughing, and threw their arms around each other as Norman trotted over wearing a grin so wide he risked dislocating his jaw. 'How about that then?'

'That was ... I just ... I can't ...' Tim's words failed him. He looked at Alkemy, her face radiant, and threw his arms around her again.

'Oh no, not you two as well?' Norman groaned.

* * *

'I didn't buy that syntho's story,' Wilis said as he and Walis watched a builder-bot replace the smashed-in studio door.

'You mean about the radiation casket?'

'No, I mean about how they escaped from the Science Council building. He said they just walked down a back stair, but we had that place sealed off. If I was Welis, I'd want to know how they—'

'But you're not, are you? You're not in charge any more.'

Wilis sighed. 'I'd also check this place out more thoroughly. I have a feeling that dumb syntho isn't quite as dumb as he makes out. But you're right, Walis. I'm not Welis, and we have to follow orders.'

A cleaning-bot edged past them dragging a container filled with broken glass from the balcony doors. More bots were at work in the lounge, repairing and re-glazing the metal frames.

'I don't like what they did to that technician,' Walis said. 'I know he was a baddy and all that, but injecting him with that brainsmash stuff was horrid.'

'Welis would say the end justified the means,' Wilis said, setting a tiny watch-bot in the door jamb.

'They could've just threatened him. He'd have blabbed if he *thought* they might use it. I reckon we could have made him talk, you and I, without doing *that*.'

'I reckon you're right, brother. But as you pointed out, we're not in charge.'

* * *

Despite being blindfolded and comms-blocked, Albert's enhanced internal navigation system tracked where Welis and the thug-bots took him. It wasn't far at all.

He was pleased to discover that one of his calculations had been correct. His analysis suggested that Krilen was most likely being held in an old biology building, now closed for renovations, in a corner of the campus. The old research facility had a number of quarantine rooms that, from the plans, would make ideal containment cells, and it seemed that's where he was being taken too.

Still, it was no use being proved right if you couldn't do anything about it.

Logic told him his best course of action was to bide his time and continue playing the simple-minded syntho who did what he was told, but that was difficult knowing the forces he was up against, when his every instinct was to lash out and fight and try to escape.

There was only one way they could have found out where he and the children were hiding. It could have come from only one source, and Andop wouldn't have given them up willingly. Which meant he had been tortured. Brainsmashed, most likely. And that told Albert two further things: that the people they were up against were brutal and ruthless, and that must not let the same thing happen to him, not with all he knew. Cooperation was his only option.

On the positive side, the way he was being treated suggested that Andop hadn't been asked the one question he should have been asked: *Who else has had neural implants?* Because if they even so much as suspected Albert had been a recipient, he'd be wearing a lot more than a blindfold and a comms-block collar right now.

'You've been with the family some time, I believe,' Welis said when the formal interrogation began.

'Yes.'

'You know all their relatives and friends.'

'Yes.'

'Places they go on holiday?'

'Yes.'

'I want a list – a complete list – of every place they've ever been and stayed. Do you understand?'

'Yes, all right.'

'And I want it *now!*'

The children had been heading for Baylev on the southern coast. A distant cousin had a holiday bach there the family had used once or twice. The fun park would keep them busy for a couple of days. If he accidentally left Baylev off his list he might get a chance to warn them before they moved on.

'Certainly.'

Wilis and Walis rejoined them from the apartment. Welis handed them the list. 'Check every one of these and set a watch-bot on each one.'

Walis studied the list, frowning. It covered half the continent. 'This could take a while, Welis.'

'Not in person, you idiot. Do it remotely. It shouldn't take more than a few hours.'

'Oh, right.'

* * *

'If it's so safe, why do you have to wear a helmet?' Coral said.

'The helmet contain the computer and control the suit.' Ludokrus rapped his knuckles against his own helmet. 'You think this will save you if you jump without the suit?'

'No, of course not, but ...' She took a breath. Her knuckles around the door jamb were white. 'You know what I mean.'

'Try on. See how it fit.'

'I know what you're trying to do, Ludokrus.'

'Just try. Then you may say at least you have worn the full wingsuit.'

'If you touch me, if you try to make me ...'

He held up his hands. 'I would not. Ever. Promise.'

Coral pulled on the helmet and clipped the buckle. Like the wingsuit, it fitted and shaped itself to her skull. Extra status lights came on in her display. All green. *Ready for flight.*

'There. All right? Now I'm taking it off again.'

But she didn't. Not right away.

Ludokrus sat on the railing facing her, his back to the view. 'The first time I jump, man, I was so scare. My parent, Albert, Alkemy – all go, no problem, but not me. They talk, encourage, say how safe, how fantastic, but in here I am like, *I cannot do this. Ever.*' He tapped his chest.

'We are here for one week, and the days go past. Every day they have adventure, but not me.

'Finally, I ask myself, where is this fear? Inside of head, right? Is normal. We should be scare. To jump off cliff is crazy. But flying does not scare, in the plane or in the spaceship, because the technology keep me safe. Like this.' He flapped the arms of his wingsuit and tapped his helmet. 'Therefore, the only difference is inside the head, in brain. You *think* you cannot do it, so you never try. All you need to change is that one thought, and maybe you can do it after all.' With that, he leaned over backwards and fell over the side.

Coral let out a startled cry and rushed to the edge, peering down, only realising where she was when she saw him hovering on an updraft a few metres below.

'Come,' he beckoned. 'Just close the eyes and jump.'

She was already hanging over the edge. It was more than she'd ever risked before, even without the wingsuit.

Oh what the heck, she told herself, screwed up her eyes and kicked off.

The sudden rush of air made her gasp. She would have screamed if she hadn't felt her arms and legs snap out into a star shape, held rigid by the suit. She risked a peek, then opened her eyes wide. 'Oh my god, I'm flying!'

46 : An Unexpected Delivery

After at least a dozen cliff dives, Coral and Ludokrus lay sprawled on one sofa, Alkemy and Tim on the other, while Norman was slumped in an armchair with the remains of another food fabricator experiment on the floor beside him.

'Who'd have thought flying could be so tiring.'

'I'm not tired,' Norman said. 'I'm resting my eyes.'

'It's not so much the flying, it's that long ride back up,' Coral said. 'They need express silkas or something.'

'A chairlift of an elevator would do it.'

'Or a helicopter.'

There was a faint knocking sound.

'Is that the front door?'

'Neighbour, maybe. Complain about the yell and scream from jumping.'

'That was Norman.'

'What about you when you went off backwards?'

'That was an accident. I slipped.'

The knock sounded again. Louder this time.

'Anyone going to get that?'

'Asker wins!' Norman said. 'Anyway, you're closest.'

Tim groaned and went to answer it. There was a peephole in the middle. He checked it first and saw a cone-shaped bot standing on the step holding a package in one spindly arm. There was no one else about.

The bot held up a package as he opened the door. 'Good evening, I have a special delivery for Kresti Alman.'

'I think you've got the wrong address. Hey, anyone here know a Kresti Alman?' Tim called over his shoulder. There was a chorus of no's. 'Not here, sorry.'

The bot apologised and trotted off.

'Since I'm up,' Tim said, returning to the balcony, 'who's up for one last flight?' There were groans from the others.

'The only thing I'm up for is a shower.' Coral got to her feet.

'Me second!' Ludokrus called.

'I come.' Alkemy smiled. 'We go together.'

Norman opened one eye, saw her take Tim's hand, and closed it again.

'Norman?'

'If you two are going to do all that hand-in-hand, soaring-like-an-albatross stuff, you'll be hours yet. I'll catch you up.'

Norman had taken up dive-bombing. By forcing his arms back as far as the suit would let him, he'd drop like a stone, watching the airspeed indicator in his heads-up display go from green to orange to red. Eventually, the suit would forcibly take back control, jamming his arms out and inflating the whole thing in an emergency braking manoeuvre. It looked terrifying, but Norman reckoned it was the hottest thing since plimp sauce.

Tim and Alkemy stepped off the railing, backwards this time, and did a somersault before their suits took full control, guiding them away from the cliff face in a gentle, sweeping arc. They preferred the flight itself, making it last as long as possible, searching out currents and updrafts that could keep them soaring for half an hour or more.

Evening was approaching. The reflection of two suns sparkled on the waters below, and the changing air currents took them far out to sea before amber indicators in their heads-up displays said they should turn back. Down below, the fishing fleet was returning to port; tiny black dots on the iridescent blue ocean.

'I think we set new record,' Alkemy called. 'The longest ever flight.'

'It's just so … wow!' Tim shook his head as they banked in a wide arc and dipped towards the beach.

They were halfway there when an odd thought struck him. 'Hey Al, didn't you say there were no bots in Kestel?'

'They are not allowed.'

'But … there was one at the door just now.' He broke off and looked up, hearing what sounded like a helijet.

* * *

Norman ambled out onto the balcony, shielding his eyes to see where Alkemy and Tim were. They'd been cruising around for ages – so long that both Coral and Ludokrus had finished their showers – but they were now, finally, heading towards the beach. Another couple of minutes, he reckoned, then with a well-aimed, high-speed dive-bomb he'd land right between them.

Hearing the whine of a distant helijet, he glanced up and watched as a black silhouette came in from the west then swung towards the town. It drew closer, looking like it was following the line of the cliffs, looking as if it would pass directly overhead. Then it slowed abruptly and descended sharply. Figures appeared, hanging out of either side. Several jumped. He was so caught up in the spectacle that it took him a moment to realise where they were heading.

'Look out! Run! We've got company,' he yelled, racing inside to warn the others.

Coral and Ludokrus had been sharing a kiss. They sprang apart at his interruption, and seconds later a fist pounded on the front door. The roar of the helijet grew, mingling with the sound of splintering timbers.

'You still have wingsuit.' Ludokrus yelled to Norman. 'Jump! Get away!'

Norman raced out again, but the helijet was now hovering over the balcony and the downdraft drove him back with hurricane force.

Four of the Military Council's latest war-bots sprang from the helijet as it approached, two from each side. They landed cat-like on all six legs then immediately snapped upright on their hindmost set. Two landed in the street outside and immediately charged at the door of the house. Two landed on the balcony, weapons at the ready.

Triple-Dub made a more leisurely exit, abseiling from the hovering helijet. Welis let go his rope a couple of metres up, flexing his legs and taking the weight of the landing in his knees. His clone-brothers made more careful touchdowns.

'Act cool,' Ludokrus told the others, adding to Norman, 'We try to make distraction. Maybe you can get away.'

Welis strode through the French doors, grinning a steely grin and adjusting the bandanna around his neck. 'Well, well, well, brothers. Look what we have here.'

Three faces looked up at him from two separate sofas. It wasn't quite the entrance he'd expected. The kids didn't run or hide or cower in terror. If anything, they looked a bit bored.

'Yeah, yeah, we heard your heli-thing *and* your toy soldiers.' Coral flicked her hair, still damp from the shower. 'You could have knocked, you know. The door wasn't locked.'

'Stand up when you talk to me!'

'Why?' Coral asked in a reasonable tone. 'Have they made you a king or something?'

Welis snapped his stainless steel teeth at her.

'Urgh! You should brush more often.'

'Where are the other two?' he said.

'What other two?'

'Search the place!' he told his brothers, but with only four rooms it barely took moment.

'I said, where are they?'

'Who?'

'Your leader and the other girl.'

'Our *leader?*'

'The other boy,' Welis snarled, the image of Tim burned deep in his memory. The boy who'd led his friends down a certain alley on Selene station. The boy who'd teased and taunted him until—

'He's not our ...' Coral suddenly twigged. 'Oh, right!'

Norman did too. 'Since you'd follow him anywhere, how

about if I told you he jumped off the cliff?'

Welis's hand snapped out and grabbed him by the scruff of the neck. 'Well, well, look who this is. The one who squirted plimp sauce in your face, Walis. Why don't you get some from the food fab and return the compliment? I'll hold him for you. Or you could just smash his horrid face in. Wilis and I will say he tripped and fell, eh Wilis?'

Wilis looked uncomfortable. Walis shook his head.

'Go on. Free shot.' Welis shook Norman like a dirty rag.

'That wouldn't be fair,' Walis said. 'Not when they're under arrest.'

Welis snorted and tossed Norman to aside, giving him a clear run at the balcony. The helijet, though still hovering overhead, had backed off, making the downdraft now more a strong wind than a hurricane. But he'd have to get past the bots first.

Ludokrus registered the situation too and got to his feet. 'Hey, leave our friend alone, tin teeth!' He squared up to Welis even though the augment towered over him. 'You were not invite. Go! You *and* your toy soldier men.'

'Yeah,' Coral said, standing up beside him. 'Clear off. You're making the place look untidy.'

Welis bellowed for the guards.

The thug-bots on the balcony lowered their weapons and advanced, arms extended, focused on Coral and Ludokrus. Norman, still getting to his feet after being cast aside, sprinted forward, dived between a pair of legs, slid across the tiled surface, then leapt to his feet and bounded up onto the railing.

'Go!' Coral yelled, but the bot he'd dodged spun rapidly and lunged, catching and tearing the webbing beneath his left arm as Norman leapt off the cliff.

47 : Deadly Plunge

'Something's happening up there,' Tim yelled as he and Alkemy came in to land, stepping lightly onto the beach with their wingsuits billowing around them. 'I just got a comm from Coral saying they had company. Then it cut out and now I can't get a signal.'

'Same also. Ludokrus say to not come back, then his comm die also.'

They peered back at the sheer cliff trying to pinpoint their house. 'It's about there, isn't it? Underneath that helijet?' As he spoke, a black dot disengaged itself and tumbled past the russet coloured cliffs. 'Is that Norman? Wow, look at him go!'

'What of the others?'

Norman's signal crackled into life as he dropped below the range of whatever was blocking it.

'Nice going, dive-bomber,' Tim told him. 'What's happening up there?'

'Triple-Dub ... suit's ripped ... can't control ...'

'Get away from the rocks!' Alkemy cried. 'Find deep

water!' But the falling figure continued its deadly plunge.

* * *

The world whirled and tumbled around him out of control. One moment it was the rocky cliff face racing past, then the sky, blue and timeless, then the wave-swept rocks below. He spiralled down with all the control of a bird with a broken wing, the last few seconds of his life flashing past incoherently. It was like being bounced around the inside of a giant tumble dryer.

Norman closed his eyes and focused his attention on his heads-up display. Tim and Alkemy were yelling over comms, but he ignored them. There was a tear in his wingsuit, not just ripped fabric but a damaged line somewhere. It was leaking fluid. He could feel it spraying around his ankles. Icy cold. Evaporating as he fell.

Left arm. That made sense. The one the thug-bot tore. But what to do?

Fluid pumped around the suit from the backpack stiffened and controlled the webbing. A broken line would soon bleed out, leaving him with no control at all. But how could he stop or slow the leak?

The answer came in a flash. He was so used to his arms and legs being thrown into a star shape and held there by the suit that he was trying to mimic the configuration himself. But the ripped webbing under his left arm made that aerodynamically unstable, causing him to tumble.

Focussing on that arm, he dragged it close to his body, keeping it in place by hooking his hand around the back of his neck. Immediately the pressure gauge in his heads-up display stopped plummeting and he felt a little stiffness return to the rest of the webbing. A couple of the dozen red lights in his display dropped back to orange.

His helpless fall stabilised a little, though it was still a wild, tumbling, out of control ride. Heeding Alkemy's cry to find deep water, he edged himself away from the cliff face in a stuttering, spiralling turn. Orange lights turned red again. The suit, trying to follow his directions, increased pressure in the still-working control surfaces – which increased the rate of leakage in the damaged one. The harder he forced the turn, the more the suit strained and the quicker the pressure gauge dropped.

There was a loud *foop*. He thought his ears had popped with the sudden change in pressure, then realised his heads-up display was gone and the suit had lost its skin-tight fit. It flapped around his shoulders like an old curtain. He was no longer falling like a bird with a broken wing, he was falling like a brick.

48 : Downward Spiral

'What's the matter? No cheeky banter now then?' Welis chuckled as a pair of thug-bots bundled Ludokrus and Coral into the helijet and strapped them in, one in the front, one in the back.

They'd both heard Norman's suit rip and saw him fall. They'd both seen the augments rush to edge and track his downward spiral. And they'd both seen them wince at the impact.

Coral felt numb and a little sick. The thought of that sheer drop sent a shiver down her spine. And she and Ludokrus had encouraged him, even provided a distraction and cheered him on ...

She had a sudden vision of Glad Smith, Norman's mum. What would they tell her?

Cuffs snapped and locked around her ankles, fastening her to the seat so tightly she couldn't turn or twist. The high seat back blocked her view of the rear of the helijet where they'd taken Ludokrus, and the comms-block collar round her neck filled her head with static when she tried to call him. Just a glance, a glimpse, would do, she thought, to reassure herself he was all right.

The side of the hovering helijet dipped as Welis climbed aboard. Pausing at the sliding door, he beckoned to his clone-brothers. 'I've just spoken with Administrator Meli. The town's locked down. No transport in or out till you round up the other two. Is that easy enough for you?' He gestured to the pilot-bot. The idling engines kicked up a notch. 'Oh,' he added, shouting over them, 'and recover that body. It's one of the aliens. Haril will want to dissect what's left of it.'

* * *

Norman hit the sea with a sound like a fat insect being stepped on by a heavy boot. Tim and Alkemy heard it from the beach, even though he was a good twenty metres out.

'Call for help!' Alkemy yelled, pulling off her wingsuit, kicking it aside and running into the surf. 'Hurry!'

The awful sick feeling that gripped Tim vanished in an instant and he started tearing off his own wingsuit as he ran and stumbled up the beach heading for the jetty while comming for assistance.

Alkemy was a strong swimmer and reached the lifeless figure in record time. Norman was floating face down, the expanded wingsuit surrounding him like a giant lily pad. She pushed it to one side and tried to turn him over, recoiling as she gripped his right shoulder. The bones were either broken or dislocated. It felt like trying to grip a bag of lumpy custard, but she *had* to get his face clear of the water.

The emergency life raft! It was right there in front of her, packed into a cigar-sized cylinder attached to the bottom of his backpack. She pulled out a rolled orange mat that looked like a burst balloon, held it underwater beneath his midriff and hit the inflator. The narrow craft expanded quickly, lifting his whole body clear of the surface.

One arm, his right, slipped off the side. It was already bent at an unnatural angle and the added stress must have been extremely painful because, even though he was still unconscious, he gasped and coughed. Treading water, clutching the side of the life raft, Alkemy carefully lifted it back in place, relieved to see he was at least still breathing.

Tim was halfway to the jetty and still bellowing into his comms when the rescue launch put out. It seemed he wasn't the only one to report Norman's fall. He slowed, hung up, then called Alkemy. 'The boat's on its way.'

'I see her. Thanks.'

'How is he?'

'Bad. But breathe at least.' She sounded out of breath herself. 'Here come the boat. See you on the dock.'

He shielded his eyes and stared out to sea, feeling a mixture of shock and helplessness catch up with him. But it was mingled with relief. Norman was still breathing.

The jetty, like everything in Lower Kestel, was surrounded by large air-filled pontoons so it floated during the area's exceptional tides. Now, at low tide, it had settled onto a series of piles driven into the beach. As he approached, Tim saw a crowd gathering at the landward end, a crowd that parted suddenly to accommodate a pair of running figures. Large running figures. Two-thirds of Triple-Dub.

Tim backed away and ducked beneath the canopy of a Basic Beachwear stall, watching as they cordoned off the jetty.

'Alkemy, are you there? There's a problem.' He told her what he could see.

'You think they look for us?'

'I'm guessing they're just after Norman, but you better stay out of sight and slip over the side when the boat docks.'

'No problem. The rescue people are busy with Norman. Meet under the jetty.'

Tim turned back towards the boat as one of the augments glanced his way. He half expected a shout of recognition or a thunder of footsteps, but nothing happened. Still, he edged deeper into the shadow of the stall's awning.

In keeping with the rest of Kestel, even the Basic shops were bot-free; the goods inventoried and replenished manually overnight. He helped himself to a towel, a big straw hat and a pair of sunglasses. Alkemy would need things too. There were stacks of gaudy shirts and shorts, beach toys and swimming aids. He found a bag and helped himself.

When he re-emerged, hat and sunglasses firmly in place, Wilis and Walis had taken full control of the jetty. He joined the back of the crowd, watching as the rescue boat docked and two waiting medics hurried aboard carrying a portable stretcher. There was no sign of Alkemy. He slipped away and headed down to the beach.

The underside of the jetty was coated with streamers of seaweed. Barnacles clung to its uprights, and a lazy tide lapped the shore. At the far end, where the rescue boat tied up, Tim saw a shape break the surface of the water and swim towards him. He waded in knee-deep, holding out a hand to help her out.

Alkemy was pale and tired and out of breath. He hugged her. She hugged him back, tightly, as if he was the last life preserver in an empty ocean. Her skin felt cold and she shivered in his arms, despite the warmth of the day. Pressing a finger to his lips he pointed up. She nodded. No point risking themselves to the augment's keen hearing.

He guided her to the shore and handed her a towel. She took it gratefully, wrapping herself in its warmth as he gestured to the bag of things he'd collected. She changed quickly beneath the towel as the portable stretcher rumbled across the floorboards overhead. They heard a brief exchange between the medics and the augments.

'You mean he's still alive?'

'Just. But we have to evac immediately.'

'The town's on lockdown.'

'This is an emergency.'

There was a slight hesitation, then, 'All right. I'll clear it.' Moments later they heard the approaching whine of an evacjet.

The craft, looking like a cross between a light plane and a drone, was highly manoeuvrable and settled on the landward entrance to the jetty. A perspex capsule on its undercarriage had room for only a stretcher and two medics, and it took off again within seconds, the blue and red lights around its sides strobing through the sky.

Alkemy held up a hand, two fingers crossed. Tim covered it with his own.

The sound of the evacjet faded. The sound of the sea

returned. Then a voice overhead said, 'Three down, two to go.'

Wilis or Walis. Tim pressed a finger to his lips again.

'Only a matter of time now,' the other augment replied. 'We've got war-bots on all the exits; the maglev station, the marina, the walking and electrobike tracks. They won't get away this time.'

49 : Conspiracy Theory

It was late evening when the helijet landed in a patch of anonymous ground surrounded by trees. Though Coral could barely turn her head, the buildings in the distance seemed vaguely familiar. Was this the university? Before she could take in any more, a black felt bag was pulled over her head.

'Oh, come on!' she cried, but her voice was muffled by the bag.

Her wrists and ankles were uncuffed, then a pair of metal hands half lifted, half dragged her from her seat. She landed on her hands and knees on what felt like grass, and for a moment whatever had been blocking her comms failed. She mightn't have noticed if it hadn't been for the bag. Her dim heads-up display brightened and the signal indicator blinked on.

'Ludokrus?' she whispered, getting to her feet, feeling a cold metal grip around her wrists. 'Are you there?'

Before he could answer, the bag was ripped from her head and Welis's glared down at her, a nasty smile on his face. 'So, the little alien has a comms piece, does it.' He snatched a handful of her hair and hauled her up till she was practically standing on tiptoes. 'Hidden away, is it? Give.' He held out his free hand.

Coral hesitated. She'd forgotten about the augment's augmented hearing.

He jerked her higher, threatening to tear her hair out by the roots.

'All right, all right. Give me a chance, will you!'

She felt behind her right ear, unhooked the earpiece and dropped it into his meaty paw.

He let her go. She slumped to the ground as he held it up between two stubby fingers and examined it. 'Very useful. Thank you.'

His stainless steel smile was the last thing she saw before the bag was pulled back over her head.

* * *

Albert's cell was painted a rather unpleasant green and contained nothing but a narrow, fold-down bed, a wash basin and a toilet. The stout steel door had a small barred window two-thirds of the way up, currently covered by a hinged metal cover on the outside, and a narrow food slot at the bottom. His built-in comms were blocked, and there was no news console or infotainment unit. Not even a mirror. Glass was banned, presumably because it could be broken and used as a weapon. A small square of polished stainless steel was bolted to the wall above the wash basin, and Albert amused himself by studying his reflection and making vision adjustments to correct for its imperfect surface.

It seemed his analysis of where they were holding Krilen had been right. Now he was being held there too. The old Biological Research Facility in a far corner of the campus of Theia University had been closed for renovations a few weeks earlier after a nasty toxic spill – right about the time of Krilen's supposed illness. A couple of decades earlier, the building had been upgraded and converted to classrooms, but a portion of its original layout had been kept as part of a historical display; six of the original basement cells reserved for dangerous mental patients.

As they brought him in, Albert noted they passed three open cells and that he was placed in the fourth. He guessed the one on the end contained Krilen, and the one between them, Andop. Or what was left of him.

He'd also been right about the corruption of Valax. There were flaws in the system, but ones of such subtle complexity that even he struggled to follow their intricacies. Which suggested they weren't of Eltherian origin.

Who then?

The Thanatos.

If you wanted to keep an eye on a species living just fifty light-years from one of your most important, longest running experiments, the simplest way to do so would be through their own planet-wide computer system. A system that stored everything and provided free access to everyone.

Was that why Krilen had kept things to himself and ran several secret projects; because he suspected their perfect system wasn't quite so perfect after all?

There was an ancient conspiracy theory that reckoned a shadowy group called the Ruling Council really ran Eltheria.

It was the stuff of legend, the plot line of many third-rate books and virts, and he'd always dismissed it as fanciful fiction. Now he wasn't sure.

The best way to control anything was from behind the scenes, and the Thanatos would only need direct contact with two or three actual agents. They would then exploit unwitting dupes, in it for whatever they could get – wealth, influence, personal power. Even here on Eltheria where nanomachines and Basic shops provided all the necessities of life, people still sought power for the sake of it. Especially, ironically, the already wealthy and powerful. It seemed they could never get enough.

A disturbance in the corridor outside roused him and he stooped to listen at the food slot, boosting the volume of his hearing as he did so. He heard the sound of footsteps, muffled voices and the banging of cell doors. Two of them. Two more prisoners. The children. His heart sank. His deception hadn't worked after all. They'd caught them too.

50 : Heavy Going

Once Alkemy was dressed, Tim took a floral-patterned shirt from the bag of things he'd collected at Basic Beachwear and handed it to her. She took it curiously and held it up. It was at least five sizes too big.

'Put this on first.' He draped an inflatable life vest over her head. She smiled, understanding at once, put the baggy shirt on over the top of it and began inflating the vest.

As the evacjet carrying Norman headed for the nearest hospital, two overweight kids in brightly patterned shirts, straw hats and sunglasses emerged from beneath the jetty and waddled away up the beach.

'I try to comm Albert,' Alkemy said when they were well out of earshot. 'No response.'

'Same here. I've been trying Coral. Oh, hold on a sec. I just got a text.'

The message simply read: *Hi!*

Where are you? What happened? Tim texted back.

'I try Ludokrus, but no response,' Alkemy said. 'What does she say?'

'She just said ...' Tim thought for a moment. 'Oh man, I'm an idiot!' He tore off his earpiece and stared at the traitorous thing. 'We *know* they've been caught! We heard Triple-Dub: *Three down, two to go.* No more comms, Alkemy. They're using it to track us.'

Behind them on the jetty, one of the augments turned towards the two fat figures on the beach and cupped his hands around his mouth. 'Oi! You two. Stop right there. Stay where you are!'

'Run! Tim yelled, but Alkemy didn't need any encouragement. She sprinted off ahead of him, heading up the beach to one of the many narrow tracks that led up the cliff. Tim followed, deflating the life vest under his brightly patterned shirt as he ran.

There were dozens of paths up to the town, some wide and well-trodden with neatly cut steps, and others like this one, narrow, steep and little more than linked patches of scuffed earth amongst the barren rock. In places, there were hand and toeholds that looked like they'd been kicked into the earth. In others, there were steep, slick slopes that could only be managed with a full-on sprint – and the hope of a rocky handhold at the end to stop you sliding back. Still, panic helped, and after five full minutes of furious climbing they reached a plateau sheltered by some thorny shrubs about fifty metres from the beach.

'Halfway,' Alkemy gasped, pointing to a wider track further up that led to the lower reaches of the town.

Below and behind them, Wilis and Walis had jumped from the jetty to pursue them, but the heavy augments were struggling to make much speed in the soft sand.

'There are plants now. They will hide us,' Alkemy said,

unbuttoning her garish overshirt. 'Keep low and move quick. They might not see.'

'No, wait. Leave that on for the moment,' Tim told her. 'I *want* them to see where we're going. I've got an idea.'

* * *

'Hurry up, Wilis, they're getting away,' Walis yelled over his shoulder.

'That jump ... this sand ... my knees. You go on, Walis. I'll comm the war-bots to head them off.'

Wilis was right. The jump from the jetty hadn't helped, and pounding through soft sand that shifted with every step made his own knees ache, but he wasn't going to let his clone-brother down. He struggled on till he reached the track they'd taken up the cliff face, started up it, then stopped, looking up at the narrow toeholds and sheet steepness of the climb. It felt like both his knees said *No!* in unison.

'Go on, Walis. What are you waiting for?'

'I'm ... blocking their retreat. I can see them up there. Tell the war-bots they're taking the farthest fork of the western track up to the town.'

* * *

The track ended at the bottom of a cobbled lane between two whitewashed houses. A hand-painted sign fixed to one of them pointed back the way they'd come. It read: *Beach (Steep!)*.

Catching their breath, Tim and Alkemy took off the oversized floral shirts, life vests and straw hats they were wearing and packed them into Tim's bag. Transformed into a pair of T-shirted tourists, they made their way up the lane.

At the intersection, they found three small children playing Eltherian hopscotch in the road. Further up, an elderly woman sunned herself on a tiny porch. A tethered silka watched them pass.

Tim paused by a wall covered in a dark green vine heavy with purple flowers that smelled of honeyed lavender and dropped the bag into a communal recycler. 'Any idea which way?'

Streets, lanes and alleys snaked away in all directions. They were in the lower part of the ancient town where houses were piled in on top of each other and there was hardly a straight line anywhere.

'The augment say they send war-bots to the marina, tracks and maglev station,' Alkemy said. 'Nearest will be the maglev.'

'So, up is good,' Tim said. 'The further the better.'

They stopped at a tiny corner store and asked directions to the nearest silka park.

'I've got a couple round the back,' the storekeeper told them. 'Where are you heading?'

'The lookout. But quick. We want to catch the sunsets.'

'If you give them a couple of palopalo each,' she pointed to the fruit display arranged beneath the counter, 'they'll sprint all the way. But be sure you hold on tight!'

They thanked the woman, led the silkas out into the street and fed them. The animals chewed noisily and swallowed as Tim switched on his comms earpiece and tucked it into a fold in one of the silka's saddles.

'There you go fella,' he told it, letting go the reigns and giving it a smack on the rump to send it on its way. 'Easy climb today.'

They watched the pair of silkas gallop away. Tim laughed. 'She wasn't kidding. They are keen!'

As they headed downhill he added, 'You know, even with no thug-bot guard, the maglev station might still be locked down.'

Alkemy smiled. 'You think the goods yard also?'

'What do you mean?'

'Ever hear of bubbletrucks?'

51 : Trick or Track

Coral was furious with herself for whispering to Ludokrus with her head in that bag. She couldn't see a thing. Welis might have been standing right beside her when she tried to comm Ludokrus! Now she had no comms at all. Worse, her headset contained numbers for Tim and Alkemy, numbers he could use to trick or track them.

She kicked at the wall of the room in which they'd thrown her, a prison cell two metres wide by three deep. There was a fold-down bed secured by chains at either end, a washbasin and a toilet behind a low partition. That was it. The floor was bare concrete and the walls were painted a nasty greenish colour.

Returning to the door, she gripped the metal bars in a small opening partway up and looked out. All she could see was a corridor painted the same pukey green.

'Hey, anyone there?' she called.

A thug-bot raced over and slammed down the metal cover on the hatch.

Coral kicked at the door then slumped on the bed. The

mattress was paper-thin. There was only one blanket and no pillow.

Time passed. There was nothing to do. She wanted to switch off the overhead light and try to sleep, but she couldn't even control that. In the end, she wrapped her head in the blanket and did manage a little sleep, but her dreams were troubled. She woke once to the sound of screaming, but it stopped as she pulled off the blanket, and in the end she wasn't certain she hadn't dreamed it. Next time she woke, a tray of food was being pushed through the lower slot in the door. Whatever it had once been was now unrecognisable; vegetables of some sort boiled to a mush. It looked like lumpy green porridge. She sneered and pushed it aside.

The upper hatch was still closed, the overhead light still on. It was hard to know how long she'd been in there or even what time it was. Late evening? Early morning?

More time passed. At one point a metal claw appeared through the lower slot and withdrew the untouched food tray.

'Hey, you!' Coral dropped to her hands and knees trying to peer out, but there was no reply except for the fading clack of metal feet on concrete.

Sometime later the footsteps returned. Coral heard them pause outside her door followed by the beeping of a keypad. The lock clicked, the door opened, and a war-bot stood beside it, silently beckoning her out.

She stepped into the corridor. The bot's bulk blocked one way and it directed her towards the far end where she saw a patch of light beyond the last cell.

She counted off the doors as she passed them. Four more

cells. It was impossible to see inside as their cover plates were closed, but she guessed their occupants nonetheless: Ludokrus, Albert, Andop and Krilen. Glancing back, she saw the two cell doors at the far end were ajar and her spirits lifted briefly. They hadn't yet caught Tim and Alkemy.

The corridor at the end turned right, opening out into what appeared to be a chemistry lab. One wall was covered with racks of test tubes, retorts and all manner of glassware, while another held an array of multicoloured chemical compounds in stoppered bottles. A stout, metal-topped bench sat in the middle of the room containing some complicated apparatus that ended at a tall glass condenser that dripped a pale blue liquid into a flask. The rest of the bench had been wiped clean and the whole place smelled vaguely of cleaning fluids and something unpleasant.

A desk sat in the far corner. The woman behind it looked up as Coral approached. She smiled and got to her feet. 'Good morning.' She offered her palm in greeting, but Coral ignored it and said nothing. 'My name is Chix Haril. I'm here to help you.' She gestured to the only other seat in the room. 'Please ...'

Coral hesitated. The woman sat back down, straightened some papers on the desk and looked at her expectantly. Coral relented and sat. 'What are you, some sort of lawyer?'

'If you like.'

'What does that mean?'

'You've gone way beyond the laws of this planet, but I *can* help you.'

The woman was of indeterminate age, had glossy black hair held back in a barrette and a rather engaging smile. Still, Coral was suspicious. There was something about that name …

'How?' she asked.

'Before I answer that, I should tell you that they've captured all your friends.'

'What?'

'Apart from the dead one, of course. The boy who jumped.'

'Norman …? Norman's dead?'

'I'm afraid so.'

Coral's breath failed her for a moment. She had wondered, worried … But to have it confirmed …

He was annoying at times, a real pain, but he could be amusing too. She thought of his food fab antics and the ridiculous pavlova he'd made. He'd even insisted on eating a slice, trying to convince the others to try it.

And he was only a kid …

She swallowed and wiped her cheek. A single tear had sneaked out.

'I want to see the others,' she said, her voice unsteady.

'All in good time. I'd like some information first. About you, who you are, where you come from.'

'No, now,' Coral said, her mind filling with the image of the empty cells at the far end of the corridor.

The woman's mouth tightened fractionally. 'I should tell you that I'm working to a deadline here.'

'Then hurry up. You said they've got all the others. Show me. Prove it. And who are *they* anyway?'

Haril. The woman's name suddenly registered. Wasn't that the name of Krilen's deputy, the one supposedly missing in the mountains? It was definitely the name Welis had used calling to his brothers from the open door of the helijet: *And recover that body. It's one of the aliens. Haril will want to dissect what's left of it.*

This was all a pretence. *I'm here to help you. They've captured all your friends.* It was a lie. *I* and *they* were one and the same.

Haril said, 'You're not in a position to negotiate, you know.'

'You're right, I'm not. So just show me them in their cells then.' Coral stood up. 'Come on. It won't take a minute.'

'They're ... not all in this facility.'

'Aren't they? Show me a vid feed then. Or haven't you really got them at all?'

'We've got them all right.'

'*We.* Hah! It's you, isn't it? *You're* behind all this. And you haven't really got them at all.'

Haril's smile turned into a snarl. For a moment, Coral glimpsed someone else entirely. 'Guard!'

The war-bot reacted immediately, grabbing Coral from behind, a single metal claw clamped round her neck.

'Want to see one of your friends, do you? Want to see what I'll do to them, all of them, if you don't cooperate?' Haril stalked from the room. Coral, gripped by the war-bot, was frog-marched along behind her.

Haril opened the viewing hatch on the second cell. The smell hit Coral immediately, a toxic mix of vomit, urine and faeces. 'Show her!'

The war-bot slammed Coral's face against the barred grille. The smell was even worse now. She screwed up her face and gagged, fighting back the urge to be sick. Then she took in the sight of the prisoner.

Andop was sitting on the bed, leaning back against the

wall and staring at the ceiling. His mouth was open, his eyes vacant, his clothes filthy. Drool ran down his chin.

'That's all he does now.' Haril's tone was jubilant. 'He sits and dribbles, in between the occasional screaming fit. But he told us everything he knew.

'He has to be fed with a spoon now. Frankly, it's too much trouble. We've decided not to bother any more. We'll leave him. Let him die in there in his own shit and vomit. And if you don't cooperate, little girl, we'll do the same to your other friends. All of them. Then you.'

52 : Degenerate Species

'Oh, my innards have slurped the other way now.'

'You know what that means, don't you?'

'That we're braking hard?'

'And that means we've arrived.'

'Where?'

'Wherever we were heading.'

'Thank you for your insight. I'm so much better informed now.'

'Well, how am I supposed to know where we are or what's going on outside? We're still locked in this wretched dungeon.'

'Is that what this place is? And there I was, thinking it was a holiday camp.'

'You're not funny, you know. Not even faintly amusing.'

* * *

Tim and Alkemy were sound asleep when the bubbletruck rolled to a stop in the siding behind Macet Upholstery Services. They'd been in it all night, partly because the lockdown of Kestel had continued for six long hours until the news nets started taking an interest, and partly because the automated *Red for Danger* code involved redirecting out-of-town shipments to other addresses in other cities. There, the tags were changed and they were forwarded on to mask any link between the sender and Macet. As a result, they'd visited Orme, Dul and Palyfusta too – not that Tim and Alkemy had seen much of them, or even been awake for most of the rocking, rolling, rumbling trip. But the sudden stop and silence now woke them both.

'What? Huh? Are we there then?' Tim's mouth was dry and he tried to stretch his legs, but there wasn't much room in the carton.

A clunk and a hiss sounded from outside, followed by a brief, wobbling roll. He opened the flap they'd cut in the cardboard and saw the interior of a delivery dock. That was all the answer he needed.

'Oh man, let me out of this thing!'

The whirr of machinery grew in volume as the outer and inner bubbles were unlatched. Welcome wafts of fresh air came in through the flap, and a minute later they were kicking away the packaging or at least trying too. Tim discovered one of his feet had gone to sleep.

'Good timing,' Alkemy said, looking up at an ancient clock on the rear wall. 'We arrive before the syntho worker open up. Best to not be seen.'

'How far is it to the apartment?' he asked, hobbling back and forth, using the bubbletruck rail for support as the tingling in his foot gradually ebbed. 'I can't wait to hit the shower.'

'Or to see Albert,' Alkemy said with a smile.

* * *

'Seen enough?' Haril sneered.

The war-bot released its grip and Coral staggered, grabbing at the barred window for support. Her knees felt like jelly, her stomach churned, but a fierce fury consumed her, one she struggled to contain. How could anyone – human or Eltherian – do that to another being?

Her instinct was to lash out, but that would be futile. The thug-bot would tear off her arm before she even got within range of Haril. Coral thought: *She's trying to scare me. Intimidate me. Well, there's another way of fighting back ...*

'Who's that then?' she said, dusting off her hands as she turned from the window hatch. 'Some smelly old wino you picked up off the street?'

Haril's mouth pursed. 'That is – or was – Andop Scolyfol.'

'Who's he?'

Coral's reward was a momentary flicker of uncertainty in Haril's dark eyes. 'The man who hid you and your friends on the university campus, right under our noses.'

'Well, I don't know where your nose points, but I've never been to one of your universities.'

She could see Haril struggling to keep her cool. This wasn't the reaction she'd expected. Coral should have been a blubbering wreck by now, begging to cooperate.

'Where are you from then?'

'Up there.' Coral pointed at the ceiling.

'Up *where?*'

'Third star system past that spiderweb in the corner.'

'How did you get here?'

'By spaceship, of course.'

'Whose?'

Coral shrugged. 'I dunno.'

Haril slapped her. Not hard, but it stung her cheek.

The thug-bot tensed, anticipating Coral might try to strike her back. Instead, she laughed and blew Haril a kiss. 'You know, where I come from that gesture means *I love you.*'

Haril sneered and shook her head, clearly thinking she was as crazy as the prisoner in Cell Two. 'Take her back to the lab and get some samples. I want to identify exactly what sort of degenerate species we're dealing with. Get me fingernail clippings, skin scrapings, saliva and blood. Use force if necessary, then throw her back in her cell.'

Haril stormed off. The thug-bot did as it was told. It was rough and the procedure wasn't pleasant, but Coral focused on the one consolation she could find: if they needed *her* for such samples, it meant she was the only one of her species Haril had access to. At the very least, Tim was still at large. And Norman wasn't dead because he hadn't been brought back for dissection.

53 : Approaching Storm

Dark clouds were building on the western horizon as Alkemy led the way from the river station. Tim saw a cloud-shrouded flash of lightning and began counting, trying to remember the formula Norman had taught him to work out how far away a storm was. Alkemy ignored it and continued on, forcing him to run to catch her up. They could have taken one of the river walkways that skirted the perimeter of the playing fields, but the shortest distance to Pyramid K was a straight line, and Alkemy was taking it.

Groups of people dotted the field talking in low voices and studying handhelds while flick discs, balls and other sports equipment lay abandoned at their feet.

'Is there a big game on or something?' Tim asked, catching her up.

'Albert will know.'

Tim smiled. The closer they got to their destination, the quicker Alkemy seemed to move.

In the pyramid's lobby, groups of people clustered around all the large vid screens, pointing and talking. But it wasn't a sports game. It looked like some sort of space exploration programme – or maybe it was just the half-time filler. Whatever it was, it gripped peoples' attention. The bar and cafe were crowded, the sports court and diving pool empty. The deep blue water looked cool and inviting after the cramped bubbletruck ride and racing across town. Tim looked at it longingly as they passed. He'd have the whole pool to himself too. A deep dive to wash off the cobwebs, then float around on one of the inflatables ... But Alkemy was already at the elevator and holding the door for him.

The passage around floor nine was deserted. Alkemy tapped the code into their door and pushed it open, not noticing she dislodged a leaf-sized bot as she did so. It drifted to the floor, broadcasting its alert as Tim stepped in behind her.

'Albert?'

The air was stale and dry and filled with a static hum from the study-slabs piled along both sides of the hall.

'Has he had more delivered?' Tim peered into the bedrooms as they passed, seeing tall stacks in each.

'Would ask, but is no one home,' Alkemy said, looking about as she reached the lounge.

'Maybe he's out watching that programme.'

'Could watch from here.'

'You reckon?' Tim pointed to the vid screen's power socket, overloaded with study-slab adapters.

Alkemy checked the balcony then returned, picking up Albert's notebook from the coffee table. 'Strange, he go out without this.'

'What's strange about that?'

'He always like to keep with him. Very precious, see?' She

opened it and flicked through pages filled with tiny handwriting and beautiful illustrations of the mechanisms of clocks and other machines.

'How does he write that small?' Tim said. 'Whoa, careful!' A small silver packet slipped out from between the pages and fell to the floor. He picked it up, turning it in his fingers. It was the thickness of a bookmark and diameter of a fifty-cent coin encased in a clear plastic sleeve. 'What's this?'

'Flexi-disc. Used to store data.'

He handed it back to her and gestured at the slab-cluttered room. 'You think he was running out of space?'

The doorbell rang. 'There he is! We can ask.'

Alkemy was halfway down the hall before Tim managed to catch her. 'It can't be him,' he hissed. 'He knows the code. Besides, he doesn't know we're back.'

She paused, peered through the peephole, then let Tim look.

'A delivery-bot,' he whispered. 'I know that trick from Kestel. We've got to get out of here!'

They raced back to the lounge as the doorbell chimed again. 'Here, help me with the sofa. We need to barricade the door to slow them down.'

Kicking aside study-slabs, they pushed the sofa into the hallway and dropped one of the beds behind it, wedging it between adjacent door jambs.

The chiming bell was replaced by a pounding fist.

'That doesn't sound like a delivery-bot,' Tim said as they sprinted out to the balcony.

Side by side, they climbed over the railing, held on as they lowered themselves on outstretched arms then let go, landing with bent knees and rolling to absorb the impact of the three-metre drop.

Welis bellowed from the floor above, telling whoever was in the apartment to give themselves up. His words were accompanied by splintering, smashing sounds as a troop of war-bots broke through the wedged door and fought their way up the cluttered hallway to take control of the place.

'Hurry, before they seal off the building.'

They darted through apartment J-8-9, past a couple of startled students watching the space programme on the lounge vid screen, and down a hallway almost as cluttered as their own. This one was piled with empty suitcases instead of study-slabs.

Alkemy reached the front door first, tore it open, let out a startled cry and lurched back. One of the thug-bots, either anticipating their move or just taking precautions, was hanging from the floor above, directly outside the apartment. The pyramid's shape meant the higher floor overhung the one below so the thug-bot was swinging back and forth in order to grab the eighth-floor safety railing with its lower limbs.

'Duck!' Tim said, grabbing the largest suitcase he could find and charging past Alkemy with it. As the thug-bot swung inwards, he rammed it into the machine's belly. Some reflex made it grasp what it thought was a solid object and release its upper limbs. Tim could have sworn it looked startled as it fell away through the empty interior space of the building, still clutching the suitcase. Seconds later it smashed to pieces on the empty sports court far below.

'We should split up,' he said. 'Make more targets. More chance to escape.'

'Good idea. Meet up later. Where?'

A metallic clatter-crash sounded from the balcony behind them as one of the other thug-bots dropped from the floor above.

'The waste ground by the crash test dummy. *Go!*'

They went. Tim ran left, Alkemy right as the second thug-bot charged through from the apartment in hot pursuit.

54 : Reason Number Three

Alkemy ran for the elevator as the doors began to close. Behind her, she could hear the thug-bot thudding through the eighth-floor apartment and cries of outrage and alarm from its inhabitants. The elevator was almost full, but someone held the doors and she ducked inside.

The trip to the ground floor seemed to take forever. Any moment she expected the elevator to grind to a shuddering halt as power to the building was shut off, but the doors finally opened and she found herself in the midst of chaos and confusion.

A crowd had gathered around the netting of the sports court where the thug-bot had fallen, smashing the hard playing surface as well itself.

'What happened?'

'Bot fall.'

'Someone could have been killed!'

'Is that one of those war-bot things?'

A couple of intrepid students pushed inside the court to examine the debris as Alkemy skirted the perimeter, heading for the nearest exit. Her luck was in. Several electrobikes were parked in the sharing area outside. She took one, trying to seem casual as she secured her helmet, but there were no running feet, no shouts for her to stop, and she rode away across the empty playing fields.

* * *

Tim raced down the stairwell taking the steps two or three at a time, focusing on where his feet landed, keenly aware that the slightest miscalculation might see him break a leg – or worse. The one thing he couldn't do was move quietly, and whether it was the sound of his footsteps or the sight of the closing stairwell door that attracted the thug-bot's attention, he didn't know. What he did know was that it was after him.

The thug-bot didn't bother with the stairs at all, it simply leapt from landing to landing. Tim could hear the thud of its impacts and risked a glance back up the stairwell. It was gaining fast. He'd never make it to the ground.

Bursting out onto the walkway around the third floor, he looked around, searching for some obstruction he could pull down in front of the thug-bot, or an open apartment he could duck inside. Nothing. The walkway was empty and all the doors were closed.

The thug-bot wasn't slowed by the stairwell door. It smashed straight through, tearing it off its hinges then sprinted after him.

The only exit was over the side. The diving pool was directly below and Tim didn't hesitate. He vaulted the railing feet first, sucked in a quick breath and held his nose.

The thug-bot didn't hesitate either. Eight floors might be fatal, but three were well within its design parameters. Even for a landing on concrete.

Tim hit the water. Seconds later, there was an enormous splash beside him.

The shock wave from the thug-bot's impact tumbled and disoriented him. He clawed for the surface. But while he did so, the machine kept sinking. With no natural buoyancy, it went straight to the bottom of the five metre deep pool.

Tim struck out for the side, dipping his head to keep an eye on the machine as it skittered back and forth like a giant crab, trying to get purchase on the tiled walls at the bottom of the pool. There was an element of desperation in its movements as if it really was about to drown. Then he spotted a faint lightning flash on the machine's back. It slowed, seeming to lose all coordination. Several more flashes came in quick succession. It stopped moving and sank to the bottom, its six legs splayed wide.

Willing hands helped Tim from the water and people crowded round. A green-eyed girl handed him a towel. 'Nice work, man. You killed it!'

'I did?'

'You see those flashes? Short-circuits. I guess they're not designed for underwater work. Why was it after you?'

'I don't know. They grabbed my friends then came for me. I just ran.'

'MC bastards! They think they own the planet. Always picking on aliens.'

Another voice said, 'Look out, there's more up there.'

Tim looked up as Welis and a third thug-bot peered

down from the ninth floor. 'Don't let them see me!'

'Come in a bit closer guys,' the girl said.

The group around him shielded him from view, but Welis and the thug-bot's attention was focused on the debris on the sports court.

'What are they doing?' Tim asked.

'Looks like the augment's comming for back-up.'

'I need to get away before it arrives.'

'No worries. Here.' More towels and some dry clothes were thrust at him. 'Get that wet stuff off.'

'Bori, you're about this guy's size. How about you take his gear and go for a run out the back way while the rest of us stroll out past the cafe?'

Bori grinned and pulled on Tim's wet T-shirt. 'Any bets on how far I'll get?'

'The speed you run, I doubt you'll make it to the door.'

'Oh yeah? Watch me fly, babe.' He gave her a peck on the cheek and took off, shoving his way past people, drawing cries of protest and attracting plenty of attention. Nine floors up, Welis tracked his movements and issued orders to an approaching helijet.

Tim pulled dry clothes over his wet underthings. The green-eyed girl handed him a hat. 'Thanks.'

She smiled. She had a small brown face with spiked yellow hair and a ragged fringe. The flesh beneath her lower lip was pierced, ornamented with a silver hexagonal nut. She twirled the stud on the inside of the piercing and made the nut rotate.

'I'm Tim,' Tim said.

'Eng.' She gave him a quick hand pat then gestured to the group gathered round them. 'And these losers are my friends.'

They were a mix of students of varying ages, but all seemed to share a common dress sense – or rather, a lack of one. Their clothes were eccentric. Some were faded, some were worn, some positively tatty – Coral would have been horrified – and their hands looked equally grimy, but many of them sported fancy gadgets Tim hadn't seen before. Digital rings, electronic bracelets, augmented necklaces and anklets, all beautifully handmade.

'Eng is the losiest of the lot,' a tall guy with a breast pocket full of tiny tools said amiably.

'I wouldn't have it any other way,' Eng replied. 'OK team, let's get moving?'

The group ambled off with Tim at its centre, joking and jiving with each other, talking as casually as they moved. As if they had all the time in the world.

'Thanks and everything,' Tim told Eng, 'I really appreciate it, but why are you doing this? You could get in real trouble.'

'A couple of reasons. Number one: anyone the Military Council doesn't like *has* to be a friend of ours. Right, guys?'

There were cries of, 'Oh yeah!'

'And number two: we're just returning the favour. Your little dive there has netted us a complete war-bot. We're engineers; SRC students. Once the heat dies down, we'll fish that baby out and see what makes it tick.'

Tim glanced over his shoulder. The formerly empty diving pool was now crowded with people and pool toys. They were swimming, playing games and splashing about, masking the silent machine down below.

'SRC? Is that the Syntho Research Centre?' Tim said. 'I

know of Andop Scolyfol.'

'An the Man?'

'He's a friend.'

His new companion clapped him on the shoulder. 'There you go then: reason number three.'

55 : New Moon

Tim brought his electrobike to a skidding halt as Alkemy appeared from one of the little beach huts. He'd barely got the bike on its stand before she threw her arms around his neck. 'You are safe! I have been so worry!'

He hugged her back, grinning.

'And your hair is wet.'

'Yeah, I stopped off for a swim on the way.' He laughed at her expression. 'I'll tell you later. Hi, Toxteth,' he called to the syntho making adjustments to a new anti-gravity platform nearby. Toxteth glanced up briefly, waved an acknowledgement then went back to work. 'It is still #263, is it?' Tim whispered to Alkemy.

'Not much longer, I think,' she whispered back. 'He say he must hurry to finish so he can show the platform off to visitors.'

'Well, I hope they like fireworks.' Tim grinned as she led him into one of the empty huts where Albert's notebook lay open on a workbench. 'Find anything interesting?'

'Much. He say what Ludokrus suspect; that Valax is

broken. It can be made to hide things, forget things and cover up.'

'But I thought your Mind of the Planet was free and open. Surely someone would have spotted that.'

'Not regular peoples. Albert say the way it is done is much complicate.' She flicked through several pages of close-packed handwriting. 'Even with enhanced brain, it take him much data and many days to work out.'

'So who could possibly have done it?'

She pointed to a single word written sideways in one of the margins: *Thanatos!*

'Oh. Wow!' Seeing the word was like switching a light bulb on in a dimly lit room. Suddenly everything seemed clear. 'Is that why Andop's research was blocked all those years ago, why he had to carry on in secret? They knew if his neural lace idea worked out, people would begin to spot flaws in Valax.'

Alkemy nodded.

'But the Thanatos didn't stop his research, your people did that ...' She waited while he made the connection. 'Which means they must have agents here. People working for them!'

She nodded again and turned the page. 'Here he talk of old legend, of group called the Ruling Council; secret peoples who really run Eltheria. No one believe this any more. Silly old conspiracy theory. But maybe it is not.'

'And this Ruling Council ... they're the ones after us ...'

'We return from secret mission deep inside Thanatos territory. Imagine if they hear of this. Would not be happy.'

'And Krilen organised it. So they got their agents here to make out he's sick and secretly arrest him.'

'Then wait for the mission to return. But we are two weeks late.'

'And when we get here, we look like the opposite of a secret mission. A bunch of kids and an absent-minded syntho. Suddenly it all makes sense!'

Alkemy closed the notebook and looked down at the worn leather cover. 'Now they have the others, we are the last ones free, and the only ones who know. You see how the war-bots come for us at Kestel, at the pyramid. They will not stop till we are found and capture also.'

Tim put an arm around her shoulders. 'It's OK. We'll be fine. We'll think of a way out of this.' But his words sounded hollow even as he spoke them.

'Hello there!' Toxteth said, coming into the hut and greeting Tim with an outstretched palm. 'Sorry about earlier. I was placing the last of the neutronium oscillators. It can get a bit tricky. All done now though and ready for our visitors.' Toxteth rubbed his hands together. 'I can't wait for the new moon to arrive.'

'New moon?'

He looked at them askance. 'You mean you haven't heard? The whole planet's talking about it. A Thanatos war globe has just arrived in our solar system. It looks like they're going to pay us a visit!'

Tim thought of the people they'd seen studying monitors and portable vid screens. He whispered to Alkemy, 'That can't be a coincidence.'

'Here, see for yourselves.' Toxteth took a dusty vid screen out from beneath the bench and switched it on. The first channel showed a robot soap opera, but the sound didn't match what was going on. He flicked through a couple of other channels and found the news. The picture changed, but the broadcast message stayed the same. After a short pause, it began again:

'Attention, people of Eltheria. This is Local Darkness #719, official Thanatos overlord and supervisor of this region of the spiral arm. It has come to my attention that members of your species have broken our joint treaty regarding a volume of space designated KSX-119; that they have invaded a protected region, interfered with important research and kidnapped a number of alien specimens.

'We demand the immediate surrender of these criminals, their accomplices and their victims. Failure to comply will be regarded as an act of war.'

'Goodness me, I hadn't heard that,' Toxteth said as the message began again. 'That's appalling! What sort of rotters would betray their planet and put us all at risk like that?'

Tim and Alkemy said nothing.

'You shall have my full cooperation in bringing them to justice, Mr Darkness!' Toxteth told the screen. 'What about you two?'

'Um ... yeah. Sure.'

'That's the spirit!' He turned down the volume and set the screen up on a shelf. 'We should keep an eye on that. No doubt there'll be more information about who the rotters really are. Pictures and stuff. I bet they're running for the hills right now, the cowards.'

Tim spotted a stack of flexi-discs on the shelf beside the monitor and remembered the one they'd found in Albert's notebook. 'Do you have a player for those things, Toxteth?'

'Why, yes,' Toxteth patted a dusty console on one end of

the workbench, 'but it's a specialised model designed to record and restore my personal backups before each test flight.'

Behind his back, Alkemy shook her head mouthing, 'I already check.'

'So ... how's the new platform working out?' Tim asked.

'Why, splendid, thank you. It's all ready to go. I shall launch it when our visitors arrive and hover up to meet them. I'm sure they'll be most impressed with Eltherian technology.'

'You don't think you should test it first?' Tim nudged Alkemy.

She added, 'Is not like it work right before.'

'No, no, I'm confident I've got everything covered now. It was those oscillators before. Slightly out of sync, you see. But I've double-triple checked them this time and everything is perfect.'

'That's great,' Tim said. 'And you're happy with your balance and everything?'

Toxteth blinked. 'My balance?'

'I remember when I learned to surf. I had a really good board, but staying on it for more than a couple of seconds took practice.'

Alkemy laughed. 'Like me when I learn the bicycle.'

'Oh yeah, I needed training wheels for ages!'

Toxteth frowned and looked back at the screen. The war globe was approaching Nol, the system's furthest planet, and braking hard. Its time of arrival was uncertain, but a best guess suggested an ETA of early tomorrow evening. 'You know, it might be an idea to get a few of practice runs in first ...'

'You think?'

'I wouldn't want to look wobbly and unprofessional.'

'Like someone learning to surf, you mean?'

'Not in front of our visitors.' Toxteth nodded thoughtfully. 'I think you're right. A little practice wouldn't hurt.'

As he went out to direct the trolley-bots to position the launch catapult, Tim ambled over to the next hut in line and jammed a length of pipe in the ground to wedge its door shut.

Backup complete, silver flight suit on, Toxteth climbed onto his anti-gravity platform and called, 'Ready? Stand back now! Five ... four ... three ... two ... one ...'

The catapult thudded, the platform soared ... briefly ... and the resulting explosion left another crater in the pockmarked ground. Alkemy wasn't watching. Even before it hit, she'd ejected the backup disc and swapped it for the one from the top of the stack. Outside, Tim was on his bike, racing through smoke and dust towards the crash site.

The door of the next hut banged against the pipe as the new Toxteth, activated by the demise of his predecessor, tried to exit.

Alkemy tiptoed away, took her bike and followed Tim. He found the syntho's head and tossed it into the basket on the front of his bike.

'I feel bad,' Alkemy said.

'Don't,' Tim told her. 'He would have dobbed us in when they broadcast our photographs. This way, where we went will remain a mystery. Besides, we saved him from making a fool of himself in front of the Thanatos.'

They crossed the waste ground, avoiding any sign of

habitation, even giving a couple out walking their silka a wide berth. The electrobikes made smooth work of the uneven ground, and the only diversion they made was to visit a recycling hopper.

With the load lightened, they headed north. The rough ground gave way to a rutted track dotted with trees while high overhead storm clouds rolled in, masking the ghostly band of Halo's ring. Beyond it, still out of sight, Eltheria's newest moon began disgorging wave after wave of fighters and battleships, sending them racing on ahead to seize control of the entire solar system.

About the Author

Geoff Palmer is an award-winning novelist and technical writer based in Wellington, New Zealand. You'll find him online at **www.geoffpalmer.co.nz**

Look out for the next thrilling instalment in this series, *The Shadow Behind the Stars*

Coming soon!